ALL THAT
IMPOSSIBLE SPACE

ALL THAT IMPOSSIBLE SPACE

ANNA MORGAN

LOTHIAN

Line from 'Stars' by Kenneth Slessor, *Selected Poems* courtesy of HarperCollins *Publishers* Australia. Lyrics from Taman Shud by The Drones. Words and music by Gareth Liddiard. © Copyright Native Tongue Music Publishing Ltd. All print rights administered in Australia and New Zealand by Hal Leonard Australia Pty Ltd | ABN 13 085 333 713 | www.halleonard.com.au | Used by Permission. All Rights Reserved. Unauthorised Reproduction is Illegal. Extracts of *The Unknown Man: A suspicious death at Somerton beach* courtesy of G.M. Feltus.

A Lothian Children's Book
Published in Australia and New Zealand in 2019
by Hachette Australia
(an imprint of Hachette Australia Pty Limited)
Level 17, 207 Kent Street, Sydney NSW 2000
www.hachette.com.au

10 9 8 7 6 5 4 3 2 1

Copyright © Anna Morgan 2019

A catalogue record for this book is available from the National Library of Australia

ISBN: 978 0 7344 1963 7 (paperback)

Cover design by Amy Daoud
Cover photograph courtesy of Shutterstock
Author photograph by Sister Scout Studio
Text design by Bookhouse, Sydney
Typeset in 12/14.2 pt Adobe Garamond Pro by Bookhouse, Sydney
Printed and bound in Great Britain by Clays Ltd, Elcograf S.p.A.

MIX
Paper from responsible sources
FSC® C001695
www.fsc.org

The paper this book is printed on is certified against the Forest Stewardship Council® Standards. McPherson's Printing Group holds FSC® chain of custody certification SA-COC-005379. FSC® promotes environmentally responsible, socially beneficial and economically viable management of the world's forests.

FOR MUM AND DAD: THANK YOU FOR A CHILDHOOD FULL OF LOVE AND BOOKS.

PART 1
THE MYSTERY

January–March

Why don't anybody feel like crying
For the Somerton somebody with the hazel eyes?
Why don't anybody feel like crying
For the Somerton nobody with the hazel eyes?

THE DRONES

CHAPTER ONE

Ash and I lay in the hammock, our legs intertwined. The light of the day was fading, taking the heat, and our freedom. It was the last day of the summer holidays: the last day of sun and warmth and free hours. Neither of us wanted to move inside.

Ash nudged me with a golden-brown, pink-toenailed foot. I didn't understand how she always got so perfectly tanned over summer, while I ended up itchy and patchy with sunburn.

'Loz, you are not taking this seriously.'

I shut my eyes and stretched. 'No one should be taking things seriously. It's holidays, Ash.'

'Not for long it's not.' Ash moved her cherry Chupa Chup from one side of her mouth to the other, sucking hard. 'Lara, school starts tomorrow. We need a *strategy*.'

'What's to strategise? Another year of being St Margaret's young ladies, avoid their brainwashing as much as we can, boom. Summer again.' It would be the best to have endless holidays. My parents thought I'd get sick of it. I thought they underestimated my capacity for relaxation.

'This is my point,' Ash said. 'If I have to tell my mother that I'm studying with you on a Friday night – and be telling the *truth* – one more time, I'm going to kill myself.' She removed the Chupa Chup from her mouth with a pop. 'Which is why we are going to sign up for the musical with St John's this year.'

I held in a groan. The Year Ten musical was legendary. I guess it made sense in an all-girls school like St Margaret's, where opportunities for interaction with the opposite sex were so rare. I felt my stomach knot as I thought of all the potential for awkwardness and the stress of an extra schedule.

'Hannah did that, right? The musical?'

'Yup.' I shifted slightly at the mention of my sister. I'd hardly heard from her since she left for her gap year: she'd deleted all her social media accounts and hadn't replied to any of my emails. I bet St Margaret's was already completely irrelevant to her.

'So?'

'I don't know. For her it's ancient history.' Hannah had been at the centre of it all, of course: I'd listened to countless teary explanations of rehearsal schedules and scene changes that would have devastating, permanent effects on her love life and friendships.

'Come on, Loz, she must have told you about it. What was it like?'

'It sounded exhausting, actually.'

'A social life, exhausting?'

'Kind of. I'd rather just relax this year, you know?' I didn't understand why Ash always had to shake things up. What was so boring about being comfortable?

'Ah well, perhaps you'll get lucky and won't get through auditions.' Ash crunched the remains of her lollipop into splinters and flicked the white stick out onto her lawn. Her lips were stained a wicked, dark red. I felt a shiver go through me, despite the clinging heat. 'Or maybe not. And we'll finally have some fun this year.'

ADELAIDE RAILWAY STATION, NOVEMBER 1948

On 30 November 1948, a man arrived at the main train station on North Terrace, Adelaide.

Ralph Craig was manning the luggage storage at the time, and at 11.45am his thoughts were firmly fixed on the pickle and cheese sandwich he had brought for his lunchbreak, due in fifteen minutes. So, when the man checked in a plain brown suitcase to the luggage storage, Ralph took little notice, and filled out a luggage tag in a hasty, hunger-fogged daze. Which was a pity for the local police force, who would have appreciated a more detailed recollection later.

The man then bought a connecting ticket to Henley Beach station, which he did not use. Nor did he ever return to collect his suitcase.

Instead, he boarded a bus to Somerton Beach, Glenelg.

It was the last journey of his life.

CHAPTER TWO

Ash became my best friend the same day my heart broke for the first time, in two neat pieces.

It happened like this: lunchtime, Year Four, a sunny day. I search the grounds of St Margaret's Primary, looking for my friends, Isobel and Charmaine. They aren't sitting in our usual spot, a tree by the tuckshop. So I look by the bubblers, by the low brick wall where we sat and ate last year, by the paved area where the Year Fives play foursquare, by the back playground where the Year Six girls sit around and talk. I have this bright blue lunchbox, covered in spaceships. I am intensely proud of this lunchbox because, unlike my uniform, my textbooks, and my teachers' opinions of me, it wasn't inherited from Hannah: I chose it myself. But as I look for my friends, I start to feel self-conscious about the spaceship lunchbox. I can see the older girls looking at me sideways, and even though I've carefully arranged my face into a distracted, casual expression, face-crumpling tears are coming on dangerously fast.

Finally, I see Isobel peeking from behind the side of a building. Her face transforms into a caricature 'O' of shock when she sees me, and I hear Charmaine's high-pitched giggle from around the corner. Relief floods through me, and I run towards them, the spaceship lunchbox banging against my thigh.

But when I get there, they've run away. I see their retreating figures across the oval. I am too dizzy with the joy of finding them to be suspicious. I guess it's a new game, I think, and sprint happily after them.

Only every time I nearly catch them, they move on. My chest is tight, my breathing short, and I am getting light-headed – I still haven't eaten any lunch – finally, I yell at them to stop. And they do, two small figures in the distance, backs to me. They wait til I catch up.

'What's . . . the . . . game . . . we're playing?' I ask, as I get my breath back. They still aren't looking at me.

'Well,' Isobel turns to me, a smile on her face. 'There isn't a *game*. We're running away from you.'

Crack. My heart starts to split down the middle.

Charmaine giggles. 'The game is, I guess, that we don't want to be friends with you.'

Snap. And there it goes, neatly in two.

They leave me there, wheezing, holding my spaceship lunchbox. They do not look back.

I try to process what has happened. But it is hard to focus, since I am suddenly finding it difficult to breathe out. I am getting air in, big gasping mouthfuls of it, but I can't get it out again – instead the air coils in my chest, pulling it tighter and tighter – my heart is beating way faster than it should, black fingers stretch across my vision –

Turns out, heartbreak feels remarkably like an asthma attack.

This may have been because I was having my first asthma attack.

'Here, breathe through this.' A girl appears beside me, holds out an inhaler.

I breathe in. My throat opens up, my vision clears. My heart begins to slow.

I look up: it's the new girl, Ashley, who only arrived this term. She watches me with her head cocked to one side, and a smile that reminds me of the chilly sweetness of icy poles.

'What's your name?'

'Lara,' I say. My legs are too shaky to stand back upright, so I sink to the ground. Through the subsiding panic I absorb this new information: sometimes, I need help to breathe.

'Lara . . .' Ash sits next to me. 'I'm going to call you Loz.'

The spectres of Isobel and Charmaine's laughing faces, their retreating figures, begin to fade.

Ash soothed my asthma that day, and also my broken heart.

Ash and Loz. Always in that order, always together. My mum hated the nickname, and loudly called me '*Lara*, darling,' when Ash was around, but everyone else called me Loz, since everyone else followed Ash's lead. She was one of the lucky ones who grew out of her asthma, only a year or so later. Mine hung around.

There were certain rules to being friends with Ash. When we were younger, the rules were easily defined; we became the queens of the patch of scrub between the line of trees and the primary school car park. No boys (conveniently ignoring the fact we were in an all-girls school), no adults, girls only allowed to come in with permission. Ash decided who had permission: Lucy Fairly, because she could do French braids; Amy Lee, because she could do a backflip from standing; and Sophie Bell, because she had a broken ankle and let us race on her crutches. Isobel and Charmaine didn't audition for entry, but they watched us from the other side of the trees, and I viewed them from my place with Ash with a distant pity.

I was grateful Ash hadn't seemed to notice that I had no special skill, no reason to be allowed to stand next to her.

I thought if maybe I stayed beside her, she'd never look at me straight on and realise.

As we got older, we settled into our position somewhere comfortably in the middle of the mix of groups at high school – friendly with enough people we'd always have someone to sit with if one of us was away, but essentially a self-contained unit: Ash and Loz. The rules also became more complicated: you must order skinny lattes, not regular – though if I was on my own I preferred long blacks; you must reject all suggestions while shopping that, 'Oh, this would look better on *you*' (correct answer – 'No, it's totally *your* colour'); and you must agree to be Team Taylor, not Team Katy.

Occasionally I would slip up. I'd know this because, on some days, I would turn up to school, say hello, and get a locker slammed in my face and a death glare. It was like a switch flicked off, and never explained beyond a vague, 'You *know* what it was'.

Sometimes I did know: it would be the sound of my own essay being read in English as an example (Ash's smile growing tighter and thinner with every word, eyes straight ahead and not meeting my anxious glance). Or I'd buy fish and chips on a Friday and carelessly offer some to Ash. When we were younger, I followed the rules because I was desperate to keep Ash's approval. I thought of those lonely gut-twisting days as a kind of friendship-tax, an exchange for the rest of our time together. As we grew up, long after Isobel and Charmaine had gone on to different high schools and I could hardly remember what they looked like, I kept following Ash's rules – maybe out of habit, maybe because part of me was scared she might one day decide to run away.

Besides, Ash was *fun*. She had a way of bouncing into a room and meeting my gaze with a wide-eyed, raised eyebrow look that would always make me grin. We made up dances to

Lorde songs and performed them in her living room, and Ash locked eyes with me as she lip-synched with ridiculous facial expressions, while I collapsed laughing, helpless, on the floor.

She had a weakness for cherry Chupa Chups (mine: Fruit Tingles, especially the multicoloured ones), and loved the way they stained her mouth dark red, so she could truthfully tell our Vice-Principal she wasn't violating uniform code as she really *wasn't* wearing any lipstick. I became more fun with her, too. She got me to sneak into our first ever gig; we snuck in through the beer garden and into the pub, and I was too busy trying to figure out if anyone could tell we were underage to enjoy the music – that is, until Ash grabbed my arm and pulled me into a crazy, limb-flailing dance, and I forgot to be nervous.

So that was Ash and me: a convoluted, twisted mix of expectations and history, cut through by our eyes meeting as we heard our song played on the radio.

I guess you'd call it friendship.

CHAPTER THREE

I stood at the top of the hill, looking down at my park. The air was heavy, the heat of the day clinging stubbornly, despite the coming cool change. The grass of the oval made a thousand sharp shadows in the sunset light, and the bark on the stretched branches of the gum trees lit up luminous gold.

And there was the tree, the one I always thought of as mine. The single fir, deep green and out of place in its little hollow at the bottom of the hill. I shrugged off my hoodie as I jogged down, and dropped it and my water bottle under its lower branches.

Ash's voice from earlier echoed in my mind, her determination to shake up our routine – as if it needed changing. Then there was my own uncertainty about tomorrow, the first day back, the last school year before the race to university applications began for real.

I pictured myself emptying all these things out of my mind, and leaving them in an untidy heap under the tree next to my hoodie.

I took my first long strides out onto the oval, and felt my breathing settle. The grass was surprisingly soft after a long summer, and the ground cushioned my runners, each step rolling from the heel to the ball of my foot with easy pleasure. I felt my muscles align, and I wasn't separate parts anymore, of ankles (too wide), legs (too short), torso (too long), arms (gangly), but all connected – a whole, a *body* designed for this, moving through the air with speed and grace. I gave myself to each breath, each step, to sun and grass and the smell of the coming storm.

I was alive, to be alive; running, for the joy of it.

There was no one else in the park, it was too close to sunset. On the fourth lap, my breathing started to catch and wheeze, my legs grew heavy, slow. I was out of shape, and the air was thick. Instinctively I pictured my inhaler, in case I needed it, next to my water bottle under the tree. I really should have taken some as a preventative before the run – oh well, I was almost there.

I rounded the last corner, and saw a girl under my tree.

A girl who was wearing my hoodie.

Hannah, I thought, for one breathless second. I pushed my legs one screaming gear faster – really, I needed to train more over the holidays – and ran closer. Could it be Hannah, back from her trip with no warning, to surprise me in the park? It would be just like her. I could almost see it, Hannah pushing back her long brown curls from her face, grinning widely, pleased with herself for pulling off the surprise, her white skin even paler than usual after a European winter. She'd jump up, laughing at my shock, and knock me over in a ferocious hug.

I put on speed, feeling a smile spread across my face – but this girl was not Hannah, and she didn't leap up. She lay under the tree, legs crossed in front of her, her black hair shot through with a streak of purple.

Not Hannah. Of course not.

My disappointment thudded inside me. I needed water. I fixed a glare on the hoodie-stealer and walked closer.

'Hello.' The girl shook back the overlong sleeves and gave a lazy wave. 'I'm Kate. You're quite fast, you know. Do you do athletics?'

I continued to glare. The girl – Kate, I guess – kept smiling.

'Uh . . . that's *mine*,' I said, finally.

Kate looked from me, down to the hoodie, and back again. 'Oh, I thought it might be . . . you don't mind, do you? It gets cool when you're sitting in the shade. And I figured we'd know each other soon enough, anyway.'

'What?' Was she crazy?

'Your running shorts . . . St Margaret's, right?' Kate spoke kindly, as if she was being understanding of my slow response.

I looked down at the pale green embroidery of the school crest on my shorts. 'Yeah . . . but how did you . . . ?' I stopped. 'Look. *You're wearing my hoodie.*'

'I'm starting Year Ten there tomorrow. How about you?'

I blew a strand of sweaty hair out of my eyes. I didn't answer.

Kate's smile flickered for a second. She reached across and offered up my water bottle. 'Here, I refilled it for you.' The water bottle shook a little as she held it out, and I noticed that her arm was covered in thin interlocking lines of blue ink.

Maybe she wasn't crazy. Just nervous. I took the water bottle.

'Is this how you always greet new people?' I asked, when I'd taken a few mouthfuls. 'Because stealing my stuff doesn't seem like the best first impression.'

'I wasn't *stealing*. Borrowing. Have a seat?' Kate patted the ground next to her. When I didn't move, she continued, 'Look, I just moved here. I saw you running as I walked home and thought it might be worth meeting *one* person before tomorrow. Sit, please?'

I sat cautiously down on the grass. 'I'm Lara. And yep, I'm in Year Ten too. What's on your arm?' I asked.

Kate pushed the sleeve of the hoodie back up. 'A kind of map, I guess. I just moved . . . *there.*' She pointed to a tiny square house with an X, near her elbow. 'Don't know where everything is yet.' She offered her arm to me. 'How did I do?'

I looked closer. The map was intricate, illustrated like something you'd find at the start of a fantasy novel. There was a house, the park with sketched triangles that could be trees, a tiny train where the closest station was, complete with arrows pointing to skyscrapers. Everything was labelled in spiky, stylised script.

'It's beautiful,' I said. I noticed a numbered tram pointing to a low, squat building completely inked in as a solid block. 'Hey, that's my tram line! Is that school?'

Kate looked where I was pointing. 'Yeah. I was in a dramatic mood when I drew this, I guess. I'm hoping the actual building is slightly more attractive. So where's your place?'

I followed the slim pen tracks of roads, tilting my head to orientate myself. I found my street and hovered my finger a few inches above Kate's arm. 'Somewhere here.'

Kate pulled out a pen and drew a small L on the spot. 'I'm just on the other side of the park – over here.' She pointed to a K up near her wrist.

'So, you just moved here?' I asked.

'Yeah. I'm sure I won't be the only new girl jumping into St Margaret's just before the VCE years – your academic results are quite the drawcard.' Kate glanced down at her phone. 'Crap, it's already eight-thirty.' She jumped up to leave. 'I'm so late. See you tomorrow, Lara.' She took a look at her arm and turned towards the road.

'Oh – okay, see you –' I turned to call after her, and Kate raised an arm to wave as she disappeared over the hill. There was a flash of purple as her hair caught the last of the sunlight, and she was gone. Weird.

I lay back down on the grass, trying to decide if I liked her or not. At least she was interesting. A rush of wind bent the branches of the fir tree – the cool change. I shivered as the last of the heat from my run left.

Damn. Kate still had my hoodie.

CHAPTER FOUR

Postcard: The Old City, Dubrovnik, Croatia, at night.

(Now used as Kings Landing in the popular Game of Thrones series! Visit our website for a themed walking tour)

Dear Lara,
I repeat: don't show this to Mum and Dad, OK? They think I'm still in Paris.
*   I attach to this postcard a splodge of klobasa-zeli-polevka –*
aka, sausage in a stew, Croatia's specialty. Lick it, please.
I hope it tastes as delicious after a trip through the postal system (I am also wearing some on my shirt, saving that for later). Croatia's men, so far, are about as subtle as their national dish. I'm spending lots of time alone looking soulful and reading novels. It's the best.
*   H xx*
*   P.S. PLEASE start borrowing my clothes while I'm gone. Last outfit Ashley tagged you in on Instagram was doing you no favours.*

I grinned as I read Hannah's postscript, curled in tiny letters around the top of the address. I sat back on my seat in the tram and closed my eyes for a second, imagining her eating stew with a view of the ocean, surrounded by different languages and people. It made my first-day nerves fade a bit, thinking of that faraway place, even if I was annoyed at her for experiencing all this without me. Not to mention annoyed at her for choosing to keep in touch via secret postcards – romantic, yes; practical, no. I'd had to become extra vigilant checking the post before Dad got home each day. And so like Hannah to pick a format with no right of reply.

I pulled out my phone and wrote her another email.

TO: Hannah_tacocat@gmail.com
FROM: laylor.l@stmargarets.vic.edu.au

Croatia sounds great. Avoid the boys = good plan. Maybe avoid the stew too? My sample had distinct cardboard notes. First day back here, so don't worry, I am in no danger of unsubtle men. L x

P.S. If you're snooping around on Instagram, why not reactivate your account and message me? Or, I don't know, reply to this?

I looked up as we passed the service station – it was almost my stop. I deleted the postscript and clicked send, adding to the collection of unread notifications in her inbox, probably.

I shoved the brown-splodged postcard and my phone into my schoolbag and pushed the button for my stop.

Ash must have missed the tram this morning – she normally didn't make the early one, but had said she would for the first day. I didn't really mind, it was kind of peaceful, going through the first-day buzz alone, part of me still with Hannah in Croatia. I left the tram and began weaving my way with the rest of the St Margaret's girls towards the student entrance.

Down the hill from the student gate there was the chaos of the official school entrance, open today only: boxy black or grey cars inched under the stone archway and around the drive, ushered by staff in fluoro vests. Only new parents (parents in need of an impression) could use that entrance: a little reassurance that the hefty school fees were worth it, I guess.

I squinted towards the new girls emerging from the shiny cars, scanning for a flash of purple hair. I still wasn't sure if I'd be seeing the strange girl from the park – Kate – or if the whole conversation had been a bizarre heat-induced hallucination. Although I *did* want that hoodie back, hallucination or not.

I shrugged my schoolbag more securely over one shoulder and walked through the student gate to the grounds, behind two chattering Year Eight girls who punctured each sentence with squeals of excitement at their reunion.

Something strange caught my eye – a small wisp of smoke, the only grey smear in the blue sky. I followed it down to the shadows of the old wooden benches on the far side of the oval. It looked like someone was there. A man. A stranger.

A stranger who was *smoking*. On *school grounds*.

On a whim, I sped up, dodged the trail of girls filling the school grounds and slipped off the path to walk behind the other side of the benches. I looked through the gaps between the seats, hidden from his view. Yes, definitely a man, and definitely someone new. I caught slices of him: long, thin, graceful hand holding the cigarette, rumpled brown hair, a jacket with elbow patches – elbow patches, really? It was like he'd dressed up for the role of teacher in a play.

I realised I wasn't the only one who had noticed the smoking. Wilson, head of landscaping, was making a determined beeline for the man across the oval, grey head bent, practically quivering with suppressed fury.

'Sir! Excuse me! You can't have that here.'

'What? Oh, hello.' The man offered a vague smile and stuck out his hand.

Wilson ignored it.

The man let his hand drop, and then scrunched some hair off his face. He followed Wilson's steady gaze to his cigarette. 'Oh . . . the cigarette, you mean? Sorry, first-day nerves – I'm David, new teacher.'

'You still can't do that here.'

'Really? I mean, we are outside . . .'

Wilson remained impassive.

'Right,' said the teacher, dropping his hand. For a second it looked like he was going to drop the cigarette on the lush, neatly trimmed grass at his feet – Wilson made an odd high-pitched noise in his throat – but then he saw the bin standing nearby and stubbed it out on the metal edge. 'All good?'

Wilson gave a snort that could have possibly indicated approval, spun round and walked briskly off. The new teacher watched him go, his lips twitching with amusement. I held back my own smile. Whoever he was, he was clearly not the usual St Margaret's type.

'Loz! I've been looking everywhere for you – where have you *been*?' Ash's voice carried from the path behind me. The new teacher glanced around at the noise, and stared through the seats, right to where I was standing. Crap.

I spun round, jogged up to Ash, heart beating a sharp rhythm in my chest. Had he seen me?

'You were *supposed* to get here early and grab us lockers.' Ash grabbed my arm and marched towards the building.

'Um, hello, good morning, yes I *did* catch the early tram alone, no problem at all, you're welcome.'

Ash groaned slightly. 'Well, obviously I ended up sleeping in, but only because I knew *you* would be on time. No point both of us making that sacrifice.'

'There is definitely some flawed logic here, Ash . . .' She was joking, so I pushed down the irritation that she had expected me to pick up the slack and tried to keep hold of the strangeness of the new teacher, that heart-stopping moment when it seemed he caught me staring. I opened my mouth to tell Ash, but stopped – I couldn't figure out how to describe it without her shrieking that I was a stalker.

'Ah, let's just get inside.' Ash linked her arm with mine and led us to the door, blocked by a group of Year Nines crowded around one girl's phone. '*Excuse* us.'

As Ash cleared the way with her death stare, I turned and looked back towards the oval.

I could just make out the smudge of grey rising to the sky, the smoke of a new cigarette.

SOMERTON BEACH, ADELAIDE, NOVEMBER 1948

November 30 was a warm night in Adelaide, and Mr and Mrs Lyons were sluggish on their evening stroll. They stopped to look down from the high-walled footpath to the beach below, observing the man slumped back on the sand. The sunset cast an oppressive orange haze, and the smell of the sea and their own sweat mingled unpleasantly in the air.

'Look at him, John,' said Mrs Lyons, pointing to the figure.

The man lay on the beach, his head and neck propped up against the esplanade wall. A small trail of smoke drifted from his cigarette, held in the corner of his mouth.

'He isn't even swatting the mosquitoes!'

She was right. A cloud of the insects buzzed greedily around the figure, landing on his hands, his face, the bit of exposed neck between his collar and hair.

'He must be very drunk, do you think?' replied Mr Lyons. He snatched a mosquito out of the air next to his ear, crushed it in his palm into a smear of blood and legs. 'Or perhaps he's even dead – dead drunk!' Mr Lyons laughed, a loud, braying sound.

Mrs Lyons' gaze drifted back to the man. She was irritated by the heat, by the mosquitoes, by the noise of her husband's laugh.

There was something about the man that was irritating her too. Something strange about the set of his shoulders, propped up like he was. He was wearing a full three-piece suit on the beach in summer. Clearly not from around here. Ridiculous, drunk, foreigner. Something odd about his shoes, too. They were spotless, so polished they reflected the evening sun: twin patches of gleaming light. Not the shoes of someone who'd been trudging through sand.

As she was watching the man raised one arm up just above his shoulder, then let it fall to his side. Like a salute, she thought, or a wave, or, perhaps, a signal for help.

'See – there you go. So drunk he can't even properly work his arm to smoke his cigarette.' Mr Lyons laughed again. 'Shall we, dear?' he said, looking ahead down the footpath and offering his arm.

Yes. Someone else will see, Mrs Lyons thought, glancing back along the empty esplanade walk behind her. She resolved to think no more of the man, and took her husband's arm. Together they turned from the beach and moved into the suburban quiet, leaving the figure alone on the expanse of pale sand.

The sun set, leaching the last of the colour from the beach. Wave after wave broke gently on the shore. The tide was coming in.

The half-smoked cigarette of the man fell from his slack mouth, onto the lapel of his expensive, inappropriately warm jacket. He gave one slow, gentle exhale of smoke into the salty air.

CHAPTER FIVE

Thankfully there were still two lockers together.

'First selfie of the year!' Ash pulled me close and got out her phone. I gave the camera a long-suffering smile, but Ash nudged me in the ribs at the last second, so I let out a real laugh.

'Hey, that's actually a great shot.' I said, when she showed me the photo. I was cracking up, hair falling in my face, while Ash looked wryly into the lens like she was sharing a joke with the camera.

'I know – your hair looks brilliant there. Maybe one for the locker door.' Ash said. She was already transferring a selection of photos from her diary onto the inside of her locker, holding them down with washi tape. There were lots from our Polaroid camera phase of a few summers back, and a few older gems we'd printed over the years.

'Not the Year Six graduation one!' I groaned. We'd gone for matching crop tops, a decision I deeply regretted.

'Are you kidding? That's practically an historical document at this point.' Ash added it to the display and stood back to survey her handiwork. 'I call it the gradual glow-up. This is going to be our best year yet, I can feel it.'

I couldn't help but catch her optimism. I decided to share the odd encounter on the oval after all. 'Come on,'

I said, 'you've got to finish this before assembly. And I've got something to tell you on the way.'

We walked quickly down the corridor towards our last class of the day, dodging groups of girls collecting books and slamming lockers. I glanced down again at my timetable: *History, Mr D. Grant*. A new name – it had to be him. David, he'd said to Wilson. David Grant.

'Eurgh, Lara, slow down,' said Ash. 'He already knows you're super keen, you don't need to be first into the classroom.'

I stopped, and Ash walked into the back of me.

'Hey –'

'What do you mean, he already knows I'm "keen"?' I asked.

'Like you said, he totally caught you spying on him this morning. And Riley said he was *super* friendly in their class in first period – bet he's already got you picked as a favourite.'

'Eurgh, I hope not.' I wished Ash wouldn't talk about it like that – spying made me sound so creepy. And she clearly cared about the teacher too, if she'd already been asking other girls about him. 'Anyway, sounds like you've been tracking him closer than I have.'

Ash held my gaze for a beat, then laughed. I fell into step next to her. 'You know,' Ash added, 'if he wasn't so ancient, I'd have a crush on him. I had a good view of him in assembly this morning. He's got that charming Ryan Gosling thing going on.'

He didn't look anything like Ryan Gosling. I forced myself to relax and go with it. 'Mmm, too scruffy and untidy for that, I think.'

'You don't really do crushes though, hey?' Ash linked arms with me. 'My little innocent.'

She was right, of course – I couldn't really count the two-week summer thing with a family friend as a 'relationship', since we'd only had one hurried kiss where I'd left my eyes open accidentally. I'd learnt to play it down too, since Ash didn't even have that level of experience. There was a lot riding on the musical this year: I wondered if the St John's boys would be able to carry the weight of our expectations.

We turned the corner into the corridor of the History class-room. At the end there were two figures silhouetted against the window, talking. One had a distinctive scraped-back grey bun. Ash's grip on my arm increased to vice-like.

'Ms Drummond,' she hissed. 'She's the director of the musical. I'll go ask about auditions.'

'But we know auditions are next week, right?' I asked, though I knew the answer. Ash had checked the date about eight times when she wrote our names on the sign-in sheet at lunchtime.

'Loz, of *course* I know when they are. But you never pass up a chance to make an impression.' Ash piled her History books and pencil case unceremoniously on top of mine and combed her fingers through her fringe. 'Save me a seat, will you? I'll be back.' She took a deep breath, and took off down the corridor. 'Ms Drummond?'

I watched her try to walk casually, but quick enough to catch the teacher. I could almost see the waves of eagerness pulsing from her figure. Nothing could be casual with her.

The books were slipping out of my arms as I tried to push past the classroom door, almost causing an avalanche of folders and pencil cases. Someone pulled it from inside and I tumbled into the room. 'Thanks –'

It was Kate, the new girl from the park. 'Lara!' She opened the door fully, stretching out her arm, and pointed to the L on the map she'd drawn there. It was mostly faded now. 'Thank God, someone I know.'

'Hey,' I replied. Kate looked different in the St Mags uniform, though I could still see the purple streak in her hair pulled back in her ponytail.

She rescued a few books off the top of my pile, saw Ash's name emblazoned in Posca pen on the front. 'So, you deliver stationery now, too?'

I dropped a mock-curtsey. 'I am a woman of many talents.'

'At least you're cheerfully exploited, I guess.' Kate pushed herself up onto the edge of an empty desk near the front of the room, legs swinging, and dropped my books beside her.

The class was almost full already, girls sitting in clusters with chairs turned so they could keep talking. It was our first class with this guy, and new teachers were rare, male ones even more so. Everyone was chatting slightly louder than usual.

'Take this seat, if you like?' Kate patted the empty spot next to her, by the window.

I hesitated, and glanced behind me to the door, where Ash could return at any moment.

'Something wrong?' Kate asked.

'No . . .' I sighed. We are almost sixteen, I reminded myself, not twelve. This shouldn't actually matter. I sprang up onto the desk next to Kate. I half-twisted to the row behind, where there was a spare seat next to Lisa Cheng. 'Do you mind, Lisa?' I asked, Ash's books hovering in my hand above the spot. She nodded okay, and immediately returned to a heated discussion with the girl on her other side. I dropped the books and Ash's pencil case on the desk.

'Great,' Kate said.

'So, how's your first day going?' I asked her. 'Get any grief for your hair colour or homemade tattoo yet?'

'Oh, only from every second teacher. I've got a lost new girl, puppy-dog look thing going on to get me out of trouble. Think it will work for another few weeks.' Kate turned to face me. 'Now, what are your theories?'

'Theories?'

'New teacher, plus he's fairly hot for someone that age? You have to have some theories. Right now, I'm going with . . . he used to be a foreign correspondent, top-secret location, but lost his job because he violated his visa.'

I stopped worrying about Ash long enough to consider this. 'Why would he violate his visa?'

Kate paused, her fingers tapping out a rapid rhythm on her desk as she thought. 'Okay, either – noble journalistic integrity, giving up his safety *for the sake of the story*, or,' she held up one finger, 'sordid love affair with government official's daughter, slash wife, to get to key documents.' She opened her hand to me. 'Take your pick.'

'Sordid affair,' I decided. 'But initiated by the daughter slash wife, so that she could control *his* story in the Western media.'

Kate let her jaw drop in mock-surprise. 'He was duped?'

'Doesn't it fit? All's fair in love, war and high school History, right?'

Mr Grant swept into the room, his arms full of folders. He kicked the door shut behind him with one foot. Kate and I slid off our desks and into our seats, the other girls swung around. The noise in the classroom settled to a low hum.

Up close, he wasn't old, but he wasn't young either – one of those vague ages between thirty and forty I could never guess. His hair was sticking up in different directions, like he'd just run his hands through it. Not *exactly* hot, then. But there was something magnetic about the way he took up space at the front of the classroom, a fizzing energy that drew me in. And there were those eyes . . . a colour I'd never really seen before, an intense pale grey-blue.

Mr Grant ignored us, and leant against the teacher's desk, flipping through a folder. He looked up suddenly, making instant and fierce eye contact. 'Lara Laylor?'

I started. 'Um. Yes?'

He went back to his folder. 'And – Katherine Wong?'

'Kate. Definitely Kate,' she corrected.

He nodded absently and returned to the folder, flipping the page over and back. I saw headshots of girls in school uniform, next to the roll. He must be trying to learn our names.

The second bell rang for the start of class.

'Right, okay. Welcome to History, everyone. I'm Mr Grant.' He perched on the edge of his desk. 'Are we all here? Anyone missing, that I need to . . . ah.' He frowned down at the roll in his hand, as if he was trying to decide whether to actually call our names or not. The breeze tugged at the edges of the papers he'd piled on the desk behind him, and he hastily moved a book to keep them in place. 'Everyone's here, right?'

The door opened again, and Ash hurried in, breathless and flushed. I felt a twinge of guilt in my stomach and tried to read her face – but she hadn't seen me sitting next to Kate yet. She looked dreamy, eyes wide and faraway. The conversation had gone well, it looked like.

'Sorry, sorry,' said Ash, primly. 'I got caught up talking to another member of staff about some of my extracurricular activities.'

I saw Kate roll her eyes in my peripheral vision and held in a smile.

'Oh, uh, that's fine . . .' he glanced back at his list, 'Ashley, yes? Take a seat.'

Ash scanned the room and saw me sitting next to Kate. The flushed, dreamy look dropped immediately. I groaned inwardly and waved at the desk behind me, next to Lisa. Ash sat down without a word.

'Sorry – no seats together left,' I whispered. Ash didn't look at me. She delicately picked up her notebook and arranged it to line up precisely with the side of the desk. Some pens had fallen half-out of her pencil case when I put it on the desk; she pulled them free with a short sigh and sharply zipped up the case.

I did some rapid calculations, trying to guess how long this freeze-out would last. Maybe not as long as the Year Eight wore-the-same-bathers-by-accident fiasco, probably longer than the bought-hot-chips-for-lunch-when-she-was-on-the-Paleo-diet punishment. Although she *had* asked me to save her a seat, and I knew she didn't know Kate yet . . . I tried to make eye contact, but she was staring straight ahead.

'Right. I'm going to start us off doing things a bit differently this term, so you can put away your textbooks for now, thanks. See, I think the thing to remember is that history isn't about truth – what "really" happened – and lies. It's not about facts and dates. It's about mysteries.

'History is like a map to the past, but it's a map that hasn't been filled in, a map with lots of gaps in it. It's about the gaps between all the things we know, and what happens when we try to fill those gaps. That's where the magic happens. Because some of those mysteries of the past can *never* be solved – unless you can prove me wrong.'

I heard Ash let out a snort of impatience behind me. But I couldn't help it. He had me hooked.

'So, that's what we're starting today, your mystery assignment,' Mr Grant continued. 'I've got ten projects here, and you'll be working in pairs.' I immediately looked over my shoulder to Ash, but she was still avoiding my eyes. I felt a knot of worry in my stomach.

Mr Grant rummaged through the folders on his desk and picked out a stack of manila folders. 'Here's how we're going to pick who does what.' He turned to face us.

'All of you, close your eyes,' Mr Grant said. 'I'm going to read you the start of these stories. Once they've caught your attention, stand up. First to stand gets the project. Don't stand up too early – you only get one pick.'

There was some shuffling and groans, but Mr Grant waited it out. I looked around, Kate's eyes were already closed beside me. I shut mine too.

Gradually the noise died down to silence, except for the rush of wind through the open window, breathing excitement into the room.

Mr Grant spoke. 'A couple, Mr and Mrs Lyons, walk along Somerton Beach in Adelaide, 1948, and see a man lying motionless on the sand. The next morning, Mr Lyons goes for a run and sees the man is still there. He calls the police. The man is pronounced dead.'

I hear Kate's chair scrape next to me. The rest of the room is quiet. I slit my eyes open; she's the only one standing. I can see a few others with eyes half open, planning to coordinate with their friends to get the same assignment, I guess. But no one knows Kate yet, no one except me. And I can't see Ash.

'He's well-dressed, neatly presented, and has no injuries. There are no signs of a struggle. His autopsy shows he is in very good physical shape, with no signs of heart failure. The coroner cannot find any cause of death, and concludes it must be an unknown poison.'

I strained my ears for another chair scraping, but nothing so far. I can almost feel Ash's glare heating my back. She probably thinks this is stupid.

'His description matches no known missing person reports, and his dental records, when sent out, do not match any Australian records.'

Mr Grant paused. I pushed back my chair a little, ready to spring to my feet if I wanted.

'All the labels were removed from his clothing, and there were no forms of identification on his person. This man, found alone on the beach, had gone to some lengths to hide his identity – or someone else had.'

I thought I heard the call of a seagull in the distance. I pictured a lonely figure lying in the sand, and felt goose-bumps spring up on my arms.

I heard whispering from across the room – was someone else about to take the assignment? I jumped to my feet, and heard other chairs scrape around me. I opened my eyes to see half the room were standing up. I felt a stab of disappointment. I already wanted to hear the end of this man's story.

Mr Grant clapped his hands and sat back on the desk. 'I hadn't even gotten to the best parts of that one yet! But tell me, Kate, why did you stand up so early?'

'You said he was found dead in Adelaide.'

Mr Grant started to smile. 'And?'

Kate shrugged. 'My grandparents are from Adelaide, I've been to visit a few times. It's a beautiful city, but kind of . . . twisted. Gran always says that they have less crime, but it's *weird* crime. Like that one time someone broke into the zoo and killed all the animals. I knew it'd be a good story once you mentioned the city.'

'Excellent. Well, you'll be well equipped for this research then. And second to jump up was, I think, your neighbour.' He smiled at me.

'Lara,' I supplied. I heard Ash snort from behind me. She was still sitting. I turned my head slightly and saw her arms were folded.

'Oh yes, Lara.' It sounded like he'd remembered me. Had he recognised me from this morning? I looked down quickly to avoid eye contact. He walked forward and dropped the folder across our desk.

'The rest of you, eyes shut again. Don't worry, many more mysteries to be solved.' He spoke over the noise as girls took their seats. 'Next: it's 1872, and a ship is found floating in the ocean. The tables are still set for dinner, there are no signs of a disturbance, but no one is left on board . . .'

Kate and I bent our heads together and opened the folder. The first page showed a grainy black-and-white picture of a man lying on a table, cropped at his head and shoulders. His forehead was crinkled, like he was having a disturbing dream. Underneath was a faded picture of a beach, showing wooden stairs leading up from the sand to an esplanade above. Next to the bottom of the stairs was a red X.

Around us, assignments were being given out, faster now that everyone knew the drill. The classroom started to buzz as everyone paired up. I checked over my shoulder for Ash. She was still sitting behind me, still staring out the window. No point trying to talk to her yet.

A shadow passed in front of our desk. Mr Grant had spotted Ash. He walked around Kate and me, and sat on the windowsill right in Ash's line of sight. I swung half around in my chair and watched, anxiously.

'Ashley Broadway, is it?'

Ash nodded.

'You didn't find any of my mysteries enticing?' Mr Grant said. His hair ruffled in the wind, and his jacket blew out for a second, like wings.

'Not really.' She waited. 'Sorry,' she added as an afterthought.

'Can I ask what's brought on this lack of curiosity?'

Ash glanced around. Other than Kate and I, a few other girls had stopped talking to listen. She had an audience. And I knew Ash *loved* an audience.

'It's not really how we normally do History here.'

Mr Grant's mouth twitched. He looked like he was enjoying this. 'Is that so? Please, do educate me on how it works here – I'd love to hear from someone who is late to class because they're so involved in . . . ah, all your extracurricular activities, wasn't it?'

Ash's cheeks reddened. 'Well, I don't think my parents are paying over twenty grand a year for me to investigate things that should be a Buzzfeed list of "Creepiest Historical Mysteries".'

Woah. I'd never heard Ash be that rude to a teacher's face. There was a collective indrawn breath around the classroom – everyone was definitely listening now. I felt nervous for Ash. This was unknown territory.

'You don't think history is mysterious?'

Ash rocked her chair back on all four legs and glanced at me, then back to him. 'I think any online source will give all of these "mysteries" boring solutions within about twelve seconds of searching. And I don't think any of it is going to help with the VCE curriculum next year.'

Mr Grant raised his eyebrows. 'It sounds to me like you're in a pretty good position then: give me a solution to any of these assignments and you walk away with an A.' His smile disappeared. 'However, your parents may be reassured to know I will be marking you on your research tactics, powers of argument and use of primary and secondary sources. And your marks this year will determine whether you have the option of the accelerated History program next year.' He took a moment to scan the classroom, still unsmiling. 'So you'd better get started, all of you.'

There was a rustling noise as everyone turned back to their assignments. I stayed where I was, willing Ash to make eye contact with me so I could give her a sympathetic look. She was staring back down at her desk, face unreadable.

Mr Grant glanced from her to Kate and me, the only ones still watching. 'Since I take it you're now on board, Ashley, you can join these two. I may be biased, but this is my favourite of the mysteries, and I would very much like to have it solved.' He clapped Ash gently on the shoulder. She started a little. 'Looks like you're going on the search for the Somerton Man too.'

Year Ten Mystery Assignment

Teacher: Mr Grant
The Somerton Man
Folder One: The Man On The Beach

Physical identifiers

- 5'11"/180cm tall
- Estimated age between 40–50
- Hazel eyes
- Teeth: 16 missing. No dentures, though it looked as if he normally wore them. He also had hypodontia – no incisor teeth (unusual, present in <2% population)
- Ears: upper cymba is bigger than the lower cavum (unusual, present in <2% population)
- Hands: smooth, unused to manual labour
- Complexion: tanned skin, of European appearance
- Muscular, well-built and healthy, with very developed calf muscles

Cause of death/autopsy

- Time of death estimated to be about 2am on 1 December 1948
- Some food – probably a potato pasty – found in stomach
- Spleen was about three times larger than normal
- Autopsy found a healthy heart, and no indication of the cause of death
- An unknown poison was suggested as cause of death, although no trace of poison was detected

Clothing and possessions

- He was dressed in a three-piece suit, tailor made and high quality

- Shoes were highly polished and well cared for; there was no sand on his shoes
- All the labels had been removed from his clothing – sometimes damaging the clothing in the process
- Cigarette: one found half-smoked on his suit
- Army Club box of cigarettes containing seven Kensitas cigarettes (NB. It was common at the time to keep the empty box of an expensive brand and fill it with cheaper cigarettes. In this case, the opposite is true: Kensitas are more expensive and Army Club cheaper)

The suitcase

- Found weeks later unclaimed in the luggage store at the station, connected to the man by a distinctive piece of thread found on the clothing of the body and in the case
- Contained personal items like toiletries, a dressing gown and slippers, and some clothing that could only be made in the USA
- Most clothing also had labels removed
- Also contained: an electrician's screwdriver, a sharpened knife, scissors, drafting pencils, and a stencil brush often used by ship officers to stencil cargo

Key quotes

'The report I have received indicates –
1) that the identity of the deceased is quite unknown;
2) that his death was not natural;
3) that it was probably caused by poison;
4) that it almost certainly was not accidental.'

Coroner Thomas Erskine Cleland, 18 June 1949

'I came to the opinion, taking all the circumstances into account, that death was almost certainly not natural, and in all probability that some poison had been taken, with suicidal intent.'

Professor John 'Burt' Cleland, 18 June 1949

'There is no fact that I know of which points towards suicide and abolishes the possibility of murder.'

Detective Sergeant Lionel Leane, 18 June 1949

CHAPTER SIX

The new Performing Arts Centre had been finished over summer, with a huge curved metal facade that was meant to imitate stage curtains. On the first day back, one girl said it looked like 'a stumpy clam', and the name had stuck: less than two weeks later, we all now thought of it as 'The Clam'.

But inside, away from the showy architecture, it felt different: quiet and dark. There was a sort of magic to all that empty space, like it was haunted by the ghosts of a future audience.

I glanced at Ash as we climbed the stairs to the stage. She didn't look nervous. Her face was set, focused on some vision she was playing in her head.

Ms Drummond was auditioning us. I'd never had contact with her but heard she was strict, and either a genius or a dictator depending on which girls you asked. She was definitely under pressure to direct a production up to a standard worthy of the new Arts Centre.

'Whenever you're ready, girls.' It didn't sound like a voice that was used to being kept waiting.

'Ashley Broadway and Lara Laylor, auditioning for any role,' called out Ash in a clear, strong voice. We'd had the option to audition in small groups or alone, and Ash had put us down to go together. I think she knew I might back out otherwise.

The first section was a role-play showing conflict and resolution, and Ash had decided we'd do two sisters wanting to wear the same dress to a party. I felt stilted as I said my lines. Ash was the older sister, the one who owned the dress in the role-play, and as she was groaning in frustration at me, I wasn't sure if it was part of her acting or if she was angry at my awkwardness.

'Okay, that's great,' Ms Drummond interrupted me mid-apology. 'Now, let's hear you sing.'

Here was where I was more confident. We belted out one of the hymns we had to sing in assembly (easy to sing, even for Ash's shaky tone), and I sang loud to cover her wavering voice. My voice wasn't amazing, but it was solid.

'Stop!' Ms Drummond held up her hand. We trickled to a halt.

'Okay girls, that's great, thank you. Last question. As you will know, this year's production is *Into the Woods*. So my final question, what is your favourite fairytale?'

I glanced at Ash, but her face was blank. Still recovering from the singing portion of the audition, I guess.

'Uh . . . *The Little Mermaid*,' I offered.

'Why?'

Because it's the first one I could think of under the pressure of these theatre lights, and I haven't considered this question since I was nine and desperate to have red hair. 'Because . . . because she's able to risk everything, all for a crazy hope. She's brave.'

'You're trying out for a musical and choose the classic voiceless heroine – how interesting,' she said, softly. 'Thank you . . .' she glanced down at her notes, 'Lara.' Ms Drummond turned to Ash. 'And?'

Ash shook herself slightly. I could see her mind whirring, like she was trying to figure out what Ms Drummond wanted to hear. She wanted this even more badly than I'd realised. 'Well, in the musical I like the character of the Witch the best.'

There was a pause. 'Ashley . . . Broadway, yes?'

'Yes.'

'You have a good name for theatre. But that's not the question I asked.'

Ash bit her lip in annoyance. 'I don't particularly like any of the fairytales more than the others. I think that's kind of the point, in the end, that all the happy endings fail in some way. The Witch is the only one who knew that all along.'

'Right. Thank you, girls, that is all.'

Ash was quiet as we left. She walked faster than normal. These were not good signs.

'Still twenty minutes left of lunch,' I tried. 'Want to get an icy pole from the canteen? Sun's out.'

'No thanks.' She walked in silence for a few minutes. '*The Little Mermaid*, Loz, really?' She turned to face me at last. 'The most pathetic romantic heroine there is. And she's *not even in the musical*.'

'Oh, come on, as if that last question really matters.'

'It might not matter to you, but it does to me. You could have put in a bit more effort.'

It was so ridiculous I wanted to laugh. For a single hopeful moment, I wondered what it would be like if I *did* laugh, and we moved on, and that was it; what would happen if I pretended this was a different friendship, one where I really hadn't done anything wrong.

'Come on, Ash . . .'

She turned to walk in the other direction, away from me. 'Oh – and you sang over the top of me!'

I was left alone in the corridor, with the choice to trail slowly behind her or run to catch up. The thought of doing either made me feel deeply tired, like my bones had doubled in weight. Instead I turned to a door leading out to a garden next to the Arts Centre.

Sitting a little way up the stairs outside was a familiar figure – the new girl, Kate. She looked up, and I'd realised she'd seen me.

'Hey, Lara.'

'Hey.' I moved closer and leant on the rail of the stairs. I noticed something was different about her. 'Oh – you changed your hair?' The purple streak was gone.

'Only after our year level coordinator wrote a letter home to my parents saying purple did not fall into the accepted spectrum of natural hair colours. I didn't *quite* comply though – look –'

Kate tilted her head to catch the sun, and I saw a faint violet sheen in the strands. 'I put a less intense wash in instead – you can't see it at all in the indoor light.'

I wondered if that was how she saw St Mags: somewhere that left you a faded version of yourself.

'Oh, Lara – before I forget, I have your hoodie in my locker.'

'Oh, right. I'd been meaning to ask . . .' I trailed off, because finishing the sentence with 'if you'll ever give it back or not' felt rude.

'Meaning to ask why a stranger stole your hoodie?' Kate laughed. 'It's okay. Sorry. I had a feeling when I saw you running. Thought you'd be a good person to know.'

'You could tell from my run?'

'Yeah. It's hard to explain. Like you weren't really running away from anything or towards something, you were just *there*. I know it sounds weird.'

'I mean the definition of running is moving towards or away from something, so yes. It is weird.' I knew exactly what she meant though. That magic suspended feeling when my mind was clear and it felt like I could run forever.

'Anyway, I might have kept the hoodie but since we're doing this assignment together I thought it would be best to keep you onside and give it back.'

'Well, thanks.' I sat next to her.

'So, what are you up to? I thought this was an unclaimed area – I'm not in your "spot" am I?'

I laughed at her air quotes. She was safe though; the area around the Arts Centre was unclaimed. It was too new and cold: concrete steps surrounded by fresh, unnaturally orange tanbark.

'No, you're fine. Looking for somewhere to be alone then? Hope we aren't that terrible already.'

'Just biding my time.'

That sounded slightly unsettling. 'Planning a takeover, are you?'

'Oh, no. I just figure if I wait long enough, I'll work out who my people are. Otherwise I could jump into a friendship with some harpy and not even realise until it's too late.' She smiled at me. 'This is my third school in three years. I've learnt from my mistakes.' Her eyes narrowed. 'You're not a harpy, are you?'

'How about you tell me, once you've observed us long enough.'

'Deal.'

'So,' I started again, 'you've had to move around a lot?'

'My mum's job, they keep sending her all over. I don't mind that much though. It takes the pressure off in some ways, when you know you might only be close for a year or so.'

'Oh, right.' I had been at St Margaret's for ten years. And she was just passing through.

'Not this time round, though. I'm staying put until I finish Year Twelve.' She glanced at me. 'Anyway, what *are* you doing here?'

'Musical auditions.' I groaned at the memory. 'So glad it's over.'

'You're into drama, then?'

'Not so much. It might be fun, but I kind of hope I did badly enough that I won't get in. Probably going to be more trouble than it's worth.'

'Why did you audition if you didn't want to get in?'

'Well, it's kind of more my friend's thing . . .'

'So?'

Clearly Kate had never had a friend like Ash. I shrugged. 'How about you?'

'Well, I used to be a bit of a singer. It's Sondheim, what you're doing, yeah? *Into the Woods*? He's kind of a genius. But I've decided to switch to art in the last few years.' Kate flipped her hair back, a gesture that looked more self-conscious than she'd seemed so far.

'Yeah, sure.' I tried to sound like I got that, like I could make a choice and switch between talents as easily as changing a coffee order. I felt like everything I did just kind of happened to me by accident.

Kate stretched her arms above her head and shielded herself from the sun. 'It is *warm* today.' She glanced at me. 'Does your canteen have anything frozen and sugary for under five dollars?'

I smiled. 'Definitely.'

CHAPTER SEVEN

After school I opened the door to the beeping of a timer, the faint smell of figs and smoke, and the sound of Mum's voice, high-pitched and false. She was probably talking to one of her ex-model friends, Abigail or Marigold or Harmony. No sign of Dad, it was too early for him to be home. I sighed and followed the noise and smells into the kitchen.

It was a mess, as usual. Mum had left about six tasks half-finished; chicken was sitting in a tray ready for marinade, soy sauce and flour and spices lying unopened; a cheese platter was piled high with wax-wrapped packages, one fig cut open and bleeding over the wooden board; and something was smoking gently under the grill. Mum wandered back into the kitchen, midway through a trilling laugh, and rolled her eyes at me. *Marianne*, she mouthed, pointing at the phone. She gestured around the kitchen and put on her best puppy-dog eyes. *Help?*

'Oh yes, completely the wrong season for that – it must be *so* annoying for you,' Mum continued into the phone, and wandered back out of the kitchen. Her hair was coming loose from her bun, falling in curls down her back and catching in her fringed bolero.

I turned the timer off, and switched down the grill – just cheese on toast in there, Mum must have forgotten about her lunch again. I rescued the half-fig and unwrapped the cheese. I pulled myself up onto the counter and helped myself to a generous hunk of brie, minimal cracker.

Mum wandered back through, sans phone. 'It's like she *knows* I'm never going to be ready when they're coming over and calls on purpose! You,' she said, pulling me close, 'are an angel.' She kissed my forehead. 'A slightly sweaty angel. Shower time?'

I ducked out of her hug. 'You're welcome, Mum. Model reunion tonight, then?'

'You know it's a book club, sweet.'

'More like a nineties cover girl club.' I popped a fig slice into my mouth.

Mum smiled vaguely. 'Only a few of us made it to the covers, actually . . .'

I rapped my heels against the counter and waited for Mum to ask me about my day at school. But she was still all dreamy and distracted. 'So Mum, have you heard from Hannah?'

Mum's gaze flicked back to me. 'Just the weekly, agreed upon, "I'm still alive" email. She needs her freedom right now, she says. Enjoying the independence.'

I felt a stab of envy. Hannah hadn't answered any of my emails. 'I still don't understand why she even went,' I said, not for the first time. 'She didn't plan it, didn't tell me until the week she was leaving – what was so bad about Melbourne that she had to just *go*?'

Mum pressed her lips together. 'I've told you, darling, I don't know. She just said she needed to get away. I miss her too, you know. The house is too quiet without her, isn't it?'

I kicked my legs harder against the counter, trying to fill the room with noise. Mum didn't seem to notice.

'Have *you* heard from her, love?' she continued.

I thought about the shoebox under my bed, where I kept the few densely inked postcards she'd sent. No return addresses, of course.

'No.'

'I really wish she'd keep in touch a bit more. Who knows what kinds of things that girl is getting up to. All I know is she's in Paris now. No address, no itinerary, but she's safe.'

'She's probably fine, Mum. Maybe she's having a perfectly normal gap year.'

'Your sister doesn't do perfectly normal.' She reached out and pushed a strand of my hair behind my ear. 'If *you* go travelling, on the other hand, I'll know I have nothing to worry about.'

I leant away from her touch. A bubble of resentment ballooned in my chest. 'Won't even need a weekly email from me, hey?'

'Oh, I'm sure Ashley's Instagram would keep us all updated on you two girls anyway.' Mum switched gears. 'Lara, darling, they're going to arrive any second, and I haven't even changed yet – I know, I'm hopeless. Could you just cut some flowers from the back garden for me? Quickly?'

I sighed, gave up on having a chance to talk about myself, and knocked the cupboard door shut with my heel as I jumped down from the counter. I took the gardening scissors and headed for the back door.

'Thank you, love,' she said, relieved, and walked the other way towards her bedroom. 'You can use my bathroom to shower when you're done – I've just cleaned the main one,' she called over her shoulder.

I let the door slam behind me.

Outside, I heard the call of a magpie from our neighbour's garden and paused, my hands full of roses. I always thought of Zeb when I heard a magpie, even though she'd been gone for years now.

I was the one who found her, but it was Hannah who convinced Mum and Dad to let us keep her, and Hannah who took over looking after her.

I spot her after a huge spring storm, the kind that blacks out the power in a whole suburb. The remains of the nest lie between two broken branches, circled by dewy grass. And inside – Zeb. A tiny magpie, scrawny, her feathers not yet grown. I google what to feed her while Hannah raids the linen cupboard and wraps her in soft flannelette pillowcases.

Zeb grows confident quickly: she spends most of her time outside, but hops in through the back window when she feels like it. She comes to meet us at the front gate when we walk up from the tram each day. I remember Hannah in a good mood, baking spice cookies or frangipani tarts, something complicated and messy, keeping a running commentary going to Zeb – her voice high and excited, flour on her cheek and falling from her hands when she gestures – as the magpie caws back. Or Hannah on a bad day, lying outside on the lawn of the back garden, her tangled hair covering her face, as Zeb occasionally brings things to place beside her: a weed, a piece of tanbark, a rusted bobby pin.

But young magpies need to find their own territory to survive. Zeb starts to leave for hours at a time, exploring. She's always there when we come back from the tram stop though – until one day, she isn't.

The day she leaves for good, Hannah stands still, looking out on the back garden. She doesn't move when I touch her back, or when I try to bring her things: a Tim Tam, a cardigan, a glass of water. She stares out into the darkening garden, her face blank.

'She might come back?' I say eventually, although I know it isn't true.

Hannah turns to me with a slight frown, as if she can't believe my audacity. 'She won't come back, Lara.'

I reach out again to touch her arm and she sighs, turns away from the garden as if it is a great effort, as if she is pulling herself back from another world. She stays in her room for days. Her sadness seeps out like an oil spill and fills the house. Weeks later, Dad finds me looking through pictures of Zeb on my phone. He squeezes my shoulder. 'Do you miss her?'

I'm surprised by the question. It had not occurred to me to miss her, since it is so clear that Zeb belonged to Hannah, not me, and so does the loss: the same way, later, that exam stress belongs to Hannah (how could I complain about my Year Nine tests when Hannah was dealing with the pressure of VCE?), or how choosing my outfit for the social is a low priority when Hannah is organising a boycott for her Year Eleven formal because they've introduced a dress code.

I love and resent Dad for asking that question. Of course I want to feel like Zeb was mine enough to miss, but I don't want to examine how much I miss her. What if it isn't enough? What if it's too much?

I can't figure out how to say all that to Dad. Instead I say, 'Yeah.'

I make sure to close the photos on my phone before Hannah walks in the door.

I heard the doorbell ring and was pulled back from the memory – crap. Mum's friends were here. I gathered the flowers and quickly left the garden, hoping to escape to my room before they came inside.

CHAPTER EIGHT

We met for our first session working on the History assignment on Friday, the week of auditions. It did not start well.

Ash was late because she saw Ms Drummond leaving for the staff car park and ran after her to ask if she had picked the cast yet. Kate and I had already been at the library for ages by the time she slipped into the seat next to me. I didn't mind, but I saw Kate widen her eyes when Ash didn't apologise for keeping us waiting.

'So, uh . . . hi?' Ash said, raising her eyebrows at Kate.

Kate smiled back. 'Hey.'

'And you are?'

Kate glanced at me. 'Lara didn't tell you? I'm new. Kate. Moved in around the corner from her.'

Kate! I groaned inwardly. Ash was not going to be happy I hadn't told her. 'Yeah, we just met the day before school. We *just met.*'

'In Lara's park. We go running there sometimes.'

Do we? Meeting once didn't seem to qualify as 'sometimes'. But it felt unkind to correct her, when Ash was being so hostile.

'You didn't mention it.' Ash turned from me back to Kate, her smile bright and false. 'And how do you like St Mags, so far?'

'St Mags?'

'St Margaret's . . . school? It's what you call it when you've been here a while. Lara and I have been here forever: veterans, right, Loz?'

'Right.' I could see suppressed laughter in Kate's eyes. It would *not* be good if she laughed at Ash now. Not if I wanted to get through this assignment intact. I tapped the folder on the table. 'Let's start. Uh, we could brainstorm some ideas, and then divide up roles?'

'Sure, I guess. I still think it's a waste of time.' Ash opened her diary, flipped to a list of names she had written in the back. She ran her pen down the names: Lachy Stranks, Guy Hasan, Jos Ghazy, Tim Fenwick, and started doodling question marks and notes next to them.

'So, what are you into then, Ashley? Not history, I guess,' Kate asked.

Ash didn't look up from her diary. 'Oh well, I'm *into* lots of things. Including not answering inane questions from strangers.'

'Ash wants to do the musical this year!' I jumped in. My voice was *way* too enthusiastic. I sounded like my mum showing off to her friends.

'Oh yeah?' Kate smiled to herself. 'I did that at my last school. It was okay, except there were all these socially stunted girls who had never met a boy before and went kind of sex mad. All the giggling and hair flipping at rehearsals, it was insane. I saw one girl from my class writing this guy's name in her diary, little hearts around it and everything, even though they'd never spoken.'

Ash slapped her diary closed.

'Right, the Somerton Man, yeah?' I flipped open the folder and turned to Kate. 'You said you actually lived in Adelaide?' I was speaking too fast. All the words were garbling together.

Kate paused, eyeing Ash's closed diary. 'Yeah, my grand-parents live there,' she answered at last. 'Glenelg, actually. Same suburb where he was found.'

'Gle*nelg*.' Ash drew out the name. 'Sounds like someone coughing up phlegm.'

'I guess, if you have a voice that sounds like you have a constant head cold.' Kate tilted her head to one side. 'That'd be difficult if you wanted to be an actor, actually. The whole audience reaching for hand sanitiser every time you spoke, front row dodging the spray.'

'I don't want to be an actor.'

'Oh, so you *are* just doing the musical for the boys?'

I realised I was holding my breath. Even I wasn't allowed to tease Ash like that.

'No. I just think there's more to life than what you do in school.'

'You mean "St Mags"?'

Ash looked murderous.

Kate laughed. 'Kidding! Sorry. The musical sounds great, really. I almost wish I'd auditioned.'

'Well, it's best to wait a bit before you do these things when you're new. It's a small cast so auditions were pretty competitive. I'm not even sure *I* got in.' Ash softened slightly. 'You should come see it though . . . it's going to be pretty good.'

'You're a good singer too, right, Kate?' I said, remembering our conversation after auditions. I was still way too enthusiastic, so relieved the conversation seemed to be turning friendly.

Kate went quiet. 'Sort of. Not anymore though.' She took the folder from me and pulled out the pieces of paper. 'Right, the Somerton Man. Okay, one of us needs to start a basic timeline of events. Someone else could start investigating the different theories of who he was. And, uh, we could think of how to present it? Like a whodunit mystery, or maybe a choose-your-own adventure . . .'

'Or, you know, a History report,' Ash interrupted.

At least we were working. The more we could do separately, the better.

❄

As we left the library I finally remembered to ask Ash about what Ms Drummond had said before we met up to study. It was a good move, she lost the furrow of anger between her eyes and turned dreamy and flushed again.

'She wouldn't tell me if I had a part. But she said I had a *compelling presence* on stage.'

'That's good, right?'

'I'm definitely in.'

'So good! Well done.' Ash didn't say what Ms Drummond had thought of my presence on stage. But maybe she hadn't asked about me. Which was fine because I didn't even want to be in the musical, really, I reminded myself to stop the bubble of hurt. 'Why didn't she tell you your part, then?'

Ash's face clouded briefly with worry. 'She said she had doubts about whether my voice could handle the part she had in mind.' Her face cleared. 'But I told her I had a cold on the audition day and then I coughed *so* convincingly. And said that I had a great recommendation from Catherine King, one of the best singing instructors in Melbourne, and she could call her any time for reassurance.'

'You mean your mum.'

'Well, yeah. But she doesn't know that.'

Ash's mum had given me a lesson once. She was quietly intense with a warm smile and told me I had a 'lovely natural tone'. The next day Ash had been distant and said her mum wouldn't shut up about how good I was. Ms King mentioned lessons almost every time I saw her, but I never went back.

'Anyway, that seemed to help,' Ash continued. 'Thank God Mum kept her last name, right?'

'I guess . . . what if you –'

'What?' Ash stopped walking and turned to face me. 'What if *what*, Loz?'

What if you can't handle the part?

'What if you don't like any of the boys on the cast? What a waste, after all this, right?'

Ash grinned. 'Oh, I don't think that's likely. My standards get lower with each year in this place.'

Suddenly she grabbed my arm.

'Ai, what?' I yelped. 'You're repressed, I get it! No need to emphasise!'

'The cast list,' she half-whispered. 'On the noticeboard. She's put it up already.'

I almost laughed at her reverent tone, but stopped myself when I saw her face. She looked . . . shy.

'Come on, Ash. What's the worst that can happen?' I pulled her towards the paper pinned up on the drama noticeboard in the foyer.

Into The Woods: St Margaret's & St John's Year Ten Musical Cast List:
The Baker – Jos Ghazy
Cinderella's Prince – Tim Fenwick

I scanned and my own name leapt out: *Cinderella – Lara Laylor.* Oh *crap.* I was in. I had a part. It looked like a *main* part. My heart started thumping. Where was Ash? Where – oh. *The Witch – Ashley Broadway.* It was near the top of the list. So, a main part? But my character had a name and hers didn't. Was that bad? How many lines did The Witch have compared to Cinderella? I really wished I'd looked up the script.

'That's – hey, we're both in!' I hedged my bets.

Ash didn't answer. Both hands flew to her face. She turned to me, starry-eyed.

'Get what you wanted?' I started to smile. I couldn't help it, she was infectious.

'The Witch, Lara . . . it's only the most demanding part in the show. And you're in too, it's perfect. Oh! I'm going to have the most *brilliant* songs.'

'Guess Ms Drummond believed the *esteemed* singing instructor Catherine King, hey?' I squeezed her in a quick hug. 'I'm sure you'll be amazing, Ash.'

'Oh, I know I will be.' Her voice was hard and final: a lock clicking into place.

CITY MORGUE, ADELAIDE, DECEMBER 1948

Laurence Elliot, embalmer, was proud of his work, although he did not usually continue to think about it as he walked home. He preferred to leave the job behind as he washed the sweet, medical smell of the embalmers' fluid from his hands.

He never could quite lose the scent of the soap itself, though. His wife said she could smell it underneath his aftershave; it reminded her of rotting fruit.

Occasionally, he couldn't completely leave the bodies behind either. Some would haunt him: the set of a woman's mouth that showed she had worried too much. The softness of hands that had not worked. Once he had to embalm a young woman, not older than eighteen, who already had lines around her eyes from laughing. His own daughter was sixteen at the time. That night he got up to listen at her bedroom door every hour, just to make sure she was still breathing.

It had been a difficult job, this one. Normally his handiwork was only on display for a select audience: police officers, family members, suspects. This man, the Unknown Man, had received quite a bit more attention, and there was no timeline on how long his work had to last. He had injected the veins with a special fluid, watched as the cool liquid, the antithesis of life-giving blood, flowed through the man's limbs. He was looking forward to sharing the results with his fellow members of the British Institute of Embalmers, and could already anticipate the satisfying correspondence discussing his methods.

But as he walked home that night, he was thinking of the man not because of the new techniques they'd succeeded in trying. It was because something had struck him as he embalmed the body – the face, in particular. The man had a kind face.

CHAPTER NINE

I sat beside Ash the next week, waiting for our first class to start, and watched as she copied something from a screenshot on her phone into her diary with green biro. She saw me looking.

'Thought I'd use witchy green to write in the rehearsals,' she grinned. 'May as well stay on theme.'

'Wait, those are *rehearsals*?' The neat green times dotted each week.

'Loz, keep up!' She slid her phone over to me. 'Rehearsal schedule went up yesterday. You've got to keep an eye on the drama noticeboard now.'

I scanned her screenshot. 'Thursday mornings . . . that's an athletics day.'

'Is it?' Ash reclaimed her phone, and kept copying times. 'I mean, I guess we did say the musical was going to be a priority this year. You knew it would be intense.'

I didn't realise it would be this intense. I said nothing, mind whirring. Athletics had always been something I'd done just for me, for fun, since other girls were mostly faster. But I had thought I might be able to qualify for some of the inter-school events this year.

'Come on.' Ash's voice was low and playful. 'You always complained about those early mornings anyway. Rehearsals start half an hour later, it's a bit of a sleep-in.'

Half an hour later – maybe I could make it work. 'Do you think Ms Drummond would let me come late to rehearsals? Maybe I could do both?'

'Loz, you've got a *main part.*' Ash turned to face me. 'Don't even think about it. Adelaide was just in the chorus and she got booted when she asked if she could skip the monthly Saturday mornings for netball.' She poked me gently in the ribs. 'Please, Loz? You wouldn't leave me all alone would you?'

I knew Ash could do the musical without me if she had to, but it would be much easier if we could do it together. Most of the others in the cast were either the drama girls who'd done every production since Year Seven, or the more popular group. We didn't naturally slot into either.

She nudged me again, right in the spot she knew would have me laughing uncontrollably.

'Okay! Okay!' I doubled over and held my arms out to protect myself from more attacks. 'No athletics, I get it.'

'You won't really miss it, will you?' Ash fixed her eyes on me, wide with worry.

I pictured those early mornings, the rhythm of my body settling into the second lap of warm-up, the soft fog of my breath and the crunch of my runners on the track surface. It was highly possible I would miss it.

'No, you're right, who wants to exercise before 7am? And it wasn't like I was going to win anything.' I tried not to feel disappointed. Ash was right, this was our only year to do the musical. And I could always run in the park after school, anyway.

'Don't forget Tuesdays, 4 til 5.30, too,' Ash reminded me, tapping the blank spot in my diary.

I told the athletics coach the next day. My plan had been to ignore her, but the route to the school building went straight past the sports offices. She caught me as she supervised a huddle of Year Sevens spilling out onto the tennis courts.

'Lara!' She beckoned me over.

I waved reluctantly and walked over. I'd always liked Ms Tallis. She got a bit of crap from the other girls because she was super tall, over six-foot-two, and didn't let anyone get away with anything – especially pretending to have your period to get out of sport. I liked the way she unapologetically took up space in the world.

'Just wanted to check in because I haven't got your permission slip for athletics this term,' she said, not looking up from her clipboard as she scribbled a note.

'Uh. I'm not actually doing athletics anymore. Or – just not this term.'

She put her pen down and looked at me. 'And why's that?'

I started to explain about the musical, but she cut me off.

'Well, I'll start looking to replace you. No need to explain, I know the allure of the St John's boys – though I'm sure you're only doing this for the theatrical experience.'

I laughed awkwardly. Teachers always thought they knew so much more than they did. 'I'll come back when the musical's over though,' I said. 'I can still run in my park after school, too.'

'Sure.' Ms Tallis sighed. 'You know, I would have expected this from your sister – Hannah never stuck with anything longer than a term – but not from you, Lara. I guess you're more similar than I thought.'

She smiled as if it was a joke, but this stung more than the jibe about being in the musical just for the boys. I didn't smile back, just shrugged and turned to walk the rest of the way to school.

CHAPTER TEN

I stood at the door of The Clam, waiting for our first rehearsal next Tuesday afternoon, absently running my fingers over the edge of my phone in my pocket. I was the only person there except for one of the St John's boys, who was sitting reading a book on the steps opposite the door, and at whom I was very carefully not staring.

He was pretty unremarkable-looking except for his hair: a light brown corkscrew halo all around his head. It was audacious, that hair.

The boy glanced up at me and then back at his book, a tiny smile pulling at his mouth.

Annoyed that he caught me looking, I pushed down an urge to tell him that I didn't even want to sign up for the musical, that it was all Ash's idea, and that it wasn't my fault he had chosen to sit directly in my line of sight.

I pulled my phone out of my pocket. Five minutes til rehearsal was meant to start. I texted Ash.

Here, where are you?

I was about to press send when I thought it might sound too abrupt, so I added a frangipani emoji to show I wasn't annoyed.

I snuck another glance at the boy, but he was completely absorbed in his book. He had it rolled up in one hand so I couldn't see the title, only the flash of orange that meant it was one of those cheap Penguin classics.

Hannah always said St John's boys were impossible to relate to, that they mistook money for personality. 'Their last party I went to,' she told me, 'everyone had to wear bow ties. At the end of the night they undid them, left them to hang loose around their necks. It was a status thing, 'cause all the guys who didn't buy real ones, who had pre-tied ones on a string, couldn't loosen them. They all sat in one corner together, looking miserable in their neat pre-tied bows. Those boys think they're being ironic but they're just a parody of themselves.'

The theatre door opened. Ash poked her head out.

'Lara you weirdo, what are you doing? Everyone is here already.'

'What? But it's only five to –'

'Which means you're ten minutes late. Everyone gets here fifteen minutes early. Seriously, keep up – I can't look after you ALL the time!' She gave me an affectionate grin and pulled me towards the door.

I felt my cheeks burn at the unfairness of this and couldn't stop myself looking back at the St John's boy. He slowly turned down the corner of a page to mark his spot and stretched his legs to get up. He didn't look worried about being late. He didn't look like he'd care what kind of bow tie he'd wear to a party, either.

We made eye contact, and he rolled his eyes in Ash's direction, just slightly. I couldn't help it: I smiled at him and gave the smallest helpless shrug, as Ash pulled me away through the theatre door.

ADELAIDE POLICE STATION, JUNE 1949

Detective Sergeant Lionel Leane pulled the letters towards himself and sighed. The stack of paper seemed to suck the air out of the small brown office. A paper pile of human misery and hope. Of the two, hope was worse.

He opened the top letter.

Dear Sir,

I believe I can assist with your request. I have not seen my husband these last six months. He returned much changed from the war, his disposition turned dark and unsettled.

He is of medium height, has brown hair and brown eyes, and I have determined from the clothes that were left behind that he was wearing a checked shirt and loose brown suit at the time of his departure. He has a small war wound on his right thigh, a scar like a crescent moon.

I believe he must be the man found on the Somerton Beach. I look forward to your reply.

Yours, Lucy Baxter

Detective Leane dropped Lucy Baxter's letter on the opened pile next to the stack of sealed envelopes. All of them would have to be responded to, he thought, and a wave of exhaustion almost overtook him. Her description did not match, of course; the man had grey eyes, not brown, and no moon-shaped scar.

He thought of his own mother. He had a memory from when he was small, of her standing at the window waiting for his father to come home on the days he was late from work. Her silhouette against the window, her attention so completely focused elsewhere from him, a tea towel twisting tighter and tighter into a dense rope in her hands.

He let his gaze drift to the plaster cast of the head and torso of the Somerton Man, as he had become known. The bust was made at the urging of the autopsy specialist Burt Cleland. Though the body found on the beach had now reached the point where it had to be buried, Burt hoped that someone may yet recognise the man from the cast. The bust was a first in the history of the Adelaide Police. And now it sat in his office, a silent white presence. The cast had been taken in such a way that the head was tilted downwards, as if the Somerton Man was avoiding the detective's eyes.

The detective tapped his fingers on the pile of letters. Letters full of missing husbands, brothers, fathers, sons. And none of them, he knew in his gut, would match the impassive white face before him, or the corpse now buried in a grave with no name.

He glared at the cast. 'Who are you, dammit?'

CHAPTER ELEVEN

By the end of the week I was ready for a break from school, but the house felt unusually quiet on Friday night. I still couldn't get used to coming home to an empty house. Not that Hannah had always been home when I'd arrived before, but there was a different kind of emptiness now that there was no chance she'd walk in the door at any second.

No postcard today.

Mum was out, and Dad had said he'd be working late this week, so I found myself wandering through the house towards the only source of noise: the washing machine, rumbling gently on its cycle.

It was cold in the laundry, on the concrete floor, but I sat there anyway. I pulled out an old jumper sitting behind a pile of clean clothes and shrugged it on. Mum's beach jumper. It still smelled faintly of salt and campfire. I held the sleeve up to my face and breathed it in: long shapeless days in the shack by the beach, splashing with Hannah in the sea, building sandcastle forts, finding shells and bits of seaweed and cuttlefish, running excitedly to Mum to show her. And nights inside, sleepy in her arms, my cheek against this jumper, Dad's warm laugh somewhere above me. Falling asleep to the sound of the sea through the open window.

The owner had sold the shack to be redeveloped years ago. We'd not been back to the beach since.

I pushed back the sleeves and pulled out my phone to start looking up some info for the Somerton Man assignment.

Heaps of links came up straight away. It looked like Mr Grant wasn't the only one captivated by the mystery. I followed the first one, a link to an ongoing forum chat about the investigation.

The first idea the police had – a missing person, possibly a soldier returned from the war – was not very popular online. But there were a lot of stories of families who had lost fathers, sons, brothers, and husbands: soldiers who came back different after the war. One day, they simply disappeared and didn't come back. I guess now they'd be diagnosed with PTSD.

There was another theory that the Somerton Man was a refugee, brought here by the war. His dental records didn't match anyone from Australia, the UK or the US, but they could have matched someone in Central or Eastern Europe.

I scrolled down to find the end of the article, but it went on for ages. I decided I'd look at it properly later on my laptop, when I could take notes.

I watched the washing machine churn in front of me. Another memory from the beach holiday came to mind –

It's my first time body surfing. Dad is teaching me and Hannah, out the back of the swell, waiting for the waves to come in. His arms are around my waist, pushing me into the wave, his laughter and cheers sweeping us in along with the sea foam. Hannah is fearless, she throws herself into the surf. I'm more cautious, but grow in confidence as I start to feel the rhythm of the water, to hit that spot where my body weight is nothing, carried smoothly along in the current.

It feels like freedom. Like how I feel running, now.

We see a set start to form on the horizon. It's bigger than any of the waves we've caught yet.

'I got this Dad!' cries Hannah. She looks like a mermaid, eyes bright with the exercise, hair stuck together with salt water in curled strands around her face.

'I know you do, Han.' Dad's voice, amused, proud.

The first of the set hits us; I hold my breath and duck under, like I've been taught. I can feel its power as the wave moves over me, like a muscle.

I break the surface and look in to shore. Hannah has done it – ridden the wave all the way. She stands in the shallows, a bit shaky on her feet, and raises her hands in twin V-signs for victory.

The next of the set is coming up fast. It's bigger than the first.

'Get ready to duck, Lara!' calls Dad.

But I'm not going to duck. I got this, too. I'm going to ride it in, fast as Hannah – faster, even.

I position my body the way Dad has told us, streamlined, ready to launch.

'Lara – no, wait –' There is a hint of panic in Dad's voice, but he is too late.

The wave sweeps the last few metres in less than seconds, and it is on me, over me, and all around me – with a roar, I'm tossed under. It's as if the sea is angry. The force of the wave is on my back and shoulders, pushing me under, it feels personal. My ears and mouth fill with salt water, my limbs pinwheel around. In the churn of sand and salt I realise how stupid I am. How small and powerless, how fragile my body is, so easy to cut open with rock or coral, my brain lying just below the surface of such a thin skull. Which way is up? I swim blindly and hit sand – the other way! – lungs screaming, I break the surface.

In time for the next wave to hit me. Then the next.

My heart beats faster and faster. Can I have an asthma attack under the water? My vision blurs. I could just give in. I could just stop. I let the next wave take me, roll me over. I'm suspended in the swirl and it's almost peaceful, almost pleasant . . . *Find the surface!* a voice screams in my mind, fighting the sleepiness coming over me, *Find the surface, or you're going to DIE* –

Two hands around my waist pull me gasping and gulping into the world again. I am in Dad's arms, as he sprints over the beach, yelling something to Hannah about my inhaler . . .

✽

I watched a sports sock in the washing machine flip round and round in the soapy wash, with an odd sort of sympathy.

That sock, flipping round and round. Me at eleven, dumped by the wave. Sometimes things just hit you like that, I guess. A force you didn't reckon with, something you underestimated, an uncaring, larger power. For me, it was the wave, pulling me under. For the Somerton Man, if he was the refugee or the soldier, it would have been a war – living his life until the conflict swept him off his feet like a wave and left him lying washed up on the beach.

The washing cycle stopped, with a last roar and gurgle.

The front door opened. 'Lara? Hello, anyone home?'

I left the laundry. 'Hey, Mum.'

'Lara! What are you doing with that old thing?'

'This?' I pulled off the jumper. 'I found it in the laundry. Hey, do you remember those holidays we used to have down at the beach?'

Mum took the jumper and balled it up absently. 'Yes, that's right . . . funny little place, wasn't it? No real floors, and the fly screens were always coming loose.'

'How come we never went back, once they did up the shack?'

'Oh, I don't know. You girls probably wanted to go off with friends in the holidays. And it wasn't exactly comfortable, there. We always got eaten alive by the mosquitoes.'

She kept the jumper, though.

CHAPTER TWELVE

Postcard: Spiš Castle, Slovakia, in evening light.

Lara,

I'm in Slovakia. They have beautiful castles here, not Disney ones but actual fairytale ones . . . everything is hazy, like I'm seeing it through this blue-green filter, like the light comes from an alien sun.

Do you remember being Lady Lilliana and Queen Helena of our own kingdom, in Nan's attic that Christmas? Sometimes I wish I could live there instead, make up the rules as we go along, with you.

Miss you. Say something passive-aggressive to Mum for me, will you? Her comebacks are probably dropping in quality with me gone. You're too easy on her.

H x

I lay on the hard floorboards at the side of the stage, and listened as Ms Drummond called Ash and Riley into the centre of the stage, again. We were in our second week of rehearsals now and I was quickly discovering how much waiting was involved. It was going to be a while before my scene, clearly. I stretched out my legs and winced at the tightness in my muscles. I hadn't had any time to run this week. Perhaps I could just slip out now and do a few laps of the oval before class . . .

'Lara Laylor!' Ms Drummond called, 'Don't waste my time and yours – read over your part.'

Kate rolled her eyes sympathetically at me from the back of the stage area, where she was drawing up sets. Ms Drummond had 'volunteered' her after scouring the arts classes for talent. She was in the background of most rehearsals now. I wasn't that thrilled about it, to be honest. My life was a lot easier when Kate-time and Ash-time were separate.

Ms Drummond swept her gaze around the rest of the students slumped around the edge of the stage. 'All of you – phones *away*, please – I want to see scripts open. And you had better be ready if I call your scene.'

I sighed and pulled my script out of my bag, and slipped Hannah's postcard in between its folds. In pencil on the back of one of the pages I started drafting a reply to her, though I'd almost given up on sending her emails.

Han,

I do remember that Christmas, though we definitely didn't make up the rules together: it was Queen H's way or into the stocks (remember? The back of Nan's rocking chair, with the carved holes just big enough for my head and arms to stick through? No? You've forgotten? Well I haven't, because you left me there for FOUR HOURS.)

Hey, instead of castle descriptions, could your next postcard include details of your return ticket? That would be rad.

Lara

Maybe it's a good thing I wouldn't send this. Sarcasm was never the way to win her over.

'Again, Ashley!' Ms Drummond called sharply. 'Your entrance was sloppy and that is *not* the line.'

I glanced up, but Ash looked like she was in her element – maybe she was trying to stretch out her scene by making mistakes. My eyes wandered to my left, where Tim Fenwick and Jos Ghazy had also given up listening in on rehearsal, and were passing a notebook to each other, laughing easily about whatever was inside. Tim's blond fringe kept falling in his eyes and he pushed it back with a casual gesture that looked like it had been practised in a mirror. He was definitely the top of Ash's list – I'd already tried to help her decode a few conversations with very little to go on. (I suspected when he said 'Hey', he just meant 'Hey'.) Most of the other girls thought he was attractive, and he knew it, but – miraculously – he still seemed to be a decent person.

Jos was the guy I'd seen waiting on the steps before our first rehearsal. He didn't feature all that much in the other girls' post-mortems of each rehearsal; he'd kind of slid under the radar. I still thought he was one of the most interesting looking guys, though. That amazing hair.

Jos's eyes were looking calmly back at me and I realised he'd caught me staring. Again. Crap. I looked back down at my script quickly, and wrote a few nonsense words as I got my face under control. *Spiral. Corkscrew. Flight.*

A notebook flopped down over the script, right next to my moving pen. I looked up into Tim's face.

'Hey, Lara,' he said, 'want to play?' He was suppressing a smile, like he was in on a joke I didn't get.

I raised my eyebrows in what I hoped was a casually inter-ested way and pulled the notebook towards me. It was full of short paragraphs, each with a separate heading. I scanned them quickly – why is boys' handwriting so universally terrible? – and read something about killer whales, axes, and blood transfusions.

'What's the game?' I asked.

Tim scooted over so he was sitting properly next to me. 'Write us a short story. Half a page, and the title has to be two words, like this –'

'And,' Jos interrupted, still watching us from where he was sitting, 'it has to be violent.'

'Violent?'

He nodded seriously. 'Gruesomely so.'

'Hmm . . .' Ms Drummond was repositioning Ash and her partner in the centre of the stage. 'Okay, if you give me a title, I'll give you a story.' Tim snatched back the book, thought for a second and printed: THE IGLOO.

I tapped my pen as I looked up at the ceiling, and started scribbling.

THE IGLOO

Once upon a time there was an Eskimo called Quinn who lived at the North Pole with all his penguin friends. One day, he decided to build a new igloo. He spent days and days collecting ice and carefully fitting the blocks together. Finally, the igloo was finished, and Quinn and all his penguin friends went to sleep in their new home. Unfortunately, though, Quinn had forgotten to fortify his foundations, so ice weasels burrowed into the new igloo from underneath, sucked his brain out through his ears and ate it. They ate the brains of all the penguins too. Ice weasels are pretty thorough.

THE END

'Here.' I slid the book back over. Tim read quickly and gave a surprised bark of laughter.

'Enjoy, Ghazy,' he said, as he passed it to Jos.

Jos got all the way through and didn't laugh, but at the end a brilliant grin split his face for a second. The smile completely transformed him, like switching on a light. 'You have to watch out for those ice weasels.'

'Right, that's it for today. We will be starting at 4pm sharp next Tuesday, which means be here by 3.45, please.' Ms Drummond closed rehearsal.

Ash turned and saw me with the boys. Her eyes widened slightly when she saw Tim was there. Maybe she was hoping I'd been laying some groundwork for her – crap, I thought, I should have mentioned her somehow. She came and flopped in the middle of our circle.

'Ugh, I thought she'd make me say those lines *forever*. What's up?' The question was directed mainly at Tim, who had reclaimed the notebook.

'Creative writing. We're thinking of publishing an anthology.' Jos was the one who answered.

'A what?' She took the book and skimmed my story. 'I don't get it.'

'Short stories, Ashley,' Tim explained. 'That's Lara's, here's mine – it's about government controlled mechanical dolphins sabotaging asylum seeker boats, see –'

'Oh, right. Funny.' Ash sounded unsure.

'Hey Ash, great work on that scene –' I tried to bring her into the conversation.

Ms Drummond coughed loudly from the theatre door and jangled her keys at us. Quickly, I shoved my notes in my bag, and we headed out.

'Nice Dylan reference in your story, by the way,' Jos said as we left.

'What?' I frowned.

'Bob Dylan – *Quinn the Eskimo*. The song?'

'Oh . . . right! Thanks,' I answered, confused.

✱

That lunchtime, I looked up Bob Dylan on my phone. As I scrolled through the album covers, I remembered being in the back seat of our car on a road trip, Dad leaning over from the front to explain that this was part of our musical education, as Hannah and I groaned and reached for the phone to put on our own favourites.

I found the song and listened to it all the way through, and for some reason, couldn't stop smiling. I couldn't remember that song in particular. I guess it must have snuck its way into my subconscious, because Quinn was just my go-to name for an Eskimo. But no need to tell Jos that.

CHAPTER THIRTEEN

Kate and I sprinted the last half-lap to the tree. My calf muscles felt like they were stripped through with fire, but I kept going – almost there – *yes*. We flopped underneath; me first, Kate a second later.

'I give in. Take your victory.' Kate gave a bow which she turned into a roll onto the grass. 'Good race.'

I laughed. We'd started running together a few times a week now. It was unfamiliar, this open competition with a friend. I was used to subtler, unspoken contests. Racing Kate was fun. Especially since I turned out to be so good at it.

I pulled out my inhaler to reassure myself it was still there, even though I'd used it as prevention before the run.

'Is it a stubbornness thing?' Kate nodded to the inhaler. 'Choosing running as your hobby, when you have asthma?'

'Nah, more a self-preservation technique. May as well try to be good at the thing nature says I'll suck at.'

Kate laughed. 'That's what I mean. Refusal to accept your natural limitations. Stubbornness.'

'You really think I'm stubborn?'

'Of course you are. You come across as all meek and pliable, but underneath there's this rod of iron will.'

'Really?' I'd literally never thought of myself like that before. I had a disorientating feeling, like when you see yourself unexpectedly in a mirror and wonder who is that girl who has your taste in clothes.

'Really.'

'If you say so.'

'See – there you go! You don't believe me. You're just pretending to agree.'

I raised myself up on my elbows and flicked a piece of grass at her. 'Well, if I argue with you, I prove your point. I can't win.'

'True that. Better just give in to my superior will.'

I took a gulp of water as my breathing settled. 'Actually, asthma doesn't restrict exercise, really. You just have to be careful. And remember things. It only takes a few times of forgetting your inhaler to get really *really* good at checking it's with you.'

'Ah, thus why you're so organised. Makes sense.' Kate paused. 'Was it scary, your first attack?'

'I don't remember.' I was quiet for a moment. 'Actually, that's a lie. I do remember. It was awful. I was chasing some girls in primary school when it happened. I felt like I was going to die. You never appreciate breathing until you suddenly can't anymore, you know?'

'Yikes.'

We lay there in silence for a few moments. I stared up at the branches of the fir tree, rustling slightly in the wind. 'We weren't playing a game,' I added suddenly. 'They'd decided not to be friends with me anymore, and were running away from me. And I kept chasing them until my chest got so tight I had to stop, and they left me there.' I tried to smile. 'Stupid, really.'

I felt Kate's gaze on me. I kept staring up at the tree.

'Huh. Do you know where they are now? I'll bash them for you if you like,' she offered.

I laughed, and turned to look at her properly. 'Anyway, what about you? You never talk about your schools before St Mags.'

This time Kate looked away and stared up at the tree. 'It was . . . interesting.' She turned to face me. 'Not this time, okay? I will tell you the whole story. Really. One day.'

'Okay.'

'Okay?'

'Yeah. Okay.' I stood up and stretched. 'Another race? Quick one? Maybe I'll let you win this time.'

Kate groaned. 'You are a freak of nature, Lara Laylor.'

I didn't let her win. But she didn't seem to mind.

CHAPTER FOURTEEN

I was the last one in the car park after rehearsal on Tuesday. Mum must have forgotten she said she'd pick me up. I shrugged on my bag to start walking over to the tram when I realised I wasn't alone. Mr Grant stood at the other end of the car park, looking out over the oval. He saw me and raised one arm in a casual salute.

I steeled myself against the usual weirdness whenever I had to interact with a teacher one-on-one, out of class, but for some reason I didn't feel as reluctant as I normally would.

'Hey, Mr Grant.'

'Lara. I was just admiring this sunset.'

It was nice, I guess. One of those soft purple-pink ombre skies. I preferred the ones that were made up of fiery, fierce colours that never came out right in photos: the summer sunsets before a storm. My park gave a great view of those, when the sun set behind the city and coloured the skyscrapers gold.

'You look unimpressed.'

I started. He was looking at me, a half-smile on his face. 'Oh, no, it's just I like the more dramatic ones. You know, the ones when it's like the sky is actually on fire.'

'Oh yes . . .' he drifted off. 'I saw a most spectacular sunset like that once. I was on holiday and completely lost, trying to read the map in my rental car, I kept being distracted by the sky. Eventually I just stopped and enjoyed the show. We had to rely on maps in those days, no smartphones.'

I nodded politely. It couldn't have been that long ago though, he didn't seem old enough.

'I miss those old maps, actually. Something magic about translating a real physical place into lines on a page. An exercise in interpretation.'

I had a mini brainwave. 'History's a bit like that, hey? Interpreting a real world of the past into . . . I don't know, timelines and dot points.'

Mr Grant laughed out loud. 'How depressing that sounds. Like I suck the soul out of the real world of the past, leaving you with timelines and dot points.'

'Oh no, I didn't mean . . .' I felt my face heat up. Maybe it was a dumb thing to say.

'Just kidding.' He cut me off with a smile. 'It's a very poetic idea, actually. History, the map to the past . . .' He trailed off. 'What leaves you in the car park so late, Lara?'

'I had musical rehearsal. I think my mum forgot to pick me up.'

'Ah, the musical. With the local boys school, I understand?' He sounded like he was laughing at me, behind those words.

'That's right.' I tilted up my chin, refusing to be embarrassed.

'I hope they prove themselves worthy of you girls.' He paused, looking again at the sunset, then turned back to me. 'So, I've been wondering – how is the search for the Somerton Man going?'

It could have sounded like he was checking up on homework, but he seemed genuinely interested. 'Pretty well actually – I mean, you can't tell too much from that first folder, but it's so interesting, wondering who he could have been.'

Mr Grant nodded. Encouraged, I went on. 'I think it's more suspicious than just any missing person's case, though.

What with the labels missing from his clothes, even the ones in the suitcase. Surely he was trying to hide something.'

'How interesting,' said Mr Grant. 'You know, you might be ready for the next instalment of the mystery sooner than I thought. What if I go over your notes with you sometime next week, after school? Then you can get a head start on the next folder when you're ready.'

'Sure, I guess.' I was kind of surprised he was taking me so seriously. 'Like, extra tutoring?'

'If your schedule allows it. I often have extra sessions with promising students who are interested. Just a half-hour or so after class, nothing too strenuous.'

I felt a glow like a firelighter had flicked on in my chest. I knew some girls had extra Maths or Science sessions before school, if they were smart enough. The accelerated classes even got to do first year uni subjects later on in school, to get a head start. I always thought I was too in the middle of things to get invited – not struggling, but not the smartest in the class either.

'It looks like the show is over.' Mr Grant gestured to the sky, a dimming violet glow, now. The sun was nearly set.

A horn sounded an angry blare and I looked out to the road. My tram was coming, I could see it a few stops away.

'So, I'll see you in class and we can make a time to go over those notes.'

'Sure – sounds good. Thanks, Mr Grant.'

'Don't miss your tram.' He was smiling.

It was almost at my stop. 'Right – thanks!'

I jogged the last little way, and just made it. I looked out the window and saw he was still there, watching the tram pull away, his shadow stretching longer and longer in the fading light.

CHAPTER FIFTEEN

We were over halfway through the term and rehearsals were starting to get more intense, but I found I mostly enjoyed my part. The early bits with Cinderella and her family was easy, it was getting Cinderella out of that situation that was the hard bit: making myself care about the prince and the ball.

We finished another round of 'I Wish' and Ms Drummond finally let us stop.

'That was . . . fine. We will move on. Lara?'

'Yes?'

'Take a break. And while you do, try and develop some passion, please. It sounds at the moment like Cinderella *might* show up at the festival, *if* her friends are going and there's nothing good on TV.'

Ash snorted a laugh. Ms Drummond glanced at her.

'Cinderella wants this party with her whole being, Lara. Think of a time you wanted something so badly you would die if you didn't get it. Teenagers are meant to be unreasonably emotional, I'm sure you know what I mean.' She clapped her hands. 'Right, now to the Baker's Wife and the Witch scene – Baker, I want you ready as well, we'll have your bit in a second . . .'

I jumped off the stage and sat in one of the front rows of the auditorium, glad my part was over. What *did* I want with my whole being? An image popped into my head: of running a marathon, a proper one, Kate and Hannah and Ash waving from the sidelines, and me, pushing my body further than I ever had, and falling over that finish line. I shook my head. I definitely would never be able to do that if I couldn't even stay on the athletics team.

Ms Drummond was right, I wasn't so sure about Cinderella's wish to go to the festival. Why not take the chance when the house was empty to steal the stepmother's jewels and do a runner?

'Rough.' Jos sat next to me. He'd left one seat between us, but one of his long legs spilled out across the space. I felt suddenly very aware of how close my arm was to his knee.

'Oh, it's not that bad,' I replied, trying to sound relaxed. 'Ash says the more she grills you, the better she thinks you can be.'

'That's only because she gets it the worst.'

'She's doing okay.' Jos was right though. Ms Drummond had made Ash sing her solo five times last week, and only stopped when her voice started to crack.

'Her voice can't take the part. I don't know what Ms Drummond was thinking.'

I sort of knew he was right, but I wasn't going to talk crap about Ash behind her back. Plus I could see Ms Drummond looking around, annoyed at the noise we were making. I pulled out my Somerton Man folder. Hopefully Jos would get the hint.

'What's that?'

I guess not. 'History assignment. Do you have to go over your lines? You're up soon.'

'I've learnt them.'

Already? We were only a few weeks in and his was a main part.

'Hey, this looks like a detective's notebook.' He pointed to the printout photo of the Somerton Man's face in my notebook. The sleeve of his jumper grazed my wrist as he reached over, leaving the skin there tingling, like a shallow graze. I had never noticed how close together these auditorium seats were.

'Who is that guy? Your killer?' Jos asked, tapping the photo.

'No . . . the victim, maybe.' I passed the notebook to him, and felt both relieved and disappointed as he sat back in his seat, extending the distance between us. 'It's the mystery of the Somerton Man, have you heard of it?'

Jos shook his head, skimming through the notes. 'Hey, this is messed up. No sign of a struggle, no ID on the body, no labels on his clothes?'

I felt myself loosen up at his excitement. 'I know, right? No one knows anything about him.'

'And possibly killed by poison . . . he could actually be a spy, you know.'

'You think? I guess so, but it's so . . . cheesy. Like James Bond.'

'I *love* James Bond.'

Ms Drummond turned from the stage to us. 'Lara Laylor, are you in this scene?'

'Uh, no.'

'Well, unless you are the Baker, the Witch, or yelling "fire", I *do not want to hear it.*'

'Sorry,' Jos stage-whispered. He didn't look sorry. He was smiling.

I took back the notebook.

'Jos Ghazy, *get up here right now.*'

He jumped up to the stage with a last grin at me. I flipped open the notebook again. Written in the back:

If you ever want help cracking the code, my services are available. – The Baker.

And a mobile number.

❋

Ms Drummond beckoned me over after rehearsal. 'I know I was a bit rough on you earlier, but that was nice work today, Lara.'

'Uh, thanks.' I smiled. Compliments from her were rare – I must really be doing okay.

'So tell me, I've been meaning to ask, how is Hannah going?'

My shoulders slumped. I should have known I'd still end up talking about Hannah at school, even if she wasn't here.

'She's doing well, thanks,' I replied politely. Ms Drummond looked expectant, so I went on. 'She finished last year and couldn't really decide what to do at uni so she's on a gap year, travelling around.'

'Yes, that's a good choice for her,' Ms Drummond said briskly, as if it hadn't been settled until she signed off on it. 'Ferociously talented, your sister, but never very good at putting up with institutions if she didn't see the point.' She flashed me a smile.

'Mmm.' I hoisted my bag more firmly on my shoulders and hoped she'd let me leave. A thought twisted uncomfortably in my stomach. 'You remember her pretty well, then?'

'Oh, she's impossible to forget. Hannah was one of the most difficult girls I've ever worked with, and gave one of the best performances.' Her smile faded. 'Let's hope it runs in the family – some of it, at least.'

The ugly thought in my gut grew. Was my audition any good at all, or had I just got the part because of Hannah? I mumbled a few more responses and left without asking her, because Ms Drummond was just honest enough to tell me the truth.

❋

Ash was waiting for me outside the Arts Centre. 'So? What did she want?'

'Just to talk about Hannah, really.' I repeated the conversation to Ash.

'Oh, great.' Ash smiled. 'I thought she was going to grill you about my singing – I felt a little off today.' She started walking off down the corridor.

I trailed after her, still thinking. 'What do you think, Ash?' I asked at last. 'The bit she said about hoping it ran in the family – do you think I only got in because of Hannah?'

She looked thoughtful. 'It does kind of make sense why she'd give you a main part – to be honest, I was a little surprised at the casting after our audition.'

Oh. I hoped my face didn't show how embarrassed I felt.

Ash widened her eyes. 'Sorry, Loz! Too honest!' She swung an arm around my shoulder. I resisted the urge to shrug her off. 'Anyway, what does it matter, really? You didn't even want to audition, probably wouldn't have, if it wasn't for me.'

I couldn't argue with that, but it didn't make me feel any better.

CHAPTER SIXTEEN

The classroom Mr Grant told me to come to for the History session was empty. I looked up and down the corridor, but even though it was only 4pm, everyone had gone. I flipped open my diary again to check the classroom: yes, I was in the right place.

'Lara!' Mr Grant came around the corner, his arms full of books, his hair standing on end, somehow filling up the space in the corridor on his own. 'Sorry I'm late. Go in, go in. Door isn't locked, is it?'

'Oh – right.' I walked into the room, feeling dumb for waiting outside. Mr Grant followed me.

'First things first, Lara – coffee? How do you have it?'

'What? Oh – um – I normally have a long black?' It seemed a weird topic of conversation to start with.

He stopped short. 'I'm just going to the staff room, Lara. You think we have café-quality coffee there?'

Oh, right. He was asking because he was going to actually get us coffee. 'Um, well, there have been rumours there's a trapped barista kept on hand.' I rallied, trying to act like I'd meant it to be a joke.

'Well, I'll do my best French press for you – no milk.' He saluted me and opened the door to leave. 'Won't be long – get comfortable.'

The room felt even quieter when he left. I looked around for where to sit. The front row felt too close to the teacher's desk, with the whole classroom to choose from. And should I leave space for anyone else who might be coming? I pulled out a seat in the second row of desks, but that felt too formal. Eventually I compromised by sitting up on top of the desk, legs swinging uncertainly in the empty space below. Mr Grant returned with a coffee pot and two mugs.

'Is, um, anyone else coming?' I asked.

'Well, I only extended the invitation to a few.' He settled the coffee on the desk. 'And one thing I didn't realise when I started here was just how busy they like to keep you young *ladies* – it's astounding how many extra-curriculars there are.'

It sounded like he'd emphasised the 'ladies' on purpose, like Ash and I did when we were making fun of St Mags. But I couldn't be sure. 'They like us to come out of the school as well-rounded citizens, that's for sure,' I agreed, with the hint of an eye-roll.

He looked at me a second longer than usual, and smiled. He could tell I was joking, too.

'I did make sure to schedule the session on a day that didn't clash with your school musical though – couldn't have my star student missing out.' He passed me a mug of black coffee. 'It was a challenge to find a rehearsal-free day – they're keeping you occupied. How's it going?'

'It's okay,' I said. Ash's words after the conversation with Ms Drummond echoed around my mind.

'Just okay?' Mr Grant took a sip of his coffee. 'That doesn't sound great.'

'Well, you know.' I shrugged. 'Anyway. It's not that important.'

'Oh, I don't know if I agree. It seems important.' His face was bright, interested. I realised he was waiting for a real answer.

I picked up my coffee, still way too hot to sip. The caffeine smell was sharper than I was used to, acidic. Like the muddy cups Dad would drink through the night when he was working on a project, steaming with radioactive heat from the microwave. A different kind of drink altogether from the delicate lattes Ash ordered after school, fern leaves inscribed in the foam, picture perfect for Instagram.

'It's just that I'm feeling a bit of pressure, I guess,' I said at last. 'Hannah did the play when she was in Year Ten and apparently she was amazing, so there's a bit to live up to.'

'Hannah?' He looked confused.

'Oh – my older sister.'

'You had a sister who went here? I didn't know.'

I felt a tingle inside me, like something numb coming back to life. 'You might be the only one in this school not to know.'

Mr Grant took another sip of his coffee, looking thoughtful. 'It doesn't sound like you're worried about living up to her reputation, to me. It sounds like you'd rather leave it behind altogether.'

'That would be a lot easier if Hannah wasn't so memorable.' My legs swung further, hitting the chair in front of me with a clang. 'Oops – sorry.' I said. 'I'd forgotten I was talking to a teacher for a second.'

'No need to apologise.' Mr Grant turned to rifle through his folders on the desk. 'In any case, I doubt your sister had the same aptitude for History as you do, Lara.' He pulled out my initial report on the Somerton Man, which I'd handed in during our class that day. 'There are some very original insights in here.'

'Thanks,' I said, feeling myself relax. 'It's so interesting – I love how the police pretty much ruled out accidental or natural death straight away . . . like they knew it was deliberate, just not whether it was his decision or someone else's.' It was a relief to talk about the mystery with someone I knew was as into it as I was. 'Which do you think it was, Mr Grant?'

'Murder or suicide?' He looked out the window, pausing before answering. 'Have you come across any other possibilities in your research?'

'Well, not exactly, but I did read about someone else – the nurse, who lived close by, I think, who the police were questioning?' I'd been curious about her story since I found it.

'Yes, excellent. I think you've hit on the central point of the mystery, Lara.' Mr Grant put down his coffee and leant forward. 'So do you think the evidence points to a tragic love story? Which could end with either of those first options, I suppose.'

'I'm not sure.' I loved how seriously he was taking my opinion. 'What I really don't understand is why the police didn't follow up the lead, if it was a good one.'

Mr Grant looked from the window back to me. 'Well, she had a young child. And – uh – she wasn't married to the man she was living with. The police were delicate about exposing her life to the press. People were less . . . enlightened about things like that than we are now.'

I felt embarrassed, though I wasn't sure why. 'Seems a stupid reason not to investigate her.'

'Yes . . . and another interesting thing about the nurse – her child had very distinctive physical features. A certain ear shape, and teeth in a different configuration to most people: both very rare, and both features shared by the Somerton Man on the beach.'

'No way.' I couldn't believe the police had missed something so obvious. 'But then – if the child was his – she must be the key to everything.' I felt my excitement start to build.

Mr Grant tapped his fingers on the pile of papers on his desk. 'This is great Lara, and you'll have to wait for the final folder to learn more of her story. But for today I think you've come far enough for us to move on to one of the other most intriguing possibilities: a ring of spies.' He passed it over: the second folder in the mystery.

It was only as I left that I realised: no one else had shown up for the whole hour.

St Margaret's History:
Year Ten Mystery Assignment

Teacher: Mr Grant

The Somerton Man

Folder Two: Adelaide in 1948 – A Nest of Spies?

Woomera

- Woomera Rocket Range in South Australia to the north-west of Adelaide was established by the British government to test long-range missiles and other sensitive military equipment
- 'Woomera' is a word from the Dharug language of the Eora people of the Sydney basin for a spear-throwing device
- Weapons were tested over a vast range of land declared 'uninhabited', despite the presence of Aboriginal peoples
- Set up in 1946 and declared a prohibited area in 1947
- Many recent migrants accepted under refugee programs were sent to work on construction of the rocket range, as a condition of entry into Australia

Venona project

- A counterintelligence project of the USA that began in 1943 and spanned four decades
- In the late 1940s, intelligence from Venona revealed many Soviet spies to be operating in Australia, and Australia was promptly cut out of any intelligence-sharing from the UK or US
- In response, the Australian Security Intelligence Organisation (ASIO) was founded in 1949, despite protests that it would impede civil liberties

Sir Henry Tizard

- The eminent British scientist and defence expert, an authority on the atom bomb, was visiting Adelaide in November 1948

Other notes

- Barbiturate poisons, one suggested cause of death of the Somerton Man, were often used as 'truth drugs' amongst spies. An overdose would be fatal

Key quotes

'The atmosphere was ripe for foreign espionage in Adelaide. This was the height of the Cold War.'

John Ruffles, researcher, 1978

'It's quite a melodramatic thesis, isn't it?'

Alf Boxall, Army Intelligence Officer, 1978

CHAPTER SEVENTEEN

I suggested a café in between our schools. It was called Alchemy, and had a kind of vintage science-lab theme: lots of coloured glass bottles and brass instruments. I'd never been there without Ash before. When I arrived, no one else was in school uniform. I took off my blazer and scrunched my school jumper sleeves to my elbows.

'Lara!' Jos was in a booth, waving at me. How long had he been calling? I weaved my way through the café and sat down on the seat opposite him, bumping the table with my schoolbag. I draped my blazer over my knees, then changed my mind and let it slide to the floor on top of my bag.

'This place looks great. Apparently the coffee is good here.' Jos knocked over the tepee of sugar sachets he'd built, and smiled.

'Yeah, Ash likes it.' I put my hands on the table, then on my lap. 'I hope you weren't waiting long. I came straight from school.'

'No, no.' He smiled again. 'History today?'

'Yeah.' I was relieved he'd brought it up, though I felt a twinge of disappointment as well. Maybe he *did* just want to talk about the Somerton Man. 'Um. So I've got my notes here, if you were serious about helping . . .'

Jos nodded vaguely.

'How about you?' I tried instead.

Jos was looking around for the waiter, his eyes sliding off mine. 'Oh, you know. School.' His hands had started building the sugar tepee again. He flicked a sugar sachet in a practised movement, it spun round and round like a pinwheel.

The barista set down two coffees in front of us.

'Oh sorry – they asked me for an order when I sat down and I, uh, panicked and got one for both of us,' Jos said when he noticed my surprised look. 'Latte okay? I guessed.'

'Long black, actually.' His face fell. 'But latte is great, sorry! Just, for next time . . .' I trailed off lamely and felt my cheeks heat up. Next time? Presumptuous much? I took a slurp of the coffee quickly to cover my nerves and spluttered.

'Crap.' I almost spat out my mouthful. I'd burnt my tongue.

Jos passed me a napkin. 'I should've mentioned. Contents: hot.'

I glanced up at him and saw he was smiling. 'Thanks for the warning.' I smiled back. 'Very timely.' I took the napkin, and dabbed at the coffee drips on my tights.

'I'll try and do better . . . next time.'

A little shiver ran down my arms at that, hair standing on end from elbows to fingertips.

Jos ran a hand over his curls. 'So.' He brought his hands together. 'Ready to solve a mystery?'

'Sure.' I pulled my folder out of my bag. 'Here – I took some new notes. The guy died in 1948, which was nearish to the start of the Cold War, right? Something else happened in 1948 – there was a spy scandal in Australia, and America and England stopped including us in their diplomatic discussions, because we weren't safe.'

'Bloody Yanks and Poms,' Jos said in an over-the-top Aussie accent, shaking his head. He pulled the folder towards him.

'Hey, I actually know about this! The Venona incident. We were leaking intelligence like mad.'

'Right. And that's when they set up ASIO – the Australian spy agency – after this scandal, which happened the *same year* as the Somerton Man mystery. Plus, one of the major atomic weapon testing sites was in Woomera, the closest town to Adelaide. Lots of reasons for people to be snooping around.'

'No way, start of ASIO? So, you reckon he was an ally spying on us – could be either British or American then . . .'

'Except his dental records didn't match any of theirs. Or so they said – maybe they lied if he was really a spy. And some people say the picture of him looks kind of Russian. Anyway. Do you know anything about spies in the forties?'

He flipped over the articles from the History folder then set them aside. 'My dad got me really into Bond movies. Brought me up on them. So, all that Cold War stuff, yeah I do know a bit . . .'

I shifted. 'They've got the blondes and the brunettes, right?'

'What?'

'Bond movies, the girls, they're either blondes to be rescued, or evil brunettes to be killed?'

Jos leaned forwards in his chair. 'Um, it's a bit more complex than that . . .'

'For the male characters, sure.'

'Have you even *seen* a Bond movie?'

'I don't have to, I know what they're all like.'

Jos stared at me. I held his gaze.

Jos's face opened up with that smile. 'Right, Laylor. You are coming to mine for dinner. 1948, you say? You're right, early Cold War era. I know just the thing.' He sprung up and offered me his hand. 'Consider it research.'

I pulled myself up, ignoring his hand. Jos tilted his head, considering me.

'What?' I asked, as we left the café.

'I'm just trying to decide which one you are,' he said seriously. 'You know, I think it depends on your mood. Today – the brunette with the gun. Definitely.'

I whacked him with my schoolbag. Jos waved me off, and jogged to the tram stop, sticking out his arm for the one coming down the hill. I liked the way he moved, like he had only just grown into his long limbs, a hint of past awkwardness that had been overcome.

I pulled out my phone and texted Mum I'd be out tonight.

It turned out Jos was short for 'Joseph'.

I discovered this when Jos's mum called out briskly over her shoulder, 'Joseph, set the table, would you? Lara can help.'

I raised my eyebrows at him, and he whipped a tea towel onto his head and did a fake holy face. The tea towel slipped off because his curls were too springy.

Jos had six (*six!*) siblings, most of them older and moved out except for two little sisters, Mira and Jana. The devil twins, Jos whispered to me. They weren't actually twins, just one year apart, six and seven. They ran up to me, asked if I was going to marry Jos, then tore away, giggling, before I could respond.

His mum had Jos's crazy-springy curls (the other way around, I guess – he had hers) and her face was so striking that I kind of wanted to acknowledge it. *Excuse me, do you know you look like a supermodel?* But her manner wasn't anything like Mum's model friends: she wasn't fake and fluttery, but brisk, easy, friendly.

Jos was so at ease at home. He ducked under his mum's arm, dodging her attempt to ruffle his curls, grinning the whole time. He grabbed handfuls of mismatched cutlery and colourful plates, handed me half to set the table.

'Wow, cool.' I stopped in front of a huge wooden bookcase on the way to the dining room. It reached almost to the ceiling, complete with a ladder on a rail.

'Oh yes. The bookcase was my grandfather's,' said Jos's mum. 'He'd probably be scandalised with the state of it, though – all those pristine hardbacks next to paperbacks, and none of it in alphabetical order.'

The bookcase *was* chaotic. Almost every shelf had a pile of books stacked in front of other books, so you could just see the tops of spines peeping out behind.

'Hey, they're totally organised,' Jos protested. 'There's the poetry section, the fiction section, the section I bought last year, and the section of books I bought last week.' He waved vaguely at a pile of books I hadn't noticed, that hadn't even made it onto a shelf but stood in a tottering pile on the floor.

'These are all yours?' I ran my fingers along books on a shelf, mostly classics. 'Do you read new books too?'

'Sure, of course. But I mostly get them from the library. These are the ones I've rescued.'

'There's a second-hand bookshop down the road that put out a fifty-cent box every week. Joseph takes them home like they're abandoned puppies,' Jos's mum explained, as she set a smoky-green glass water jug on the table.

Jana and Mira ran up with matching tumblers, setting them one by one next to the jug in a solemn relay. I watched Jos's face as he watched them.

Jos's dad was adorably excited at the idea of watching the Bond movie with us.

'Lara's never seen one before, Dad,' Jos said, over dinner.

Mr Ghazy's mouth fell open. 'Well Jos, this *is* a responsibility. Connery, do you think, to start? Or perhaps *From Russia With Love*, a real classic –'

'Um, it's actually for research, for school,' I jumped in. 'I don't know if I want to watch more than one . . .'

'Oh no, no, my dear.' Mr Ghazy shook his head at me seriously. 'This is more than *research*. This is the start of something wonderful.'

'*Lara* thinks they're just sexist explosion movies.'

'Oh, no, I didn't mean –'

'I think Lara might have a lot of sense,' broke in Jos's mum, smiling at me as she loaded more salad onto her plate.

'We will win you over.' Mr Ghazy waved his fork at me. 'You'll start watching out of politeness, but 007 will get you in the end.'

❋

There was a three-seater couch in the lounge room and a big squishy armchair. I tried to go for one end of the couch, but Jos was sent to bring in coffee and chocolates, I was sent to help, and when we got back Mr Ghazy had firmly installed himself full-length on the couch, legs up. He waved us to the armchair. It was big enough to seat two, just, with a centimetre or two between our elbows. Jos seemed completely comfortable, with one arm on the side of the chair, and as soon as it started, he was completely absorbed in the movie. I kept my eyes on the screen. It was difficult to focus on the dilemmas of James Bond though, since I had my own issues, i.e. how to stop myself from collapsing on top of Jos, and how to know if I was breathing at a normal speed, or too fast, or too slow, or creepily in sync with his breathing.

It felt like that moment between jumping off a pier and landing in the sea. Elation. Fear. Weightlessness. But stretched over two hours, rather than half a second.

The movie was okay, I think. Mostly, I was thinking about that little sliver of space between Jos and me. Those few centimetres between elbow and arm that seemed to pulse with energy: our own tiny force field.

SOMERTON BEACH, ADELAIDE, NOVEMBER 1948

Olive fanned herself lightly as she sat on the bench. She was still hot and sticky from her shift at work as a typist, and the sea breeze was too weak to offer much relief. Gordon didn't seem to mind the heat, and shifted to close the space between them, lifting an arm to lie casually across the back of the bench around her shoulders. She caught a heady scent of leather, motorbike fuel, and a deeper, tangy smell that was just him.

She leaned away from his arm, not because she didn't want to touch him – she did so want to touch him – but because touching Gordon opened up a kind of shivery, star-filled space inside her that was dizzying and exhilarating, and she felt she could only take small doses.

As she leant forward to avoid his embrace, she caught sight of something on the beach.

'Look, Gordon.' She pointed. Two legs in brown men's trousers, stretched out on the sand. Because of the angle of the sea wall that separated the beach from the esplanade where they were sitting, she couldn't see the rest of the man, just his legs. 'Do you think he's all right?'

Gordon smiled down at her, as if pleased by her concern for others. He leaned forward to check, although his view still couldn't have been better than Olive's. 'Must be sleeping something off, poor fella. He looks dead to the world.'

Olive sat back and tried to relax. She turned her head to smile at Gordon, and froze. Up on the esplanade wall was a man, standing eerily still. She could not make out his face, only the silhouette of his hat ringed in red by the setting sun behind him. He was looking down at the man on the beach.

She watched him for a few minutes. He did not move. As if he was a sentry, she thought, as if he was standing guard.

Gordon sighed and tightened his grip, pulling Olive into his chest. And she found she very quickly forgot the man on the beach and the man in the hat.

CHAPTER EIGHTEEN

'So, are you going out again?' Kate asked me quietly, glancing surreptitiously at Mr Grant. He was mid-explanation about the storming of the Bastille, summarising our French Revolution module as term wrapped up.

'Don't know if it really counts as "out", though, right?'

'Definitely not,' Ash offered from behind us, a bit too loud. We'd kept our seats from the first class, and sometimes I think Ash made a point of speaking as if she had to yell at me from a great distance.

'Something to share, Lara?' Mr Grant turned to look at me.

Ash snorted and leant back in her chair.

'Uh –'

'It was me, Mr Grant,' Kate broke in. 'I was just commenting on your description of the different kinds of revolting peasants. I think maybe we need a visual?' She offered her hand.

He raised his eyebrows. 'Sure.'

Kate jumped up and took the whiteboard marker from him. 'Right, so you've got the san-culottes, right, and they want blood? But then there's these other guys . . .' she sketched a few figures on the board, complete with era-appropriate outfits.

'Hmm, yes, quite good.' Mr Grant reclaimed the pen. 'I think this one needs a pike, head included, though.'

'I'll add it!' Mia jumped up from behind us, clearly keen to extend the distraction as long as she could. I'd gotten to know Mia a bit through the musical – she was one of those super outgoing people who's so gushy to everyone I never knew whether to trust her friendliness. We were minutes from the bell.

Kate slid back in beside me.

'Cheers.'

'Any time. Thought you wouldn't want to have your love life discussed along with bloodthirsty peasants.'

'What there *is* of a love life,' offered Ash.

'More blood, Mia,' called someone from the back. Mr Grant handed her a red marker for effect. She was still adding to her artwork when the bell rang.

'Lara, a moment, please?' Mr Grant came over to my desk as the classroom began to clear.

Damn. I guess he had noticed me talking. Kate squeezed my shoulder sympathetically as she left.

For a second Mr Grant just looked at the board. 'Talented, Kate, isn't she?'

'She is.' With a few strokes of the marker Kate had given her revolutionaries personalities, intentions. Mia's head on a pike was less sophisticated, if more colourful.

I paused. 'Uh, sorry for talking in class, Mr Grant, I didn't mean –'

He waved a hand to stop me and turned to me with a smile. 'Lara, what did you think of today's lesson?'

I scrambled to think. 'Well . . . it is interesting, actually. I always thought that Bastille Day was about fighting for freedom. But you seem to say it was more about how expensive bread was that morning.'

He nodded, and waited until I said more.

'But it's kind of both, maybe? Because the peasants needed the political idealist type people to give them something to centre around? . . . I don't know. It's all part of the same thing, but I don't know what's more important.'

He tilted his head. 'I kind of like your maps idea from that day in the car park. It depends what kind of map you use – one that shows street names and highways, or one that shows contours and height above sea level. Different representations of the same thing. But if you try to get something that shows everything at once, like a satellite image – then it's not a map at all, and kind of useless if you need it to tell you which road to take.' He laughed. 'Sorry, I don't know if I'm making sense.'

'I think I get it. Sort of. Too many details start to get in the way, but the less you have the further from the truth you are.' I did feel like I was starting to get it, and it felt like Mr Grant was really listening to me, happy to figure out these ideas together.

'One last thing, Lara.' Mr Grant's eyes were suddenly intent on mine. 'I don't think you realise that – other than showing an impressive ability to multitask personal discussion with analysis' – his eyes crinkled in amusement, – 'these insights you have are quite unique. You have an intelligent and perceptive way of seeing the world. And I think anyone who doesn't recognise that quality, may not deserve you.'

I wondered if he was talking about Jos. Had he overheard us? I definitely didn't want to talk to him about that. I felt the warm buzz of interest at talking about history fade, replaced by an uneasy feeling in my stomach.

'We can choose our friends, Lara. It's one of the great freedoms of getting older, that realisation.' He glanced point-edly at Ash's desk, behind me.

Oh – he meant Ash, not Jos.

There was a cough from the doorway.

'Sorry, hope I'm not *interrupting*, am I?' Ash said coldly. 'We've got rehearsal, Loz.'

'Right – sorry, Mr Grant. And, uh, thank you.'

I don't know if she heard what he said or not, but Ash barely spoke to me the rest of the afternoon.

CHAPTER NINETEEN

Kate sat opposite me, the table wobbling dangerously as she stowed her bag.

'Oops. The cost of rustic décor.' She pulled out a napkin and disappeared under the table to secure the uneven leg.

I was about to help when my phone pinged three times in quick succession.

Totally forgot about today!!! I got caught running lines with Mia.

I'm sure you don't need me anyway, you've got this covered right?

Soz Loz xxxx

Ugh. Somehow I knew it was too good to be true when both Kate and Ash had been free this afternoon to go over our Somerton Man notes. I'd thought the lure of doing it with lattes instead of in the library would get Ash here, but clearly not.

'What happened?' Kate's muffled voice came from under the table.

'Nothing.' I tapped out a quick reply to Ash.

All good!! Hi to Mia.

She sent back a kiss emoji. I turned the phone over.

'It's not nothing if it makes you sigh like that.' Kate emerged and rocked the table experimentally. My phone slid dangerously close to the edge, I reached out and caught it.

'Damn, I overcompensated.' She ducked back down to readjust. 'Who are you texting?'

'Just Ash. She's not coming.' I realised how blunt that sounded and carried on quickly. 'She forgot she had a clash with stuff for the musical.'

Kate didn't say anything, but I noticed her back and shoulders tense.

It would be so much easier if Kate liked Ash. 'It's not her fault, I know the part is really full on,' I continued. 'And I don't think she's that into this mystery assignment, to be honest.'

Kate sat up and tested the table. 'There. Stability restored.'

'Should we do it anyway, do you think?' I asked her. We'd been planning on pooling our individual research, before my next meeting with Mr Grant tomorrow, the last one of the term.

'Sure, that's what we're here for.'

I wanted to say more in Ash's defence, but couldn't immediately think of anything. Kate and I were quiet as we pulled out our laptops and got our notes up on screen.

'Oh yes, they all have to sit in the same positions when they have dinner, it's hilarious.' A woman's voice from the table next to us carried over. 'Roy took Carol's spot which left her a bit bewildered, but she respects him, so that's okay.'

'Ah, the pecking order,' said one of her friends, wisely.

It seemed an odd way to describe a dinner party. I looked up and caught Kate's eye, she also looked puzzled. She grinned and rolled her eyes, and some of the tension between us eased.

'So how much do you need to have done for Mr Grant tomorrow? Is he checking in on our progress?' Kate asked.

'Kind of. I mean, I don't think they're graded or anything. They're just extra sessions for people who are keen.'

'Isn't there one person from each group though? Who else was in your first session with him?'

'Uh, it's optional, so there isn't necessarily one from each group . . .' I'd been vague to Kate about the fact I was the only one who showed up. But Mr Grant had said how hard it was to schedule a time around the musical. Maybe it was just a coincidence I was on my own.

'I could ask him if you could come along, if you wanted?' I offered. My heartbeat quickened, and I realised I was worried what would happen if she said yes. Somehow I couldn't picture the meetings with Mr Grant working with someone else there.

'That's okay – to be honest, I'm not hugely interested in the mystery either.'

Oh. I felt a mixture of relief and disappointment and reached out to close my computer.

'I didn't mean that! Like, obviously it's fascinating, but it's your thing – I'm not extra-school-time level of interested.'

The staff put down our coffees and Kate pulled hers towards her.

'So why did you come today, if you're not as obsessed as me?'

Kate looked at me over the top of her flat white. 'Because you asked me to come, Lara.'

I didn't know how to respond to such a simple answer.

The woman in the group next to us kept talking, still about the same dinner party guests. 'Yes, it all improved once Carol gave Roy a little nip – nothing serious, just to assert her dominance.'

I widened my eyes at Kate, whose mouth had dropped open.

'She's normally the gentlest little thing – even though dachshunds do have that reputation –'

Kate's eyes met mine. *Dogs*, she mouthed.

Not people, I mouthed back. I tried to stop myself from laughing and let out a very unladylike snort. The woman gave me a look. Kate held up her hand, she was shaking with the effort to hold back her laughter, and sketching something furiously in her sketchbook. She slid it over to me; she'd drawn a cartoon woman in pearls, labelled Carol, nipping the arm of a surprised gentleman in suspenders labelled Roy. Carol's teeth were particularly large.

I let out a shriek and the women on the table turned around to stare. Kate grabbed my arm. 'Don't make them mad. What if they have rabies?' And we both collapsed onto the table, laughing so loud the group actually got up and moved in a flurry of handbags and glares.

It was the best study session I'd had in a long time.

CHAPTER TWENTY

'Coffee, Lara?' Mr Grant held out a mug to me. Like last time, he brought me one from the staff room when we had our tutoring. This was only the second session, and I was looking forward to today: he'd decided it was time to pass on the next folder of material on the mystery.

He settled on the edge of the teacher's desk. 'So, how are play rehearsals going?'

'Oh, okay. Ms Drummond is pretty tough.'

'And the St John's boys? Are they living up to expectations?' He raised his eyebrows slightly.

I started to laugh and stopped myself, thinking suddenly of Jos. 'Uh, some of them are all right, I guess.'

'Mmm. Nothing quite as damning as faint praise – poor boys.'

'Oh no, they're okay, really.'

'Some of your classmates seem a bit more enthusiastic.' He took a sip of coffee. 'Is it just me, or does Ashley seem a bit giddier on rehearsal days?'

I smiled properly then. Ash was pretty much impossible to talk to about anything else on rehearsal days. 'It's definitely not just you.'

He chuckled quietly. I felt a warm satisfaction at making him laugh mixed with a twist of guilt that I was laughing at Ash.

Before I could think of how to change the subject, I was distracted by a staccato clip of heels that stopped outside the door. Mrs Lamby, our year level coordinator, opened it.

'I thought I heard someone. You're here late, David –' she saw me sitting on the desk, '– Mr Grant,' she corrected quickly. 'Hello, Lara.' Her gaze took in the piles of paper, our coffee mugs.

'Mrs Lamby!' Mr Grant smiled easily. 'Lara and I were just reviewing her assignment.' He reached behind him to a stack of folders, clearly untouched, and rifled through to find the one on the Somerton Man assignment. As he did his eyes met mine for a second and he raised his eyebrows in a subtle 'whoops' expression.

I laughed and turned it into a cough. Mrs Lamby glanced at me.

'Oh – looks like I've misplaced it. I'll bring it next time, Lara.'

Mrs Lamby's smile turned rigid. 'You know, Mr Grant, we have some new study areas in the refurbished library that would be perfect for these . . . sessions. I'll show you how to use the booking system on the intranet for next time.'

'That's so helpful of you, Mrs Lamby, thank you,' Mr Grant replied, earnestly.

I stared at my lap so I wouldn't laugh again.

'Right.' She nodded, and seemed to realise she had no more reason to be in the room. 'Nice to see you, Lara. Drop by my office any time you like, okay?'

'Sure . . .' I didn't know what she expected of me. 'Thanks, Mrs Lamby.'

She turned to go. As she opened the door, she reached out with her foot to move a spare chair to stand in front of the door, holding it open. The chair scraped across the floor as she moved it in place. It was an awful sound, a grating squeal of metal on plastic. Mrs Lamby's cheeks reddened at the noise, but she didn't say anything, didn't look up at either of us, she just left through the propped-open door and clipped back along the corridor.

I didn't feel like laughing anymore. I pushed down the worry that Kate had expected more people to be here too. Mrs Lamby's interruption felt like when there's a lull in a conversation and someone says 'well, this is awkward', making the silence curdle into something far worse than it had been before. I hate it when people do that.

All the warmth and ease of chatting with Mr Grant now felt tainted somehow. We hadn't been doing anything wrong, I knew, but the way Mrs Lamby reacted made me feel like I had. I resented that. Mr Grant was the only one who treated me like an adult, like someone who wasn't Hannah's sister, and now she was ruining it.

The way I was sitting seemed suddenly exposed and obvious, perched on the edge of the desk opposite Mr Grant, like my limbs were all too long for my body, like I was taking up too much space. When I looked at him again he seemed unfazed by the interruption, and gave me a conspiratorial smile.

'Well, I hope you have enough to be going on with until I get you the next instalment of the mystery, Lara.' He reached out for my coffee mug. 'I'd better take that.'

I handed it back to him, my arms swinging weirdly by my sides.

'Lara.' His tone forced me to look at him. He still had that warm, inviting expression on his face. 'It's been a pleasure, really. It always is.' His smile widened. 'Looking forward to continuing the discussion – maybe in the faculty-approved library room.'

I felt my shoulders relax and the tension drain out at his comment. I took my books from the desk. It didn't look like he thought there was anything wrong – maybe it was okay. Mrs Lamby did care way too much about stuff like booking the right rooms for things.

'Thanks, Mr Grant.' I left. Despite the weirdness of the meeting, I was looking forward to our next one – and the last folder of the mystery.

CHAPTER TWENTY-ONE

Everyone is a little bit louder, funnier, friendlier on the last day of term. Even the colours are brighter. It was the last hour of the day, reserved for clearing out lockers, and what the staff euphemistically called 'taking responsibility for the school community' – i.e. cleaning.

Ash and I sat on the desks in our form classroom, legs swinging. She was listening to music on her phone. Normally I'd pull out one of her earphones for myself and we'd share, but things had felt a bit weirder between us, with Kate around lately. So I just sat next to her, tapping my fingers to the tinny overflow of the song.

'Oh good. You're not busy.' Mrs Lamby spotted us and pounced with sanitiser spray and Chux wipes. 'Graffiti in the girls' bathrooms needs to be removed. Off you go.'

Ash removed her earbuds. 'You know, I'm not sure "slave labour" was what my mum had in mind when she forked out for an "innovative and inspiring educational experience".'

'The ones at the end of the hall, first door on your right, please, *ladies*.'

Ash swung down from the desk and started walking. She didn't look to see if I was following her. I tried not to read into it.

✳

We worked in uncomfortable silence. I struggled to think of a way to break the tension as I scrubbed out a very creative rendering of Mrs Lamby with a pig snout. Something at the bottom of the cubicle caught my eye: *Ash & Loz, BFFs.* Each word was carefully outlined in bubble letters. And in purple glitter-ink pen.

'Hey Ash, check this out.'

She came over. 'Huh.' I saw the start of a smile. 'I'd forgotten we did that.'

'Year Seven, surely,' I said. 'I *hope* it was Year Seven, considering the "BFF". Do you think we were using it ironically?'

'I wouldn't count on it. How good are my bubble letters, by the way?'

'No way, I'm sure that's my work. I was always the master of a good bubble-letter script.'

Ash laughed properly at that. I took a step closer to her and bumped her on the hip. She bumped me back. And suddenly, we felt okay again.

I set up her phone with an empty toilet roll as a speaker, and we had a mini-dance party as we cleaned the rest of the graffiti.

'Hey, check out this genius,' called Ash. 'Underneath a "Vegans Do It Better" sticker she's written, "I don't know why vegans are so judgemental. I love animals. I mean it's not like I want animals to die just so I can eat meat."'

'Logic. Nice. I've got an arrow pointing to the loo saying "This way to the Ministry of Magic".'

'Let's leave those ones.' Ash emerged from her cubicle and redid her hair in the mirror. 'Come on, Loz, not like she'll check anyway.'

'One sec,' I made sure all the phone numbers with gross comments were scrubbed out – no one needed that – and joined her. 'Holiday plans, by the way?' I asked. Weird that I didn't know already.

'Up the coast with the parents *and* the grandparents. Going to be eye-gougingly boring, but hopefully the weather will still be good up there. You?'

'Nah, staying here.'

'Ah well, guess you'll have Kate for company, right? Or . . . Jos?' She wiggled her eyebrows at me in the mirror.

'He's away too, for the whole two weeks. Cousin's wedding overseas I think.' I wondered if my voice sounded as disappointed as I felt. 'I don't know, though . . . I mean, can it really count as a date if his parents watched the movie with us?'

'Definitely not. But maybe, like, a quarter of a date. And going for coffee and spitting it all over him could qualify you for another quarter date. So, all up, half of a real date?'

I leaned against the mirror to try and cool down my blush and groaned. 'Where are all the underage drinking scenes our parents are terrified of? Just one. I'll get myself to one drunken party to try and figure this out.'

'Well, if you find that scene *please* let me know. Failing that, there's always the musical afterparty.'

❋

We walked back to our lockers, arm in arm.

'Urgh, it's like he's stalking you.' Ash stiffened beside me.

'What?' I thought she meant Jos – but it was Mr Grant, leaning up against my locker, a phone to his ear. He was standing in an odd way, back very straight, and almost leant away from his phone, as if his arm holding it belonged to someone else.

He hung up and his arm fell to his side. His face was completely white.

'Coming, Loz?' Ash was looking towards our classroom, where everyone else was chilling out, waiting for the final bell of the day, and the term.

'One sec. I need to grab something from my locker.'

'Sure you do.' Ash rolled her eyes and left me. So much for the good signs of the last few hours.

I walked over. 'Mr Grant?'

He turned to look at me slowly 'Oh. Lara. Hello.' He was staring right through me, eyes wide.

'Hi. Um. Are you okay?'

'What? Oh. Yes, yes. I was just walking back to my office when I got that call . . .' He shook himself slightly, and his eyes focused on me, looking a bit more like himself. 'So. How's the search for my Somerton Man going?'

'Uh, okay, I guess.' I waited, but he didn't look like he was going to explain any further. 'I had someone help me work out one of the theories the other day.' I thought of Jos at the café, talking about James Bond.

'Kate, was that?'

'No just – just another friend.'

'I see.' Mr Grant pressed his lips together. 'A friend. And what theory was that? Your favourite frontrunner?'

'The spy theory. You know, how he died the same year as a big intelligence leak in Australia – and there was that nuclear weapons testing site – and plus, if he was a Russian spy or something, that could explain why his dental records didn't match anywhere in Australia, the US or the UK.'

Mr Grant nodded. 'Good reasoning.' He narrowed his eyes. 'But you don't believe it, do you?'

'I'd like to. But it does seem a bit unlikely – a bit too neat, too much like a movie. I don't know if I think history is like that.'

'Oh really?' Mr Grant shifted a little closer to me. His eyes lit up with interest. 'And what do you think history is like?'

My first time body surfing at the beach – crushed between saltwater and sand, disorientated, gasping for air.

'Like being dumped by a wave in the surf,' I said.

Mr Grant laughed aloud in surprise. I felt myself smile cautiously in response.

'Okay, you're going to have to unpack that one for me.'

'Well . . .' I searched for the words, trying to keep him interested. 'I keep thinking of another theory of the man – the refugee, let into our country, forced to work on some manual labour project with other people who don't speak his language, until maybe the loneliness and strangeness got too much . . . he's just this one person, you know, completely swept away and crushed by war, politics – by history. Just like being dumped by a wave, nature, something bigger than you . . . something that doesn't care about you.'

'Yes . . . yes. And the tide keeps coming in and out, doesn't it? The decades, sweeping in and out . . .' Mr Grant trailed off, staring away from me. He twisted his phone in his hand, spinning it around. 'Still, either way he died, didn't he? Spy or refugee, it got him in the end. History caught up.'

I nodded uncertainly. It was a depressing note to finish on. I waited for Mr Grant to say something more, but he just kept staring into the distance, like he'd forgotten I was there.

'Uh, Mr Grant?'

'Hmm?'

'Sorry, but . . . I kind of need to get to my locker.'

'Oh, this is your locker? Right. Sorry, Lara.' He stood up, moved off the wall. 'You know, there's even more to the mystery than that – I'm really impressed with what you've come up with so far, and in a way it's a shame . . .' He stopped.

'What's a shame?'

He smiled, shook his head slightly. 'Nothing. Sorry, I'm clearly not making sense. In need of the holiday, I think. Thanks for the chat, Lara.'

'Um, no problem. Thanks, Mr Grant. See you next term.'

'Yes . . .' He tapped the phone again in his hand. 'Goodbye, Lara.'

He turned and walked away as the final bell rang and everyone burst out into the corridor.

CHAPTER TWENTY-TWO

Postcard: Hostel Orzigula, Bucharest. Very nice rooms here, acceptable and light!! Please be visiting.

Lara,

I don't know why this place can afford printed postcards of their crappy rooms when they can't get plumbing that works, but hope you like it! I've had a flu of epic proportions and have finally had to accept that wandering these little streets high on cold and flu meds and low on language skills is not a good combination, so I've retreated to my luxury recovery suite (aka single bunk bed in a dorm of 16).

Anyway, I just got up from my bed-cave for long enough to buy this from the reception lady (she smells like smoke and regret, and acted like I was asking her to give up her firstborn when I wanted a postcard).

H x

I dropped my bag in the hallway, wriggled out of my school dress and pulled on some shorts and a T-shirt, then shoved my feet into runners, ready for my end-of-term run. It was a weirdly sunny day for March, like the weather was celebrating the end of school too. But first, part one of the end-of-term ritual: peanut butter, Nutella and banana sandwich. Heavy on the Nutella. I took the first squishy, salty, chocolaty bite and felt my mouth instantly glue shut.

'Lara, I didn't know you were home already.' A voice came from the lounge room. 'What *are* you eating? It sounds disgusting.'

'Mmph?' I managed. What was Dad doing here? He came into the kitchen, and poured me a glass of water. I gulped it down.

'Dad! You're home early.'

'Can you believe it – we had a client who didn't want *any* changes to our plans. I gave the team the afternoon off. Part celebration, partly to recover from the shock.' He eyed the components of my sandwich construction, strewn across the counter. 'Seriously, what *are* you eating?'

'End of term ritual, Dad. Remember, Hannah used to make them for me?'

'Right.' Dad's smile faded at her name. He missed her too, I knew. He looked down and started to flip through the post from today. Wait, today's post. I hadn't thought he'd be home, I hadn't checked in time –

Dad went completely still. Slowly, he tidied the pile of bills and charity letters and placed them on the counter. He was still holding a small, rectangular coloured card. A postcard. Crap.

'Lara?'

'Yeah?'

'Can you explain, please?'

My sandwich felt like PVA glue in my mouth. I made a big effort to swallow. 'What's there to explain?' I took a gulp of water. 'Hannah's writing me postcards.'

'But we thought she was in France. This one is from –' He flipped over the card. '*Romania*.'

'Well, it's not like she's going to be eaten by vampires, Dad.' I tried to say it lightly, but it came out sarcastic.

'Lara, this is serious. We need to know your sister is safe. Why would she lie to us about where she is?'

'I don't know. Maybe she figured her money would go a lot further out that way. Or she just wanted to. No one cool goes to Paris anymore, Dad.'

'No one cool . . . since when is *Paris* not cool? They invented cool.' Dad closed his eyes, and gripped the bridge of his nose between his fingers. It was dangerous when he went quiet. That was when I knew he was seriously mad.

I felt a spark of frustration at Hannah flare up in my stomach. I never asked her to send me the postcards. I hadn't even known about the gap year until pretty much the week she was leaving. And now *I* was the one getting in trouble.

'Or maybe, Dad, Hannah just couldn't have a normal gap year, because she needs to turn everything into a one-woman drama starring herself.' The words came out before I could stop myself.

Dad opened his eyes, let his hand drop. 'Lara . . .'

'What? You know it's true.'

'We aren't talking about Hannah right now. This is your responsibility too. Why didn't you tell us what was going on?'

I dropped my sandwich. 'Maybe because I knew that I'd get blamed for Hannah's stuff, even though she isn't even *here*.'

'Lara, don't be ridiculous. This is not how we have this conversation –'

'Yeah, well I'm done with this conversation.' I didn't wait for him to reply. I was out the door and down at the park in minutes. I launched into a run round the oval, letting out the strange energy of the day with each step.

One lap, and the echo of slammed lockers and shrieked goodbyes faded in the call of a lorikeet and the beat of my footsteps. A second lap, and the image of Ash rolling her eyes disappeared as I focused on the pattern of the trees against the skyline. A third lap, and I left behind Mr Grant's pale face and odd tone at my locker; another lap, to erase Dad's fingers turned white as he gripped the postcard, the disappointment in his eyes; until all that was left was grass under my feet, sun on my neck, air through my lungs.

PART 2
THE SEARCH

April–August

Don't nobody wonder where he's been?
No tags, no wallet
And his brains dry-cleaned

THE DRONES

CHAPTER TWENTY-THREE

What with Ash sending me nauseatingly sunny selfies from the beach, Jos being away, and the weirdness of a house without Hannah, the holidays seemed endless. The one bright spot was the messages from Jos – I'd noticed myself smiling instinctively every time my phone dinged, before I even knew it was him. He'd given himself the task of finding the weirdest title in a second-hand bookstore over the break, and enlisted me to judge: current frontrunners were *Teaching Your Cat To Whistle* and *The Do It Yourself Lobotomy*. With that and the thought of more rehearsals, I was actually looking forward to being back at school by the time term began.

I sat between Ash and Kate in our start of term assembly, and was so relieved that they seemed happy enough to be in that close proximity to each other that it took me a while to tune in to the announcement from the front.

Mrs Lamby was saying something about staff changes, but she was struggling to get her words out.

'Due to unavoidable personal reasons – unavoidable personal health reasons – unavoidable reasons that will not be further discussed, that is, that do not need further discussion –'

At this point the principal coughed. Mrs Lamby sped up. Her hair was frizzing out of her bun even more than usual, she seemed distracted; her glasses swung from their beaded chain like an erratic pendulum.

'Mr David Grant will not be returning to his post as History teacher this term, or indeed for the foreseeable future. His classes will be redistributed amongst relief staff, until a suitable replacement is found.'

'No!' I said. Too loud. People turned to look.

I wasn't the only one though. There was a definite reaction, a general startled murmur and a few clearly outraged cries. Even some of the teachers seemed surprised, conferring with each other in their seats on the side of the hall, before they sat up guiltily and shushed us.

By St Margaret's assembly standards, it was pretty much an uproar.

CITY MORGUE, ADELAIDE, JUNE 1949

Burt Cleland was tired. A good kind of tired, the sort after a day (or, in his case, a lifetime) of strenuous and satisfying work. He was seventy-one years old, and had performed over seven thousand autopsies. Despite this, when the police requested his help with the case of the Somerton Man, he agreed.

In truth, he would not have come out of retirement for anything less than the man found on the beach with no name, no cause of death, no history: Burt would no longer rouse himself for a dead body, but he could not resist a lost soul.

He stretched his hands in front of him, shook out tired muscles of body and mind, and set to work.

The movements so familiar: scalpel, cut, examine. His hands were gentle and precise. He imagined his patients would appreciate his care, if they could. And as he pulled apart the meat and bones, examined the skin and hair and organs, stories appeared from the physicality. Stories, and mysteries.

'A dancer, were you?' He murmured, feeling the high, bunched calf muscles of the man's legs. 'Or a runner? A distance runner, perhaps.' The feet of the man were elegant, long, very well cared for. 'Good show, chap. Some of the nicest feet I've seen,' said Burt, glancing at the man's face.

The face, even after months of embalmment, retained a remarkable expression. Something of sadness, or was that pain, regret?

Burt turned from the body to the man's clothes, laid out on a separate table. He blinked rapidly to clear dark spots from his eyes. His eyesight was beginning to go. 'Too old for this, too old. The last one – you're my last sad soul, you know that? The end of a long line.'

Burt picked up and ran his hands over the man's shoes. The leather was smooth and soft, stitching tiny, perfect, even. No manufacturer's label inside, but they were clearly of the highest quality. Bespoke, perhaps. Burt blinked away his distorted reflection in the shined surface, and carefully placed the man's shoes back on the table.

'You'll give me something, won't you, my friend?' he asked, as he turned to the rest of the clothing. 'Something for old Burt? You don't have to fear me. For an old man out of retirement, one last expedition into a life – I've known so many lives, you know that?'

He examined the man's jacket, looking through stitching for hidden pockets. There was no label on the jacket either. 'Some lives ended obviously, crude bruises clear for anyone to see. And others were hidden, insidious, secret wounds carried to the grave, pain they would share with no one, no one but old Burt. But you, you're different.'

Burt moved to the trousers. Some sand was left in the cuffs. 'You have no bruises. You have no slash, no cut. You have no sign of who you are at all, or how you ended.' The manufacturer's label was missing from here, too. No labels on any of the clothing. 'But you can tell me. You can show old Burt.'

He began searching the pockets, pockets that had already been searched by sergeants and the coroner's doctor. 'Unless, of course, you don't know,' he mused, glancing back at the impassive face on the body. 'Have you completely lost yourself, my last soul? Were you gone before I arrived, wasted away even in life?' He shook his head. 'A terrible thing, to lose yourself while you're right there.'

He reached the final pocket, a small fob pocket of the trousers, smaller than usual. And Burt Cleland reached in with practised fingers, fingers that had dipped into countless pockets, and found . . . something.

'Ah . . .'

A small, tight roll of paper. With utmost care, he straightened it out. Torn from a page of a book, two words. *Tamam Shud.* His old eyes squinted to read it.

'Tamam Shud . . .'

He smiled back at the body, the man laid out on the table. Naked, and now, at last, vulnerable. 'Thank you.'

CHAPTER TWENTY-FOUR

I walked slowly towards my locker. The school felt drained of colour: the lockers a grey blur, the fluorescent lights a dull pulse above my head.

My phone vibrated in my pocket. A text from Jos – my finger hovered over the spot to open it, but I put my phone away instead. I couldn't stop thinking about the assembly. He's just sick. Teachers get sick all the time. But I could feel this was different, something was off in the way Mrs Lamby had told us. Almost as if she was embarrassed . . .

There was a note at my locker.

I looked around, but this bit of the corridor was empty. I'd walked so slowly everyone else was in class. There it was, a small brown square, jutting out from the crack where the locker door closed.

I dropped my books to the floor and pulled it out. Ash and I used to leave notes for each other years ago, back when it was the thing you did with your friends. But she knew my combination, and would leave those inside. Could it be from Kate? But why, when we'd just seen each other . . . I unfolded it, the paper crinkling in my hands.

On one side, there were the lines of a poem:

Whether the Cup with sweet or bitter run,
The Wine of Life keeps oozing drop by drop,
The Leaves of Life keep falling one by one.

I turned over the paper. *Keep searching, L – Tamam Shud.*
'Tamam Shud'. My heartbeat sped up. I had no idea
what the words meant, or the poem, but I recognised the
handwriting from the notes I got back on my History work.
It was him.

CHAPTER TWENTY-FIVE

I sat under my tree, dressed and ready to run, but I couldn't move. It was like my mind was going too fast, so my body froze to compensate. Mrs Lamby's words kept bouncing around in my mind – 'unavoidable reasons', 'will not be discussed further' – it was weird. Nothing like the normal end-of-term list of names of teachers retiring or going on maternity leave – then we'd all clap for them and, if a teacher was popular, the girls in their classes would chip in for flowers.

But this had been so abrupt, so cold.

And then – my fingers went again to my pocket, felt the soft edges of the note he'd left me. I'd checked online and found the lines he'd copied out were from a stanza of the *Rubaiyat* poem.

Whether the Cup with sweet or bitter run,
The Wine of Life keeps oozing drop by drop,
The Leaves of Life keep falling one by one.

Some of the trees around the park were ready to lose their leaves, but not yet. They were still trying out the variety of autumn colours: deep cherry, wine-stain, terracotta, lemon-yellow. Soon they'd pile up in the gutters in drifts of dusty brown. What did he mean by that note?

For the first time, I wondered about the family of the Somerton Man. Did they know he was leaving? Did he leave behind a partner, children, or parents? Did they watch him go, get on that train to Adelaide, from wherever he came from? Or did they get separated in some desperate escape from war, did they lose each other in a moment of confusion on an unfamiliar land? Or maybe his family never knew it was him at all, and to them it was a story of everyday tragedy, or international intrigue, not personal heartbreak.

And if he was a spy, would it make a difference to them, if they knew? He'd still be gone. Their house still empty.

Did Mr Grant have a family? None of us had ever found out if he had a partner or not.

I untied and pulled my laces tighter until I felt the insistent pressure across the bridge of my feet. Get up. Run. It will make you feel better.

I lay down instead and tried to use logic to sort through my thoughts.

Option one: school was telling the truth. He was sick. But Mrs Lamby's speech was too weird for that. There had to be something more.

Option two: he had to leave for some mysterious reason, bigger than teaching at St Margaret's – was it so ridiculous to think he could be in political trouble of some kind – ASIO coming for him, like they might have for the Somerton Man? This made me smile but I couldn't quite get myself to believe it.

Or what about the other possibility of the Somerton Man, the saddest and in some ways simplest? Option three tugged at me like dark shadows seen on the edge of your vision. A goodbye note. A permanent goodbye. '*The leaves of life keep falling one by one . . .*'

I stood up and started to run, feet pounding on the oval as hard as they could.

CHAPTER TWENTY-SIX

Our first rehearsal back at school, Ms Drummond had an announcement: she was arranging a cast trip over the long weekend in June, partly for some cast bonding time, partly to catch up on how 'woefully behind' our rehearsal schedule was. Predictably, this caused a flurry of immediate discussion on where it would be and who was going to share rooms with who, and made the rest of rehearsal time effectively useless. I turned to Jos and Tim, the only ones who didn't seem surprised.

'Did you know about this already?'

'Yeah,' Tim acknowledged. 'It's my family's beach house, down at Mornington. I think Ms Drummond has co-opted a few of the others' holiday houses too so she could fit everyone – I know Guy's family has one across the road – but mostly it'll be at our place. Massive enough for three lots of my family, can hold like twenty people. Mum and Dad like to justify their extravagance by offering the place for anything resembling a community service, Ms Drummond wanted a location, everyone's a winner.'

Tim smiled easily, but I could tell he was nervous talking about his family's wealth. St John's had a lot of scholarship students – I wondered if Jos was one actually, he did seem scary-smart – and being rich wasn't the norm as much as other private schools. Thankfully. Tim was so blond and likeable, it was easy to see how he could have been moulded if his parents had picked a different school: a footy/cricket/hockey captain jerk with no self-awareness and great networking skills, a future politician or CEO. Instead he was just Tim, sweet and quick to make space for others instead of claiming it as his own. And still with the hook-ups to awesome beach houses.

❋

Ash wanted to talk beach outfits and weekend strategy with me as we left, but I was distracted – I still couldn't get the note from Mr Grant out of my mind. I dropped back to trail behind the others, leaving Ash to discuss the pros and cons of the purchase of new bathers with Mia instead.

The others were well ahead when I passed the staff room, just as a teacher was leaving.

'Oh, Lana! Excuse me. Lana – excuse me!'

I turned around, even though she hadn't said my name. It was the substitute History teacher – Ms Walsh, I'd say, if I had to guess? I probably couldn't blame her for forgetting my name too.

'Thank you,' she said, relieved.

'It's Lara, actually.'

'Oh.' She reddened. 'Sorry – it's terrible handwriting. Stay there a second, please. I've got something for you.' She ducked back into the staff room and emerged with a manila folder. She squinted at the note pinned to the front.

Wait. 'What's that?'

'Lana – sorry, Lara, it must say – Laylor, right? I was meant to give it to you in class, but missed it. I'm still catching up. His in-tray is such a mess.'

'It's from Mr Grant?' I tried to keep the hope out of my voice.

'The note here says it was for an ongoing assignment –
I thought you'd know what it meant?' She frowned, looking
again at the folder. 'Unless it is for someone else . . .'

'No, it's for me, for sure,' I said quickly. I held out my hand.

'Okay, great.' She handed it over, looking relieved. 'I don't
even know what assignment it is yet, I'm sorry. Still getting
up to speed. It looks like he took a lot of creative licence with
the curriculum but didn't leave any lesson plans behind – it's
completely chaotic. He must have left in a hurry.'

'Some of the girls heard he might be sick?'

Ms Walsh tilted her head. 'Sick? I don't think so . . . but
I'm just the substitute teacher. They don't tell me much.' She
smiled at me. 'Anyway, let me know if I can help with the
assignment.'

She turned and walked back to the staff room before I
could ask anything else.

I looked down at the folder.

He had left me more than the note.

I knew if I didn't leave now, I'd miss the next tram. But I
didn't move. I sank to the floor and started to read.

St Margaret's History:
Year Ten Mystery Assignment

Teacher: Mr Grant
The Somerton Man
Folder Three: The *Rubaiyat*

Tamam Shud

- Weeks after the initial autopsy, a second examination found a tiny slip of paper rolled up in a trouser pocket. The slip of paper was torn out from a book and said 'Tamam Shud'
- The words were from a book of Persian poetry and mean 'It is finished' or 'The end'

The Rubaiyat

- After a public appeal, the book which the slip of paper had been torn from was handed into police: *The Rubaiyat of Omar Khayyam*
- The book was missing the last two words of the poem: *'Tamam Shud'*, and was an exact match with the torn slip of paper found in the Somerton Man's pocket
- There was a page of handwritten letters in the back of the book that many speculate could be a code:
    WRGOABABD
    ~~MLIAOI~~
    WTBIMPANETP
    MLIABOAIAQC
    ITTMTSAMSTGAB
- On the back page of the book there was also a handwritten phone number for the home of a local nurse

The nurse

- Jessica Ellen 'Jo' Thomson (name given to police, although she was not married to Prosper Thomson at the time), also known as 'Jess' 'Tina' and 'Jestyn' (a combination of her nicknames)
- Lived in Moseley St, Glenelg – less than a five-minute walk from where the body was found
- She had a two-year-old in 1949, Robin Thomson, who had the same distinctive ear shape and unusual teeth structure as the Somerton Man, each of which occur in <2% of the population

A second Rubaiyat & the Army Intelligence Officer

- When asked why her phone number was in the *Rubaiyat*, Jestyn revealed she had given a copy of the book to an Army Intelligence Officer named Alf Boxall about a decade ago when they met in Sydney
- Police thought Boxall must be the Somerton Man, but found Boxall alive and well in Sydney, still with the copy of the *Rubaiyat* that Jestyn had given him – a different copy to the one handed in to police in Adelaide
- Boxall denied any connection with the case

Key quotes

'In a fob pocket which was rather difficult to find . . . I found a piece of paper. After I found it and put the paper back, it took me a good deal of time to find it the second time, as it was a pocket which could be easily missed.'

Professor John 'Burt' Cleland, June 1949

'The poem itself simply means that we know what this world has in store for us, but we do not know what the other world has in store, and while we are on this earth we should enjoy life to the fullest, and when it is time for us to pass on, pass on without any regrets.'

Detective Leonard Douglas Brown, on the *Rubaiyat*, June 1949

'A. There are insufficient symbols to provide a pattern.
B. The symbols could be a complex substitute code or the meaningless response to a disturbed mind.
C. It is not possible to provide a satisfactory answer.'

Code-breaking computer program, when fed the letters written in the back of the *Rubaiyat*, 1978

CHAPTER TWENTY-SEVEN

Despite what Ms Drummond said, I thought the musical was coming along okay-ish, with the exception of Ash's solo 'The Last Midnight', which Ms Drummond had taken to skipping half the time 'for the sake of her mental well-being'. Some parts even seemed pretty good. Enough for everyone to focus their attention instead on the main event: the afterparty. I guess most normal schools just had it at some house where the parents were relaxed about underage drinking. But St Mags being the place it was, we had to have a theme. And a committee. And Ash had to be on it.

They'd gone with 'twisted fairytale'. Appropriate.

Ash and I did our initial outfit search on Saturday morning a few weeks into the term. We stopped at the op shop out of habit, not because we actually thought they'd have decent options for the party. I let my hands run over the dresses, each one either an odd pattern or a weird fabric. Hannah could always make these things work, I'd never got the knack.

'Yes – Loz, this would look perfect on you.' Ash held out a hideous sea-green dress. 'It's got the trifecta: ruffles, shoulder puffs and . . .' she turned it around with a flourish, 'a butt bow!'

'No way.' I shook my head, though I could feel a smile tugging at the corner of my mouth. 'I love it, but no.'

'Sorry, you're trying it on. No arguments.' She reached into the rack with her other hand and pulled out the dress' twin, in lavender. 'Because I'm wearing this one.'

'How are there *two*?' I asked in wonder.

'Bridesmaid dresses, must be.' Ash grinned at me. 'What do you think they did to the bride?'

'Whatever it was, it could *not* have been bad enough to deserve this.'

'Come on.' Ash pulled me into the dressing room and tugged the curtain across.

'Ah, this fabric is *literally* making my hair stand on end.' I started to laugh as the static pulled out stray hairs around my face, giving me a deranged halo.

'Oh my God, they are *so* much better on.' Ash's eyes sparkled as they met mine in the mirror. 'Hang on – props.' She turned to the nearby accessories table and gathered beads, sunglasses and two floppy hats.

She held her phone up to get a good angle and we posed for photos as she clicked. She flipped it round to show me. The dresses were ridiculous, but I kind of thought we were making them work.

'What should I caption it?' Ash asked, her thumbs hovering over the keys.

'Best-looking ugly stepsisters you'll ever see?' I offered.

Ash laughed. 'Yeah, that's good!'

I had an idea. 'Hey, we could actually do this, for the party? Go as a group? Maybe we could even find a third dress, for Kate? She could be Cinderella . . .'

Ash put down her phone. 'Hm. I have to actually look *good* at the party, remember?' She flicked at the puff of fabric at my shoulder, which began to deflate. 'And after only one date, do you really want to see if Jos will appreciate you in this?'

'I guess not . . .'

'Come on. Let's try the shops further up.'

We moved on to the chain stores, where none of the outfits Ash pulled out seemed to have any connection to the theme.

'Blue, or the red?' Ash held two dresses out for my consideration. Both were short with strange cut outs in the back.

'How would you wear a bra, though?'

'Stick on boobs, of course.' Ash held out a plastic packet.

'Oh, I thought those were to stuff *into* your bra.'

'Psh. Like I need the extra help. Anyway, which one?'

'Uh . . . the blue, I guess.'

'Hm. I think I'll try them both on.' She disappeared into the change room.

I ran my hand along the fake 'vintage' section. All the chain shops seemed to be getting on that now, re-working stuff from op shops then selling it at ten times the price. They had kind of cute overalls here though: they'd used old men's ties as suspenders. One of the ties had bright red and white stripes, like a barbershop pole. Mr Grant had one just like it, I remembered it from first term. I reached instinctively for my pocket, where his note lay folded tight inside my wallet.

The tie reminded me of something else too – old mint candies Nanna used to give Hannah and me whenever we were sick. They tasted exactly like toothpaste and made your mouth fizz up in the same way. The taste of spearmint was always associated with head colds, bed, being allowed to sleep in. The pleasant/unpleasant feeling of being sick.

I would have preferred chocolates though . . . chocolates, that's what people should give you when you're sick. And flowers . . . but it would be weird to give him flowers . . .

I dropped the suspender tie.

A get-well package – it was the perfect way to try and get more information from Mrs Lamby. If she really thought he was sick, then she'd react normally. If not, I'd know she was in on it, and then I'd have another lead to follow up.

'Okay Loz, slutty or hot? Or both?'

Ash stood in the red dress. The back gaped kind of weirdly, around the cut out. It was made for someone with no boobs.

'The colour looks good . . . but I'm not sure about the fit. Hey, is there a nice chocolate shop near here?'

Ash swung around to look at herself from behind. 'I don't know . . . maybe you're right. God, who is meant to be able to pull off this style?'

'I think it only ever looks good on coat hangers.'

'Right. I need something more secure if I'm going to dance all night.' She ducked back into the change room. 'Can you have a look for something in this colour? But *tight*.'

'Okay, but I actually do want to buy some chocolates before we go. And a card. Mum asked me to, and I forgot.'

'Ugh, why can't your mum ever do any of this stuff herself? Hey, I thought your parents were still mad at you after they found Hannah's postcard. What happened with that?'

My mind closed up at the thought of Hannah. 'Not much. I guess Mum and Dad can't do too much til she's home. I promised to let them know when I heard from her from now on. Other than that, we haven't talked about it. Which is pretty classic.'

'Hannah will run out of money and then she'll be back, you'll see. Here – put this back while you're out, will you?' Ash swung the rejected red dress over the stall door.

I turned and began trawling the racks, already rehearsing what I'd say to Mrs Lamby on Monday.

CHAPTER TWENTY-EIGHT

'I'm going to go at the start of lunch. And we'll have a whole hour of free time, so she has no excuse to cut the conversation short.' I rearranged the card and the chocolates in my locker, balancing them more securely on top of my books.

'Uh-huh, good plan, Lara,' Kate said. 'It was a good plan the other three times you rehearsed it out loud too.'

I shut the locker.

'Lara?'

'Yeah?'

'Are you okay?'

'Of course I'm okay. Why wouldn't I be okay? As you've just said, I'm over-rehearsed.' I tried a grin on her, but the worried crease did not budge from her face. 'Hey, Kate, I'm fine, really! I want to find out, that's all.'

'Well, this is your official warning that your eyes are getting a freaky glazed look. Okay? This is the intervention before you need an intervention.'

'Oh come on, I don't need an *intervention*.'

Kate put her arms on my shoulders and spoke in a mock-sincere voice, looking deep into my eyes. 'You have an addiction to fascinating and hot young History teachers, and it is beginning to hurt your friends and family.'

'Come on, you're killing me here.'

Kate released me. 'Hey, want me to come with you? Second pair of eyes on the devious deceptions of the Lamby?'

'Would you?'

'Yeah, for sure. Better let me sign the card too, in that case.'

Oh. I bit my lip.

'Come on, what did you write in it?' She smiled at me. 'No declaration of undying love in there, right?' Her smile disappeared. 'Lara? Is there?'

'Uh . . . there may be some poetry.'

'Lara! Ew!'

'It's from the assignment! He'll get it.'

'The *Rubaiyat* poem?'

'Yeah. It's practically homework I'm quoting at him.'

'I'm not sure that's exactly the point. And which bit of the poem? Half of it is about sex and wine!'

'Sex and wine? Who's having sex and wine?' Ash appeared. I swung my locker shut quickly, too quickly maybe, to hide the gift. I'd decided it was better not to share my amateur spy plan with Ash. Not only because she never really liked Mr Grant, but also because she never had a problem embarrassing me when she thought I was doing something dumb. Ash's eyes narrowed. 'Excuse me, Kate, could I get to my locker please?'

'Oh – sorry.' Kate shifted aside. She gave me a look that said *this is not over* and went into our form room.

Ash started to unpack her stuff. 'So, you and Jos have progressed beyond half a date, I guess.'

'What – oh! No! No, that's not . . . we were talking about homework. Uh, poetry and homework. I swear.'

'Because you could tell me, you know. Just 'cause I don't have a boyfriend doesn't mean I won't get it.'

'Ash, of course I'd tell you . . .'

'Not that I'm that interested in your fumbling high school sexcapades, of course.' Ash swung her locker shut. 'But I do have older sisters. I can advise.'

'Poetry. We were talking about poetry.'

'Whatever.' She headed for the classroom too. 'You'd better get some Clearasil action happening if you are planning on it though, Loz. That volcano on your chin is going to blow any second.'

My hand jumped to my chin before I could stop myself. She was right, a pimple was coming through. I hadn't noticed.

CHAPTER TWENTY-NINE

I had never been in Mrs Lamby's office before. I knew Hannah used to go to counselling with her for a while: she'd manufacture a breakdown whenever she was sick of going to Latin class. She said she stopped when she realised that talking to Mrs Lamby for fifty minutes was the only thing worse than Latin class.

'Go on, then.' Kate said, and gave me a little push closer to the office door.

As I reached up to knock, Ms Drummond came around the corner.

'Oh good, Kate! I need to see you, please. I've had some new set designs drawn up and I need a second opinion.'

'Sorry, I've just got to drop something off with Lara . . .' Kate held up the present and card.

Ms Drummond glanced at her watch. 'Well, Lara is perfectly capable of doing that on her own. After Year Eight we expect you to be able to interact with staff members solo, instead of in pairs.' She turned to walk down the corridor.

Kate looked at me helplessly.

'Go, go. I'll be fine.'

'Okay. Sorry.' She handed me the present and ran to catch Ms Drummond.

I took a breath, and knocked.

'Come in,' called Mrs Lamby. 'Oh, Lara – take a seat, I'll just be a second.'

The office was full of brightly coloured posters and pamphlets about 'teen issues': though there were many more about the danger of over-work and stress than drinking or drugs. None on teen pregnancy, I noticed.

The centrepiece of her office was a round fishbowl, full of stress balls, each the round yellow face of a different emoji. She'd probably bought them without knowing what emojis were, thinking they were just handy counselling aids. A hand-written sign taped to the fishbowl said 'Need to express your feelings? Have a squeeze!'

I reached in while I waited for her to finish tidying away the folders she was working on when I came in. The stress balls squeaked softly against my hand, frowns and tears and manic grins bumping together. I did not see how this activity could make you feel *more* emotionally stable.

'Lara Laylor! An unexpected pleasure. What brings you here today?' Mrs Lamby's face softened as she saw my hand in the fishbowl. 'Turbulent emotions, perhaps?'

'Uh, no.' I retracted my fingers quickly, and looked away to avoid her sympathetic eye contact. There was a postcard of an old-fashioned railway station, pinned to the board behind her. It looked familiar. 'Is that Adelaide Railway Station?'

She turned to look. 'Yes, yes it is. Have you been to Adelaide?'

'No. I recognised it from . . . from a class assignment.' I wasn't ready to bring up Mr Grant yet.

'I studied there, back in my bohemian youth.' She smiled fondly. 'Kept in touch with some friends from those days. They're all quite respectable now though – the friend who sent me that postcard is in local government, I think.' She turned back to face me. 'Anyway dear, what is it that's troubling you today?'

'Uh, I'm not actually here for me.'

'Oh, coming for a *friend*, are you? Well that's very kind of you to ask on their behalf.' She gave me a knowing smile and leaned forward, hands twirling in her scarf.

'No – really, it's not about me. It's about Mr Grant.'

Mrs Lamby sat up straight and her fluttering hands went very still.

'Mr Grant?' I tried again. 'The History teacher who's left?'

'Sick. He's . . . sick, yes.'

'Exactly.' I waited, but Mrs Lamby was silent. Her eyes looked glazed. Normally I was used to trying to avoid the over-intimate eye contact with her, but now it was like she couldn't even see me.

'Uh, well . . . some of the girls and I wanted to get him something. You know, a get-well gift.'

I handed over the wrapped package. I'd chosen fair trade chocolate, because I thought he might like that, if it all turned out to be true. The guy at the shop had wrapped it in old newspaper and raffia, which looked cool in there but here in Mrs Lamby's garish office, next to the bulbous emoticons and neatly stacked binders, it looked . . . childish. Kind of like I'd wrapped it myself.

I felt heat rise to my face. *Pay attention*, I reminded myself. You're here to *spy*.

But I didn't feel much like a spy. I felt exposed.

'You . . .' Mrs Lamby reached out and touched the package, like it was something precious but also slightly unseemly. 'You bought him a present?'

'Just chocolate. And a card, from, um, a few of us.' I was so glad Kate had signed the card.

'Chocolate . . . and a card.' For a second, it looked as though she might cry. 'I'll – I'll take care of these, dear.'

'So, you know where to find him? Is he in hospital, or at home?' *Just how serious is it?*

'I'll – yes. I'll see to it. He's not in hospital, no. But I don't think he will be back. Not for a long time.'

I felt something twist inside me. 'He's not . . . is it really bad?' I pictured Mr Grant at the window to our classroom, jacket ballooning out in the wind like bat wings, sparring with Ash and smiling. He really talked to us, like people, not like students. Not like *young ladies*. I couldn't imagine that figure in a hospital bed, skinny and alone, eyes unfocused instead of sharp and interested.

'Oh dear.' Mrs Lamby tried to push a packet of tissues towards me subtly, and knocked over a set of pamphlets. Any need to cry vanished when I saw the sickly sweet smile on her face.

'Why can't you tell me what's going on?' My voice was back to normal now. Mrs Lamby's smile disappeared.

'Well, young lady, that is private information.'

'But, I just want to know if he's okay, if he'll be coming back –'

'That's enough.' She fingered the card, flicked it open almost absently.

'Hey, that's –'

Her eyebrows shot up. 'Poetry?'

'It's from class –' I didn't understand why everyone found this so odd. 'I'm still working on the assignment, actually, he left behind some –'

Mrs Lamby's face grew dark. 'What did he leave you?'

I didn't say more. I knew if I told her about the note she definitely wasn't going to tell me what was going on.

'Lara, if a member of staff gives you a gift of some kind, you have to tell me – that kind of favouritism is highly inappropriate.'

'No. I just meant I was still working on the assignment from last term.' I knew I couldn't say anything about the note now. 'Could you tell me where to send the card, and stuff? If he's not sick, where is he?'

She shut the card with a neat snap, quite unlike her normal dreamy self. 'Lara, I said I'd take care of this. I will. I don't want any more discussion.'

I stood up to go. 'Fine. I'd like it if you could pass on the gift though. It's not just from me, it's from a couple of us. Lots of us miss him.' I felt this was important to say. 'He was the best teacher I've had so far. For sure.'

Mrs Lamby pressed her lips together and sighed. 'Thank you, Lara. You may go.'

I paused at the door.

'He's really not coming back?'

She looked at me. I was pushing it, asking this last question. I knew it. But it wasn't frustration in her face, looking back at me. No, it was that look again – guilt.

'Lara, if there's one thing I'm sure of, it's that Mr Grant will not be coming back to teach at St Margaret's. Ever.'

SOMERTON BEACH, ADELAIDE, 1948–1949

George noticed the book on 1 December: the first day of summer. He had parked his car next to Somerton Beach for his customary stroll, and like most motorists of the time left his window half-open to ease the heat. When he returned, there was the book: lying in the back seat of his car. Someone must have thrown it through the open window. *The Rubaiyat of Omar Khayyam*: a Persian poem currently in the collections of all well-read families. Fashionable, gaudy, ornamental.

He had never read poetry before.

He was a thorough man, and would commit to see a thing through whether or not he was enjoying the experience. So, when his enquiries with locals did not reveal a rightful owner, he decided to assess the book on its own merits before disposing of it. He sat out the front of his office on the park bench, ate his ham-and-cheddar-on-white, and, as he had for fifteen years, read the entire *Adelaide Chronicle* from start to finish. But instead of then sitting in quiet for the final ten minutes of his break, George began to read the *Rubaiyat*.

It was somewhat of a revelation.

He read about flowers blooming and dying, about sunrises that burn and illuminate, about veils and gardens and hand-thrown pottery; lines in praise of 'the season for wine, roses and drunken friends', lines of despair and passion and reckless abandon to live for today.

He read, 'Be happy for this moment. This moment is your life.'

He looked down at his current moment, the wilted sandwich and the grey park bench, and he began to think.

Is *this* moment the best my life can do?

That evening, he accepted an invitation to go for a drink with a friend, and met a young woman with a warm, quick smile.

He began rushing through the *Chronicle* in his lunchtime ritual, skimming or occasionally completely skipping articles, impatient to return to the wisdom of Omar Khayyam.

(On 9 June 1949, he overlooked a small article on the case of the man who had been found dead on Somerton Beach the previous summer. A second examination of the body had revealed a clue: a note with the words 'Tamam Shud', most likely torn from a book of Persian poetry. Police urged any members of the public with further information to contact them immediately.)

Another month later, George was a new man: giddy, prone to whistling and smiling at strangers. He read passages of the *Rubaiyat* to Elena, the girl with the warm, quick smile. Together they shared in the urgency, the intensity of Omar – because they were in love, and their lives were intense and urgent.

It was Elena who pointed out the damage to the slim pamphlet. The last quatrain ended, and then the page had been ripped, like someone had torn out the last few words. And scrawled on the back page: a series of letters and numbers, some crossed out. And a phone number.

George nodded absently to Elena's speculation on the previous owner – why they abandoned the book, who the phone number was for – a past lover? Secretly, George resisted the evidence of previous ownership, of a claim other than his to the *Rubaiyat*. It had come to him, mysterious and perfect. How could it belong to someone else?

On the 25 June in the *Chronicle*, on the front page where even love-struck George could not miss it, MYSTERY MAN:

INQUEST INTO SOMERTON BEACH DEATH PROVIDES NO
ANSWERS.

The article re-hashed many of the facts George remembered reading back when the man was first discovered in
December last year. There was one new piece of information
however: a second autopsy had discovered a small, torn piece
of paper bearing the words 'Tamam Shud', which translated to
'It is finished'. The words came from the last page of a book
of Persian poetry. Unfortunately, said the article, despite a
media call to the public, the book had not been handed in
to authorities before the inquest. The clue was determined
to be a dead end.

George put down his sandwich. He read the article again.
He reached into his coat pocket and picked up the tattered,
loved, faded copy of the *Rubaiyat*. Flipped to the back page –
the torn ending. The last quatrain stopped, and then nothing.

Tamam Shud. It is finished.

But I'm only just getting started, he thought.

There was after all, no way to know for certain that the
Rubaiyat was the same. There were many copies floating
around, it was true. And George, never before a whimsical
man, was encountering his first bout of superstition. He kept
the poem.

One month later, Elena came to visit George on that park
bench in his lunchbreak and haltingly, clumsily, broke his
heart. There was someone else. She was sorry. She hoped
he'd understand. She left him alone with his sandwich, his
paper, and his small book of poetry.

George handed the *Rubaiyat* in to the police that afternoon, 22 July 1949.

He asked that his name be kept anonymous.

CHAPTER THIRTY

Postcard: Black sand beach in winter. Vík, Iceland.

*Instruction: go stand in front of the open freezer and play
Sigur Ros as you look at this postcard, for the full Iceland
experience. I'm here, Lara, and good news, the hipsters
have not ruined Iceland like I thought! This country is still
small and weird and cool. The horizon is bigger here, like
it threatens to swallow you up at any second, and I've never
seen the kinds of blue of this sky – blue like the inside of a
diamond. It's so expensive here that I can only afford half a
meal – if I find a friend at the hostel, we go halves on a meal
out. Tried to make spag bol but seriously you should have seen
the tomatoes in the supermarket – tiny and $6!! No space love
you H xx*

Our History class with the hopeless substitute only lasted
thirty minutes, so we were let out early. It was now over a
month since Mr Grant had been missing.

The rest of class dispersed quickly, but I walked slowly
along the corridor next to Kate, my mind going over the
possibilities. He could have quit, but then surely the school
would have just told us? If he was sick, why did Mrs Lamby

react so strangely to the card and chocolates? Normally she'd have praised such a classic display of manners and thoughtfulness, right in keeping with the St Margaret's image. So that left the stranger options: spies, death, mystery. And I couldn't help feeling that there was some *other* reason he'd given me the Somerton assignment, some reason why he'd encouraged my conspiracy theories . . .

'Lara. Hello?' Kate flicked the front of my pile of books, so that *Deutsch Macht Spaß!* hit me in the nose. It was clearly not the first time she'd tried to get my attention.

'Oi! Uncalled for.' I rubbed my nose. 'Did I miss something?'

'Oh, just me sharing my opinions on the silver-grey hair trend for about ten minutes, followed by your lack of response, followed by me saying, "Lara if you don't make a noise right now, I'm going to hit you with your German book", followed by nothing, followed by hitting, and here we are.'

'Right. Sorry.' I leant back against the wall. 'Just thinking about Mr Grant.'

'Again?' Kate joined me leaning against the wall. There was an office opposite us, door slightly open, but the corridor was empty. The others from History were outside already, enjoying the early lunch, and everyone else was still in class.

'Well, it *is* weird, don't you think? Mrs Lamby's announcement in assembly was bizarro, even for her. She said "sick", but you could tell that wasn't what she meant. And her eyes kept darting all over the place.'

'Yeah, but that's just her. Probably on the lookout for signs of sub-par school spirit, even while delivering news that a colleague is on his deathbed.'

'You really think he's dying?' I felt my voice shake, unaccountably.

Kate glanced sharply at me. 'No, God no! Sorry. Stupid joke.'

I decided to try my theory on her, even if it did sound crazy in my own head, let alone out loud. 'I have an idea. And I know you're going to laugh, but just don't, okay?'

Kate gave me a pouty frown. 'Serious face: applied.'

'Okay.' I took a breath. 'So, when I had that meeting with her, Mrs Lamby mentioned she used to study in Adelaide, when she was young and carefree –'

'*Please* don't make me imagine it –'

'*And*,' I continued, 'she still has a friend there. Who works in the *government*.' I paused, hopefully.

Kate's face was blank. 'So . . .'

'*So*, you know how so much of the Somerton Man case has been lost over the years? The suitcase was destroyed, they lost the *Rubaiyat*?'

'Yeah . . .'

'Well, if there *was* some government cover-up because of the mystery, she could totally be involved! Maybe she heard that he was asking questions about the Somerton Man, getting us to investigate it, and told her friend, and they decided that something needed to be done –' I broke off. Kate's mouth was held so tight together it looked like she was trying to do a ventriloquist routine, and her eyes were lit up with humour. 'Look, if you're going to laugh, just laugh.'

'I'm *sorry*,' Kate burst out, 'it's just, Mrs Lamby as an undercover spy agent?'

I folded my arms. 'Could be! Maybe she's undercover, with this *friend*. Like a *Mr & Mrs Smith* romance thing?'

Kate grinned. 'I think she's far more likely to have an animal as her partner in crime. A cat maybe?'

I relented. 'Or seven.'

Kate paused, considering. 'You know, I think cats are too normal for her. What's one step crazier than a crazy cat lady?'

'My cousin has rats,' I offered. 'She carries them around in her pockets.'

'Ooh, crazy rat lady. Bit too gothic though.' Kate picked unconsciously at the chipped nail polish on her fingers. 'I've got it. Gerbils. With their twitchy noses and their little pink eyes. *Perfect.*'

I started to warm to the idea. 'I bet she'd get them in St Margaret's colours for sports day.'

'Yes! Dress them in tiny green gerbil vests.'

'Tell them off for gnawing with their mouths open.' I was laughing now.

'I bet her house is full of them, just her and gerbils, watching TV on the couch together every night.'

'Dressed in matching frilly nightgowns for bed.'

Kate shrieked and sank to the floor. 'You've imagined her in a nightgown?'

'It fits, don't you think?' I joined her on the floor, laughing.

A strange, choked noise came from the office opposite us.

We looked up, then slowly, horrified, to each other. There was someone *in* there?

The bell rang for the start of lunch. The office door swung open. Mrs Lamby burst out, hair frizzing out of her bun, a long, thin scarf trailing behind her.

She waved an arm distractedly at Kate and me, didn't meet our eyes.

'Better get outside, girls . . . beautiful day –' Mrs Lamby broke off, turned and walked quickly down the corridor.

I suddenly wondered what her first name was.

Kate opened her mouth to speak, but before she could say anything throngs of students from the nearby classrooms surrounded us, and the corridor was full of slamming lockers and chattering girls.

CHAPTER THIRTY-ONE

The cast bonding trip was scheduled for the Queen's Birthday weekend, when the winter was just starting to hit its stride. I always appreciated the monarchy on this weekend, the only little oasis of rest in Term Two.

It was a cold and sunny day when we left. From inside the minibus, with the sun streaming in the windows, it almost felt like a summer road trip. Ash pulled out a cherry Chupa Chup for her and handed me a pack of Fruit Tingles, and one earbud to share her music.

'Ugh, why is she here?' Ash nodded to the front of the bus. Kate had just got on. Ash had come around to tolerating Kate, but I guess sharing an unexpected weekend with her was still too much to handle.

'Don't know . . . Kate! Over here!' I waved her to a spare seat in front of us. 'Didn't know you were coming.'

'Ms Drummond decided to include any members of the crew who were keen, which includes set painters apparently. And I had no plans for the weekend.'

'Surprise, surprise,' Ash muttered.

'Oh, Fruit Tingles? Yes please,' Kate said, ignoring her.

I handed her some, and crossed my fingers for a short drive.

✸

Tim's holiday house was about an hour and a half away, though it ended up being more like two in the shuddery minibus. We broke out in spontaneous cheers when we finally turned into the driveway.

The house stood on a hill looking over a steep rush of bush-scrub down to the sea. One of the smaller back beaches that not many people used – wilder, open onto the ocean rather than the quieter bay that lay between here and Melbourne.

'Woah, nice view,' Ash said.

'Shotgun master bedroom!' called one of the boys from the back of the bus.

Ms Drummond opened the minibus door. 'Okay, unload your bags onto the deck first, then I'll distribute room assignments . . .'

'Tim, give us the tour!' Kate said, as we piled our bags on the deck and spilled into the house.

'Woah . . .' the main room was a big, friendly kitchen-and-lounge area that opened onto a veranda, with windows that showed the sea glinting in the distance.

'Hey, cool, table tennis!' a voice called from downstairs, followed by the light pop-pop of a game.

I wandered further into the main room. It wasn't as mansion-ish as I was expecting. It looked like Tim's family actually used the place: it was full of life-clutter, stacks of CDs, an old movie schedule for the local cinema stuck to the fridge –

'Hey Tim, what's this?' I said as I picked up the photo I'd found next to the movie schedule. A seven-year-old Tim doing Nippers surf training, big ears sticking out adorably from under his swim cap.

'Ah, no – Mum promised they'd clear away the embarrassing stuff before we got here.' Tim reached for the photo. 'Oi, Lara, give it.'

'No chance. Jos, have you seen this?'

'Wow, lucky you grew into those ears, mate.' He grinned at me and passed on the photo before Tim could reclaim it.

'Right, now you've had a look, can we unpack? *Now*, please,' Ms Drummond called us back from the deck.

Most of the cast were staying at Tim's, a few at Guy's a few doors down. Boys were crammed into bunk beds downstairs, next to the games room with table tennis, and us girls got the upstairs rooms. Ms Drummond had organised everything in her trademark regimented way – rooms assigned (Ash and I together, thankfully), and the days broken up into break-fast, drama activities and rehearsals in the morning, lunch, rehearsals all afternoon, then two hours' free-time til dinner.

It's funny how when you're at home in the holidays the days just slide past without you doing anything much – I'll realise I've done nothing except have breakfast and get dressed and it's already 3pm. But the moment the days have some structure the time goes forever, especially the free-time bit from late afternoon until dinner.

On day two, in this strange empty time, Tim dug around in a cupboard by the front door and pulled out a dusty red frisbee. 'Ultimate on the beach, anyone?'

If it was just me and Ash, we'd probably spend the free hours lazing on the beach with the occasional wander in search of ice cream. But with all the boys here I felt full of energy, and weirdly inclined to be social. Even social enough to overcome my private one-woman protest against team sports (running alone = mind-space and peace; running to put a ball in a hole while everyone is yelling at you = misery).

'Sure,' I said. 'I'm in.'

'Same,' Kate said, and threw down her book on the couch. We walked down to the beach together.

A few of the others were already at the beach when we arrived. Ash had gone on ahead, and lay on a huge, soft, red-and-white Country Road towel I knew she'd bought new for the weekend. A couple of people were bobbing half-heartedly in the sea, but most were dotted around Ash in differing levels of boredom and contentment.

'Ultimate frisbee anyone? Yes? I saw you thinking yes, Ash,' Tim called, drawing lines in the sand with his feet, further down from the sunbathers where the sand was wet and firm. Ash just waved at him with one hand, not looking up from her phone.

I squeezed onto the towel next to her, leaving Kate to run down to join the boys near the water. Ash followed her with her eyes.

'Come on, Ash. A game could be fun?' I tried. Maybe now would be one of the moments when she'd snap into her fun self.

'I appoint myself team captain, and pick the two athletes on the towel,' Tim said, pointing at us.

Ash glanced up at Tim. 'Fine,' she said out of the corner of her mouth to me. She went over to join him.

Well, at least the chance to flirt had got her to play.

Once we started, I fell into the sport. It was pretty easy to pick up; and even if half my throws went wobbly, at least I could run. Tim and I found a good rhythm, and though no one was really keeping score I was fairly sure we were winning.

I kept trying to pass to Ash, but it was like she was being deliberately terrible. She screamed and giggled when she dropped the frisbee, until she realised Tim wasn't really finding it funny. After that, she stood in sulky solidarity with Mia, who was on the other team but also didn't seem that

interested. I glanced over, worried. I knew Ash could be good
if she wanted to.

'Ghazy! Come join – they need the help.' Tim waved to
Jos, who was walking towards us across the beach.

'*Please*,' said Kate, who'd been single-handedly leading the
attack of her team with Mia and Guy.

Jos jogged the last few metres and threw down a paperback
on the piles of towels we'd left further up the beach. 'What's
the score?'

'Eight to three,' said Kate.

I guess someone had been keeping score.

'Whew,' Jos exclaimed, and joined her.

With them together it was a whole new game. The scores
got closer.

A sharp whistle stopped us mid-play. Ms Drummond stood
on top of the wooden stairs down to the beach. 'Six o'clock!'
she called. 'Dinner duty group back at the house now, please.'

'Okay, Ms Drummond – last score wins,' Tim called back.
He looked at me out of the corner of his eye and nodded
slightly down the field. I took a few steps backwards, giving
myself space to run.

Ms Drummond came down the stairs and blew her whistle
again, happy to take on the momentary role of referee. And I
started to sprint, round the outside of the group and towards
the score zone at the far end.

Tim let the frisbee go, a sweeping arc towards our end,
where no one was, yet.

'It's Lara – get Lara!' Kate yelled, and I saw her and Jos
start to sprint towards me, but it was no good, because I was
running, running just like in my park at home, bare feet
kicking up the sand, and Jos was sprinting next to me now,
trying to beat me to the frisbee in the air, and I had time to
look sideways and grin at him as I put on that final burst

of speed, left him behind, dived the last few metres, hand outstretched for the frisbee –

Tim whooped as I slid into the sand. We had won.

I grinned at him and flung the frisbee in the air and caught it. That had felt *good*.

Jos flipped into a victory handstand, even though he'd just lost, and his top fell over his face. He kicked his legs to balance and fell, spraying sand over everyone nearby.

The dinner duty group brushed themselves off and headed towards the house. Ash left with them, yelling back something about getting in first for one of the showers. I felt the victory sour slightly in my stomach. Maybe I'd been showing off. I could have held back a bit.

Kate, Tim and Jos flopped down on the sand around me. The tide was starting to come in, waves getting closer to our feet.

'You are *really* fast,' said Kate. 'I don't know why you didn't sign up for athletics.'

'Or you can join my ultimate frisbee team,' Tim said. 'I've decided it's my next business venture. Get it into the Olympics, sponsorship deals, the lot. We could be cereal box stars, Laylor.'

I laughed. They were completely exaggerating, but it was nice.

Tim kicked Jos. 'Who's that guy with the wing feet we were doing in Latin the other day, Ghazy?'

'Hermes, messenger of the gods.'

'Yeah, the one with the wings. That's you, Lara – Flying Feet Laylor,' Tim said.

Jos smiled quietly. 'God of athletics and sport, and a peacemaker, too. He's caught negotiating between the humans and gods. Maybe it suits you.' He sketched a wing in the sand.

Kate tilted her head sideways to consider. 'That's right, one on each foot.' Kate pulled out her marker pen from her shorts pocket – she'd even taken it to the beach – and grabbed my leg.

'Oi!' I tried to twist around to see what she was doing.

'Just a second.'

She brushed the sand off my ankle, and I felt the cool, quick liquid strokes of the pen.

'There.'

On the outside of my ankle, she'd drawn a tiny, feathered wing, sweeping out to my heel.

'Perfect,' Jos said, with a nod.

And for a moment, lying with them on the sand, with the sound of waves crashing in our ears, I did feel like I could fly.

CHAPTER THIRTY-TWO

After dinner, I snuck out down to the beach for an evening walk. No matter how much I was enjoying myself, after a solid day and a half of 'bonding' I needed a people break.

I stood for a second and breathed in the air of the sea at night – dank seaweed smell, sharp salt, eucalyptus from the gum trees behind me. The constant crash and suck of the waves sounded louder in the dark. A black shape stirred in the corner of my vision; a shag bird, flapping out to sea.

There was someone else on the beach too. I could just make out a haze of hair in the moonlight.

Jos.

'Hey. Needed some fresh air?' I asked.

'Just had enough of socialising for a little while.'

'Me too.' I sat down, then realised that might have been a hint. 'Oh, sorry, should I go . . . ?'

'No, no. You're all right.'

I made myself comfortable on the sand, staring up at the stars. You could see so many more, away from the city. Like a spray of spilled sugar on a black sheet.

Stars, sea, air. Why would you leave this behind?

'Why do you think he chose to die – the man on the beach?' I asked after a few minutes.

'Your Somerton Man?' Jos replied.

'Yeah.'

Jos's hands drew lazy shapes in the air. 'Well, who says it was his choice?'

'You still think it was a spy conspiracy?'

Jos shot me a look. I couldn't quite see in the dark, but I was pretty sure he was smiling.

'Well, I'd like to think so.' He was silent for a second. 'Looking at these stars makes me think of a poem we studied in English last year.'

I didn't know if he'd changed the subject or not. I let the silence stretch a little.

'*I could not escape those tunnels of nothingness / The cracks in the spinning Cross,*' Jos quoted suddenly. He rolled his head to look at me. 'Slessor. It's about the spaces in between the stars.' He leaned back, looking up. '*Tunnels of nothingness.* It stuck with me.'

I looked up at the sky again. The stars looked cold now, burning pricks of ice. In between, all that impossible space.

For some reason I thought then of Hannah, lying on a hotel bed in Sofia, and the loneliness of it almost made me gasp.

'Maybe that's why he did it,' I said. 'He finally realised that it's just . . . he realised the huge *nothingness* there is out there, and he couldn't take it anymore. And he covered up his decision to die with this – this *detail*, this obscure quote from a book and all this mystery and removing the tags from his clothes, just to . . . to give himself something in between. All these details and secrets and codes were something to hide behind, to put between himself and those . . . those tunnels of nothingness.'

Jos didn't say anything. I bit my lip to stop myself from saying more, to try and explain this thought I had half-captured.

'Maybe,' he replied softly. He continued in his normal voice, 'Or maybe, it was just to screw with people. Whatever the reason, it's one messed up History assignment.'

'He's a great teacher,' I said. 'I think it's brilliant.'

'Yeah, yeah.' Jos sounded sleepy. 'He's still sick, right?'

'Or something.' I didn't feel like going into more detail just now. I was sleepy too; the weekend was catching up with me. I fought back a yawn. 'We should go back. The others are probably in bed by now.'

'Yeah,' Jos said, slightly strangely. He moved his arms from behind his head, drawing circles in between the stars again. He showed no sign of moving. His hands fell to his sides. I closed my eyes, waiting lazily to gather the energy to get up and walk to the house.

Jos's fingers grazed my pinkie finger.

Suddenly, I was not at all sleepy. Did that just happen? Cautiously, very slowly, I moved my little finger outwards, just a little – his hand was still there. My finger jerked back, it could have been an accident, but if his touch wasn't then . . . and his fingers brushed mine again, a good few seconds longer this time.

I opened my eyes, and stared straight up at the sky. There was a strange, shivery electricity going right through me, radiating out from my pinkie finger. Surely, the stars hadn't been this sharp a second ago? The silence felt like it was ringing, vibrating the air around us. And then, Jos tentatively, slowly, slipped his fingers between mine, and I twisted my hand just enough to let him.

The crash of the sea was loud, so loud – and not nearly as loud as my breathing. I listened for his. The sound of our breathing filled the vibrating air.

Lightly, his thumb was stroking the back of my hand. We both sat up and he pushed my hair back from my shoulder.

Jos Ghazy kissed me carefully and awkwardly under the stars and the gaps between the stars, and it felt exactly right.

CHAPTER THIRTY-THREE

It was hard to believe we'd only been at the beach for three days, as we all piled into the bus to go home on Monday afternoon. Everyone was a bit looser and louder than they'd been on the way in – legs were spread out over the aisle, people shared their food and passed phones and headphones around to play 'that song I was telling you about' to each other.

Ash and I grabbed seats near the middle, and I tried to stop myself looking around for when Jos walked in the bus.

'Why do you keep looking at the door then out the window?'

'What? No, I don't.'

Ash cocked her head at me. 'Did I hear you sneak in late last night . . . ?'

There! He'd just walked in. Was he looking around for me? 'Um, I'm not sure –'

'Laylor!' Jos slid into the seat in front of us and swung around to lean over the back.

'Hey, Jos.' I could feel myself grinning like an idiot. I tried to dial it back. His smile was getting bigger too. It was like we were trying to out-grin each other.

'Shove over, will you?' Kate slipped in next to him. 'Hey, Lara. Ashley.'

Ash nodded and turned to stare out the window. Oh well. At least she'd acknowledged Kate's existence.

'So, Laylor. I've been thinking about your Somerton Man.'

'Is that right?' I guessed that meant he'd been thinking about me, too. I felt like my face might split apart with all the smiling. How come no one ever warns you about cheek pain when they tell you about this stuff?

'Yeah. More I think about it, the less I like the spy theory. I'm now thinking he was a refugee. But that doesn't mean he couldn't have been murdered, right?'

'Who'd want to murder a refugee?' Ash asked.

'Oh yeah, because we treat refugees so well now, right?' Kate chimed in. 'We've watched refugees be murdered. By guards. Under our care.'

'You know, I was reading about where he could have been from, as a refugee, after the war – and it wasn't much better back then. Everyone talks about how good our post-WWII program was, but it was kind of terrible,' said Jos.

I knew this, too. 'Right, like the Snowy Mountains scheme. They shipped all these refugees in to do dangerous or menial construction work as a condition of their visas – and they were often separated from other people from their home country, totally alone. These camps of lonely, isolated men who had just been through awful trauma. Heaps of them died too, working on those projects.'

'Yeah, but,' Kate was clearly sceptical, 'they died from forced labour. Not a cigarette laced with some undetectable poison.'

'It does seem unlikely . . . and what about the code on the back of the book?'

Jos shrugged. 'Code? Or was he just trying to figure out a crossword puzzle and needed somewhere to doodle? That would help explain all the weird letter clusters, particularly if it was a language other than English. Oh, and I still think there was some connection with Jestyn, the nurse whose phone number was written in the poetry book. Maybe *that* was the murder motivation. Some kind of love triangle?'

'Urgh, can we please talk about something else?' Ash turned around from the window. 'I'm so sick of hearing about the wonderful Mr Grant and his dumb assignment. He isn't even around anymore. *You are doing homework for no reason.*'

'But Ashley, learning is so much fun,' Jos said, mock-seriously.

'I knew it was a bad idea doing the musical with the only school nerdier than ours.' She pulled out her headphones and popped one earbud in. 'Well, if you're not going to change the topic, I'm out.'

'Oh, please, no, we're devastated,' Kate said, quietly. I pretended I didn't hear. Life was sometimes easier if I was semi-deaf.

'So, he's really gone? Your teacher?'

I turned back to Jos. It was kind of like staring into the sun, talking to him right now. How do people sustain this for the whole length of a relationship?

Kate coughed and answered for me. 'Uh, yeah, since last term. And no one knows why.'

'Huh. Have you tried looking him up online?' Jos asked.

Kate and I looked at each other. 'What an . . . obvious idea.' I laughed. 'We are terrible representatives of our generation. We could google him right now.' I reached for my phone, weird excitement building in my chest. What if the answer was that easy?

'Oh, no – I mean, you can look it up when we're back, right? I'm kind of enjoying talking to you.'

'Oh. Okay.' I slipped the phone back in my pocket.

'So, tell me, Lara,' Jos got more comfortable with his arms on the back of the bus seat, 'other than the History teacher, any other mysterious missing people in your life?'

I was so surprised by his question I answered without thinking. 'Actually, my older sister is on a gap year. She's been gone since just after Christmas, and isn't replying to any of my emails.'

Kate watched me closely, her face suddenly interested. I guess I didn't talk about Hannah very often, now I thought about it.

'I didn't know you had a sister,' said Jos.

I tried to be casual. 'Yeah. You're probably the only one who doesn't. Hannah's reputation definitely precedes her, and me.' I stared up at the skylight, and spoke in a rush. 'And she's having a great time, I think, although she doesn't like Croatian men, but I miss her.' I took a breath. 'I miss her like crazy.' I hadn't said it out loud before, not even to Mum or Dad. To my shock, I felt tears form behind my eyes.

Great. I'd kiss him and smile weirdly at him then cry on him. I had this flirting thing down.

I felt two warm, comforting hands on my shoulders, over the back of the bus seats. One was Kate's, one Jos's.

'That sounds really crap, Lara.'

'Yeah.' Jos nodded. After a second he continued, seriously, 'Although, I think the real victims here are the Croatian men. *What* exactly is wrong with them?'

So. He could make me laugh, too.

CHAPTER THIRTY-FOUR

I smoothed out Mr Grant's note, let it sit on the computer keyboard. I was in the library after school, the first chance I'd had on my own to google his name – but I soon felt my hopes of finding an answer fade. There were so many David Grants. After two pages of unrelated LinkedIn profiles and articles about a soccer player, I took a break. I checked in on one of the Somerton Man blogs I'd been following, instead.

As you can see from my YouTube demonstration; it's clear that the code of the Rubaiyat included 'micro letters', common use for Russian intelligence agents of the time.

I picked up the note and held it close to my face. Could *this* have micro letters? I started to go cross-eyed and let it fall. I wished he'd been a bit clearer in the note. What did that poetry mean? Was it a clue? Was the Somerton Man himself a clue to what happened to him –

Someone's arms wrapped around my shoulders, grabbing me from behind.

'Woah! Oh, hey Kate. Don't *do* that.' My heart was thumping to a crazy beat.

'Got you.' She slid into the seat next to me. 'Hey, you look really white. Sorry, didn't mean to actually scare you.'

'No, it's okay. I've just been reading about spy assassination theories, that's all. Easily spooked.' I tried a quick smile.

'You're still looking up Somerton Man stuff?'

'What? It *is* an ongoing assignment. Technically.'

'But you know he's never coming back to check it, right?' Kate reached over to scroll up the page so she could read, and her hand brushed the note.

'What's this?' She picked it up before I could stop her. 'Lara!'

'What?'

'Is this from who I think it's from?'

I didn't say anything. Kate dropped the note back on the keyboard. I resisted the itch in my fingers to reclaim it.

'No wonder you can't stop thinking about this. Why would he do that?'

'Exactly! Why, unless there's something weird going on, right?' I replied, relieved.

Kate was silent. Her eyes were wide, full of worry.

'What?'

'I don't know Lara . . . it feels off. Why would he leave a note just for you? And so vague? Like he's trying to mess with your head or something.'

'What do you mean?' I felt impatient. Couldn't Kate see the need to find out what the note meant, not criticise him for leaving it?

'Come on – it's not normal for a teacher to do that. And why did he have all those one-on-one sessions with you anyway? This was meant to be a group assignment, remember?'

'You sound like Mrs Lamby.' I tried to laugh but it came out like a snort. Something cold and powerful was flowing through my body. 'I didn't realise you were jealous of the extra sessions, Kate.'

Kate's face went blank with shock.

'Lara . . .'

'If you don't want to help me, that's fine. Could you just leave me alone, though?' I turned back to the computer. I kept my eyes focused on the screen, though I could feel Kate's gaze.

'Lara. Stop it. I'm on your side.'

I didn't acknowledge that she'd spoken. A powerful feeling spread through me, like coffee on a cold day. Warm and buzzing.

It felt good.

I wonder if this is how Ash feels. The buzzing feeling disappeared.

I turned to Kate. 'I just – look. I don't know what you think is going on. But I *know* something weird is happening and the school is keeping it from us. So, you don't have to help me, but I'm going to try and find out.'

Kate hesitated. 'Okay.' She didn't sound convinced. I opened my mouth to say more but she put up her hands to stop me. 'I said okay. Now I'll help you, but only if you don't go all ice-queen on me again, right?'

'Okay.' I tried a shaky smile. 'Sorry.' The anger had gone as quickly as it came, and now I felt kind of nauseous.

'I mean it's unsettling, you're normally so cuddly. Like being told off by a Teletubbie.'

I started to feel more normal. 'Hey, Teletubbies are horrifying.'

'I know,' said Kate. 'And now we're even.' She pulled her chair closer to me. 'So, what have you found out so far?'

'Well, I took Jos's advice and googled him but nothing's come up so far.'

'Hang on. There's this site my parents use to check out new schools . . .' Kate reached across me and started typing furiously.

I breathed out and felt my shoulders fall, so relieved to be finally sharing this.

'Okay so . . . here we go. This looks like him on GradeYourTeacher.com.au for Kingswood Grammar, Adelaide – must have been his old school before us.'

We started to scroll down the page.

'Wow, lots of reviews.'

'Good ones too . . . look at his average rating, all fives! They liked him, then.'

I started reading the individual reviews. Most were short and positive, a few backhanded compliments like, 'I never thought someone could actually make history interesting'.

'Okay, end of the page – this is the last review.' It had been posted anonymously just two months ago.

He was always a great teacher. It's a shame what happened to him.

Kate and I stared at the screen, at each other.

'But that was when he was teaching here . . .'

'April . . . about when he left.'

We looked back through all the reviews, but there were no other clues.

'Okay, what about the school website?' I said, trying to ignore my growing worry.

'Right. Okay . . . they've got some old newsletters here . . . no mention of Mr Grant – oh wait, this one, from last year.'

We farewell a much-loved staff member in Mr David Grant, who is moving to Melbourne to take up a History post at St Margaret's Girls' School. We wish him all the best in his future endeavours.

'Uninformative.' I sat back in my chair. 'But – much nicer than the send-off he got here.'

Kate bit her lip. 'Okay. I admit there is something weird going on.'

'More than just off sick, right?' *It's a shame what happened to him.* Was it a threatening, or sympathetic, post? What did that person know?

'Girls! I didn't see you there. It's past five-thirty, the library is closed.' Mrs Calder, the librarian, stood at the door, keys in hand.

'Five-thirty? Crap . . .' I pulled my phone out of my pocket. The screen was flashing with missed calls and texts, one from Jos, the rest from Ash.

I'd completely missed rehearsal.

That night, I couldn't sleep. Ignoring all the articles Mum kept sending me about the evils of screens and blue light, I opened my laptop. The Somerton Man document was still sitting open, pages full of my notes and ideas.

The reviews I'd found in the library today swirled around my brain. I opened a new document, and started typing. *The Search for Mr Grant.* As a joke to myself I copied the Somerton Man folder format: *Physical characteristics: blue-grey eyes, estimated age 30–40, no missing teeth.*

I started a new heading: *What does the school know?* and wrote down a few notes on Mrs Lamby's strange announcement in assembly. I paused, then described the gift I'd got him, the card, and what happened in her office.

Another heading: *The note.* I felt a little weird about this one. For some reason, writing about his note to me felt like I was betraying his trust in some way, exposing something soft and fragile. I reminded myself that this was only my laptop, for me. I typed out the text. I even pulled out my phone, took a photo of each side of his note, sent it to myself and pasted it into the document. Now, it did look a little like the Somerton Man folder on the *Rubaiyat*, with the pictures of the handwritten code. Finally, *Kingswood Grammar*. I typed out the details of the review, when he was there, the date he left.

I flopped back on my pillow, my head throbbing from the laptop glare. Gathered all together, the information looked more promising than I thought. At least, it looked like a start.

CHAPTER THIRTY-FIVE

Ms Drummond was that terrifying kind of angry where she seemed completely calm.

She didn't say anything as I babbled about why I'd missed rehearsal – and the longer I talked the more ridiculous it sounded. 'So, I guess, I just got caught up working on this extra assignment, and lost track of time . . .'

Ms Drummond was silent. I looked to Ash for support, but she was standing in the corner whispering something to Mia. Probably thought I deserved this for not answering any of her texts.

'I really didn't mean to . . .' I tried again.

'Lara Laylor, were you working on this assignment at a computer?' Each word was a sharp sting, like angry little insect bites.

'Yes . . .'

'Did that computer have a clock? Or was it some model I have never seen before with no method of telling the time?'

I shrunk into myself. 'It had a clock.'

'And do you own a watch? Or, failing that, a phone, which among its many uses also, miraculously, can tell the time?'

'I've got a watch and a phone,' I mumbled, stupidly. Out of the corner of my eye I could see the entire cast was watching now, no one was even pretending not to notice. Ash was looking at Ms Drummond, not me.

'So. You had ample opportunity to "keep track of time". I can only assume you did not think it important to be here, and instead felt it appropriate to disrespect my time, the rest of the cast's time – none of whom had any problem attending – by wasting our rehearsal period.'

'I'm sorry –'

She cut me off. 'I don't want to spend any longer on this today. Speak with the rest of the cast later to catch up on what you missed. I assume I can trust you with that responsibility, at least?'

'Yes, Ms Drummond,' I said quietly. I was surprised I had the ability to make my voice audible at all, I felt so small.

Kate came to stand beside me as I joined the rest of the cast. 'Alchemy Café, after school, okay?' She whispered. 'Jos is coming too.'

And I felt a little less small.

❦

'Okay, so new theory,' Kate put a water jug and three glasses on our table, 'and I know you might not like this Lara, but go with me here okay?' She settled herself on one side of the table and took a deep breath. 'It was Voldemort.'

'Huh?' Jos tilted his head.

Kate rolled her eyes dramatically. 'Who killed the Somerton Man, Jos. Obviously.'

'Okay.' I smiled at her theatrics. 'Tell me more, I'm listening.'

'Right.' Kate started ticking off points on her fingers. 'One: it solves the cause of death mystery – it was clearly the Avada Kedavra killing curse, which leaves no marks. Two: there were no medical records of the Somerton Man because he was a wizard, and would have never been in a Muggle hospital. Three: the clue is probably written in Ancient Runes. And four: they never found the killer because he could just apparate out of there.'

'Hmmm, look, you make some convincing points,' I pretended to consider her idea. 'You've forgotten one thing, though: it's 1948. Pretty sure Tom Riddle was still safely at Hogwarts then. So, Voldemort is probably NOT your best choice of suspect.'

I spread my hands out in victory and sat back in my chair.

'Damn, Lara, you out-Pottered me!' Kate shook her head in admiration.

Both of us turned to look at Jos, who was looking between us.

'Uh . . . Voldemort is the one with the big beard, right?'

Silence. Kate and I stared at each other.

'You mean . . .' I started.

'How –' Kate sounded outraged.

'There's so many of us, we didn't really go see movies as kids!' Jos looked desperate. 'My parents made us play board games instead.'

'Didn't go to the movies?'

'Do you think Harry Potter is just a *movie* series?' I asked.

'Were you allowed to *read*?' Kate said, her voice straining.

'I mainly read the classics . . .' Jos looked down at his hands.

Kate widened her eyes at me and slowly shook her head.

'Okay. Okay, this is okay,' I said quickly. 'You've missed the greatest cultural movement of the century, but that's fine, we can fix it.'

Jos scrunched up his face. 'Well, would you say the *greatest*?'

'Nope.' I held up my hand to stop him. 'If you don't know the difference between Voldemort and Dumbledore you do not have a right to comment.' He held eye contact, a slight smile playing on his lips. My heart was beating a staccato rhythm.

Kate jumped in. 'Solution. Marathon. Next weekend.'

Jos threw up his hands in surrender. 'Fine. But I'm teaching you two to play Settlers of Catan in retaliation.'

CHAPTER THIRTY-SIX

At our last rehearsal of the term, Jos slipped in to stand next to me as I waited in the wings for my cue.

'Psst. Lara.'

'What?' I was distracted. It was nearly my scene and I kept screwing up my opening line. Plus, I was still recovering from the lecture I'd got from Ms Drummond about missing rehearsal. I looked down at my script again, but Jos's proximity to my elbow made it difficult to focus on the words.

'I think you may have been too quick to dismiss that Voldemort theory.'

'Huh?' I re-read my line desperately, willing the words to stick in my brain.

'Voldemort. You said he was in Hogwarts at the time of the Somerton Man's death, right?'

Ms Drummond walked out onto the stage, demonstrating to the others *exactly* where they were failing the choreography. 'Again!' She demanded. I had another minute.

'Yeah, he was at Hogwarts, okay.'

'Well, I think you might be wrong.' Cause Tom Riddle opened the Chamber of Secrets fifty years before the book, which was set in 1992, right, so that's 1942, and he was a sixth year' – Jos took a deep breath – 'which means that by 1948, Voldemort was a few years out of school and maybe ready for an Australian holiday with a casual mysterious murder before he completed his quest to be the Dark Master.'

'Dark Lord,' I corrected automatically. I stared at him. 'Wait. You *read* them already?'

'Just the Wikipedia summaries,' he admitted. 'Couldn't get caught out by you again.' Jos blushed – he blushed just under his cheekbones, I noticed, like he'd over-contoured after a makeup tutorial.

I felt my own cheeks warm up in response. I was kind of overcome by the image of him googling Tom Riddle and doing the maths of where he'd been and when.

Ms Drummond poked her head around the curtain. 'Lara Laylor, are you expecting the audience to call your name three times on opening night before you'll make your entrance, or is that a privilege just for me?'

'S-sorry.'

She gave a final glare and disappeared.

I widened my eyes at Jos. 'You've got me in trouble now. *And* we are going to talk about you reading Wikipedia before opening the books.'

'DO NOT MAKE IT FOUR!'

I tried to tamp down my smile for the sake of Ms Drummond, but she still remarked sarcastically that my take on Cinderella that day was 'particularly giddy'.

On the last day of term, I opened the door on an empty house and heard the echo of my schoolbag hitting the floor. Thud, *thud*.

I had never noticed that echo before this year, though surely it must have happened sometimes when Hannah was home. But it always felt like, even if she was silent in her room, she filled the space with energy.

I'm learning lots of new things about the house, with Hannah gone. Like the fact she must have been the only one to eat Sultana Bran – the same packet has been sitting there, almost but not quite empty enough to throw out, for months.

The weirdest part though is something I can't even pin down. Not a silence – though it is kind of like a silence, like the ringing in your ears you get when you know there's nothing to hear – not a smell, not something I see; it's absence. Hannah's mood used to fill this house. Fill it up from behind the closed door of her room, tainting the house with a sense of her. Now – nothing. No emotions to watch out for, no smell of unexpected baking experiments, no Hannah.

Instead, the echo of a schoolbag on the floorboard. I lifted it again, just to check. Thud, *thud*.

My phone vibrated. Ash. *Have you picked your afterparty dress yet? Don't want to clash! X*

I shoved the phone back in my pocket and, on a whim, went into Hannah's room.

The emptiness was even more obvious here, since the room was so much tidier than usual. My gaze drifted to the wardrobe, doors neatly shut instead of her habitual half-open, clothes-spilling-onto-the-floor-and-flung-over-doors décor. Right. A dress. For the party.

I opened the wardrobe and riffled through her collection. Most of it was sourced from op shops, crazy floral prints and velvet creations I could never see myself wearing. Probably one of the reasons why we didn't end up killing each other – though Hannah had never had the same reluctance over stealing *my* stuff.

She'd cut the labels off most of her finds, she claimed because they itched her neck. I suspected it was so her friends didn't see that half the clothes were big-name brands just like theirs, only a few seasons older.

That was a possible motivation for the Somerton Man to remove all his clothing labels that no one had considered.

My hand stopped as it passed through the wardrobe. I felt something pleated. Layers and layers of it. I pulled out the dress – a shimmering bronze skirt, right to the floor, fanning out in glinting folds.

I remembered this dress. Hannah had seen it in the window of an op shop as she was dropping me at an athletics event, and stopped the car so fast we almost had an accident.

She bought the dress without trying it on. When she got home, she realised she was too tall, it didn't sit right on her body. But she kept it anyway.

'I'm meant to have it. I know it.' And she'd put it in her closet for later.

It was the *perfect* Cinderella dress. I touched it again. It felt like a mild electric shock on my fingertips.

I'd look *brilliant* in it.

So brilliant Ash might kill me.

I needed Hannah here. Hannah would force me to get into the dress, she'd spin me round even while I rolled my eyes and groaned, and she'd draw me into the theatre of it despite myself. She'd know how to wear it, how to make it cool, twisted – fun.

There's no way I could pull it off without her help.

The dress looked kind of faded actually. More brown than bronze. I threw it so it lay in a heap at the end of Hannah's bed. I wandered back out to the kitchen and sent Jos a message.

My house is lacking in siblings. Send me some of yours?

He replied straight away, not even pretending he wasn't watching his phone.

Laylor. A house of no siblings is a wonder to behold. In fact, I think you're making it up.

Nope, can confirm. My schoolbag echoes around the house, it's so quiet.

Echoing schoolbag? You are less and less credible.

A minute later.

Cannot spare siblings, they are all occupied being insane/annoying/too old to live with me. But will come in person to investigate outlandish house emptiness & schoolbag echo claims.

I felt a smile form on my face. I tapped out a reply.

I am insulted by your lack of trust in me.

After a pause, I added:

All will be forgiven if you supply chocolate for the investigation. Especially mint-flavoured dark chocolate.

POLICE STATION, ADELAIDE, JULY 1949

Paul Lawson did not have high hopes for today's visit. He exchanged pleasantries with Detective Leane as he carefully manoeuvred the bust cast of the Somerton Man onto a table, ready for another viewing. It's not that he minded helping police with their investigation, he thought, it was just that some members of the public could be so stupid.

One woman last week, when she came in to see if the man could be a wharf worker who had walked off the job in late October, had been particularly irksome – when he revealed the bust cast, she'd tilted her head on one side, so that her squashed-looking hat threatened to slip off her head, and said, 'Well I suppose it could be him, but it's not a very good likeness.'

Not a good likeness! She should have seen what kind of conditions he had to work under to make the bust. He was a taxidermist by trade, used to dealing with animals, and to take a plaster cast of a body six months after death – well, most people in his trade would not even have attempted it. He would have liked to see the woman do better when the body had started to thaw, and in between the work taking a cast of each section – first the neck and shoulders, then the face and back of the head, and finally, each of the ears – he'd had to wipe down the body and his own hands with towels to wick off the moisture. The result, all the detectives who had been involved in the case from the very beginning had agreed, was an extremely accurate representation of the man they had found on the beach. Not a good likeness, indeed!

Lawson had been satisfied when the rude woman with the squashed hat had revealed that the man she was searching for was only five-foot-five. The frustrated police had patiently informed her that he couldn't possibly have been the man Lawson had taken the cast of. Lawson had not been able to help noticing what a fine specimen the man was, almost six-foot tall, broad shoulders, nicely defined muscles, and smooth hands that did not look used to manual labour.

Lawson shook out a white cloth to cover the bust. 'Do you think you have a lead with this one, Detective?' he asked.

'Hard to say, hard to say.' Detective Leane looked more animated than he usually did on his visits, rolling forward onto the balls of his feet as they waited for the witness. 'She does have more of a solid connection to the case than most.'

'It's not –' Lawson paused in arranging the cloth. 'Is it the woman whose phone number was in the poetry book? The nurse from Moseley Street, so close to the beach?'

'Ah, you've been reading the papers, Mr Lawson.' Detective Leane could barely contain his smile. 'Then you'll know that the woman asked to remain anonymous, so there's nothing more I can say on that front.'

The two men heard footsteps approaching down the corridor.

'That will be our witness.' Detective Leane moved to the door and opened it, letting in a small group of people – a woman, flanked by two detectives. The policemen moved to stand by Leane in line with the bust, facing the woman. She remained by the door. Quite a striking face, thought Lawson. She had dark eyes, and sharp features. Her mouth was set in a polite, somewhat sardonic smile, as if she was sharing a private joke with herself.

'Mr Lawson, if you'd be so kind.' Detective Leane gestured to the table where the bust sat.

Lawson removed the white sheet from the bust.

The woman looked at the bust and took a step back, as if she'd been struck. She looked immediately down at the floor.

When it became clear she was not going to speak, Detective Leane cleared his throat and asked, 'Do you know this man?'

'No.' Her reply was barely audible.

'Was this man the man you gave a copy of the *Rubaiyat* to, in Sydney?'

'I don't know.' She swayed slightly, as if she would faint, and Lawson automatically lifted an arm to support her, though he was too far away to reach. He let his arm fall back to his side.

Leane asked his next question with his jaw clenched. A redness was forming across his forehead. 'Mrs – Ma'am, do you really mean to say you do not recognise this man at all?'

'I don't know. No.'

'Perhaps you'd like to take a closer look at the bust –'

'No.'

Before she left, she looked up just once, glancing to her right, away from the bust. She made eye contact with Lawson for a second. Her face was drained of colour, and her eyes were full of a loss of such intensity that Lawson had to look away before she did.

It must be a very good likeness, he thought in wonder.

CHAPTER THIRTY-SEVEN

Ash wanted to squeeze in some extra musical rehearsal time during the first week of the holidays and, after some nagging from me, agreed to let Kate come to read the other parts. I arrived a bit early, to make sure I was there first.

I paused for a second at her front garden, remembering having Jos over a few nights ago – how fun it was, even though all we did was hang out and watch dumb videos online, until his mum called him to go home and look after the twins. I felt like part of me was still there, sitting next to him on the couch with our hands loosely woven together – like when you're reading a really good book and half of you is going about your daily life while the other half is still living in the story.

A cool breeze shook me out of my thoughts, and I pushed open Ash's side gate. I found her outside in the hammock, shivering in shorts and a crop top.

'Brave of you.' I was cold enough in my long-sleeve tee and jeans.

'Forecast said eighteen and sunny today. Thought I'd try for a bit of last-minute tan.'

'Yeah, and we know the forecast never lies. Shove over?'

Ash moved her legs to make space for me, but there wasn't quite enough. I squished in anyway, legs bunched up uncomfortably to my chest.

A gust of wind blew through the garden, making the hammock sway.

'Fine.' Ash tumbled out. 'Help me bring it in then, would you? I guess winter is officially here.'

'Sure.' I felt a slight pang as I climbed out after her and began to fiddle with the knots at my end. The summer days of lounging and gossiping here felt like forever ago. Actually, I hadn't been here since the day before school went back at the start of the year.

I untied the last of my knots and half the hammock slid to the ground. Ash was still picking at her side.

'Do you want a hand?'

'I got it, Loz.'

'Okay.'

Ash yanked at a bit of rope with extra ferocity, and the hammock slithered down, coming to rest in striped coils. I reached down to pick up an end to fold it, but Ash grabbed it before I could, and bundled the material into an untidy ball. She kicked open the back door and dumped it on the floor, then sat on the couch, looking out over the back garden.

I followed and perched cautiously next to her, trying to think of what to say. I could tell something was wrong, but if I asked her straight out what it was, she'd say 'nothing' and it would only get worse.

Ash swung around to face me, bright smile suddenly on her face. 'So, we never really debriefed about the weekend away?'

'What?' It had been a few weeks since the weekend. We'd definitely talked about it. But I could tell she was getting at something. 'What's there to debrief?' I ran back over the weekend again, worried there was an interaction between Ash and Tim I'd forgotten to ask her about.

'What happened with Jos, of course?'

'Jos?' I couldn't stop a smile forming on my face.

'I *knew* it.'

'Knew what – what are you talking about?'

There was something hard and glittery in her expression. 'Mia and I got talking after rehearsal the other week – you know, the one you missed?'

The time I was in the library looking up research for Mr Grant.

'Anyway, she said someone was making out on the beach on the last night of the weekend away. And I heard you sneak in late.'

I felt panic rise in my chest, I tried to backtrack. 'It wasn't really making out . . .'

'What, was he that bad?'

'No, he wasn't bad –'

'I know he's a nerd, but it's nothing to be ashamed of, Loz.' Ash smiled kindly. 'He's even sort of cute, if you're into that kind of thing. I just don't understand why you wouldn't tell me.'

'I didn't tell anyone, I hadn't thought –'

'I mean, now Mia is telling everyone it was you and Jos, because of course when she told me I said you'd come in late, and that he'd been flirting with you all weekend. I was so surprised. I didn't know it was a *secret*.'

My head was spinning. 'Wait, Mia is telling everyone what?'

I thought back to that funny, strange night under the stars – the awkwardness, the heat and *rightness* of our hands twisting together – it felt like such a delicate, insubstantial thing, and now Ash was picking it up, turning it over, packaging it into a neat piece of gossip. *Someone was making out on the beach on the last night.*

'Loz? Aren't you going to apologise?'

'What?'

'For keeping this from me.'

I stared at her. Her smile didn't waver, her eyes were hard.

'I . . .' I didn't know what to say. I knew she expected me to apologise, but I couldn't bring myself to say sorry. The only thing I knew for sure was that I didn't want to talk about it with her, not now.

'Ash – I didn't mean to keep it from you – it wasn't really – I didn't know what to think about it. It didn't feel like a big deal.' Maybe if I brushed it off, she'd let it go. I needed time to process.

'Well, it's a big deal now. You two are the first to couple up in the cast.'

She reached over and pulled me into a hug. My arms stayed by my side. 'And you're forgiven. I want to hear *all* the details now, though, okay?'

The doorbell rang, and she released me. 'Oops, that'll be Kate. I guess I won't say anything in front of her, right?' She skipped towards the door.

She left me sitting on the couch, staring out over the back garden at the empty hammock frame, and the black branches of the trees twisting in the wind.

CHAPTER THIRTY-EIGHT

I hadn't exactly started training with Kate. It just happened that most evenings we would both end up at the park, running together, and then suddenly we were doing about four laps every evening – even now, in the winter holidays when the ground was hard and the air sharp.

Tonight was not a good night, though. Ash's sneering words nudged at me, niggled, like a stinging insect bite I was longing to itch. *Someone was making out on the beach on the last night. Mia is telling everyone. Aren't you going to apologise?*

'Okay. I'm calling it.' Kate slowed to a walk. 'Enough today.'

'Thank God.' I could tell I wasn't going to achieve that mind-body escape today. We walked back towards the tree, and our water.

'Ugh, I don't want to walk up the hill to my house,' Kate said.

'You just ran, like, three times that distance.'

'Yeah, but that was by choice. I resent being forced to do exercise out of necessity.' We sat down on the ground. Kate flicked me with a piece of grass. 'Would you rather be able to instantly teleport anywhere you like, or be able to transform into any animal?'

'Teleport. How is that even a question?'

'Seriously?'

'Wouldn't you? Imagine . . . winter day in Melbourne, poof, go off to some Spanish beach for the afternoon.'

Or, when I picked up a postcard in the mail, I could be there instantly, into the city square of Prague, looking up at the cathedral in real life instead of a plastic image on cheap cardboard. And then maybe I could walk across the square, find a girl with a backpack and dark curls writing in a café . . . I snapped myself out of it.

Kate shook her head. 'No way. How about winter day in Melbourne, I become a dolphin. They don't mind the cold. Have a cheeky swim.'

'Or a seal. More of a layer of fat.'

'Thank you, Lara, so flattering.' She lay back on the grass. 'I'd rather be an eagle actually. Imagine. *Flying*.'

I looked up at the tree, the top branches where I used to climb with Hannah, sitting and swaying in the wind. We felt almost like we were flying, then. Like we were creatures of the air. Unafraid. 'I'll still take my instant Spanish beach, thank you.'

'Fair enough.'

We lay on the grass for a while in silence.

'So, are you going to tell me what's up?'

'What do you mean?'

'Just – you seem off. And Ashley's passive aggressive skills were particularly on fire today. Every time she offered you something to drink, I felt like I should check it for poison first.'

'She doesn't mean anything by it,' I said automatically. I sighed. 'She's mad because I didn't tell her about Jos.'

'Ah.'

I glanced at her. 'Did *you* know about Jos?'

'I've heard rumours of his existence, yes.'

'Kate.'

She shrugged. 'I don't know if there's anything to know. A few people were asking me stuff after the weekend. I figured you'd tell me, if you wanted to, and I told everyone else to shut up if they didn't know what they were talking about.' She paused. 'Is there something to know?'

'Yes. No. I don't know. There was definitely no extreme making-out on the beach on the last night. None that involved me, anyway.' I felt a smile tug at my lips. 'But we did kiss.'

'And?'

'And it was nice.'

Kate started laughing. 'What a review. Poor Jos.'

'No – not like that. It was just – just what it was. I don't know how to explain it.'

Kate was still smiling. She lay back down. 'What makes you think you need to explain it?'

I opened my mouth to reply, and realised I didn't have an answer. Who *did* I owe an explanation to?

'Anyway. We've hung out a few times since, but I haven't really told anyone yet, and I don't think he would have.' I pulled up some tufts of grass. 'I'm seriously *dreading* rehearsals next term, now I know everyone's been talking about us.'

'Huh. I see. So explain to me the part where Ashley's mad at you for the nice kissing?'

'She's mad at me for not *telling* her about the nice kissing.'

'And her way of showing you this was by telling everyone you guys were making out on the beach?'

I felt exhausted suddenly. 'She just didn't know what to say, I guess. Because I hadn't told her anything.' I groaned. 'I normally do tell her this kind of stuff. I wasn't keeping it a secret on purpose.' I just hadn't worked out how to think about it properly. To answer the questions I knew she'd ask. To react and squeal and laugh in the right places. I wanted to keep it as my own thing, strange and weird and slightly magic. 'I think she was kind of hurt, actually.'

Kate made a non-committal *mmhmm* noise.

'Anyway, it'll blow over in about a week, I guess. Now I've just got to figure out what to do about what everyone else is saying.'

Kate was quiet for a while. 'You know Lara, there's no law saying you have to stay friends with someone forever. You could just . . . stop.'

I smiled slightly. 'You make it sound so easy.'

Kate took a breath as if to say something else, but didn't. 'Ah well,' she continued finally. 'I guess some people are better as friends than enemies.'

I snorted. 'That, I can believe.'

CHAPTER THIRTY-NINE

Ash and Mia sat chatting together before rehearsal on Tuesday afternoon. Out of habit I went over to join them.

Ash nodded towards the door. 'Ooh – look who's here.'

I sighed, and stopped myself from looking. It would be Jos. They'd started doing this every time he came in.

'She's all quiet – so shy!' Mia squealed. 'Cute.'

I bit my lip. I wasn't shy. I just wished they'd stop. Rehearsals in the week and a half since term went back had been excruciating. Tim worked jokes about Jos and me into practically every conversation, and Ash encouraged him with this shrieking high-pitched laugh that prompted Ms Drummond to make a scathing comment about witches' cackles, and how it wasn't necessary to stay in character *all* the time.

I looked up at Jos to see if he'd noticed Mia's squealing. We made eye contact and he smiled his light-switch-flipped-on smile. He was coming over. Crap. I looked down at the floor again.

Ash gripped my arm, slightly too tight. 'He can't wait to see you! Adorable.'

'Hey, Lara,' Jos said.

'Hey,' I mumbled to the floor. The quicker he left, the less chance Ash or Mia would have to do something embarrassing.

'Do you want us to give you two some *privacy*?' Ash stage-whispered, loud enough that the group next to us also stopped talking to listen.

Something embarrassing like that.

'Yeah, Ghazy – player!' one of the guys from the group called. Another wolf-whistled. I hated them both.

'What?' asked Jos, confused. 'Hey Ashley, Mia.'

'*Heeeeey.*' Ash drew out the word like a cheesy pick-up artist. Mia didn't reply, just collapsed into giggles.

'Is there something I'm not getting . . . ?' Jos looked at me, waiting to be let in on the joke.

'Nope.' I smiled tightly then looked away. There was an awkward pause. I wished he would leave, and I could come find him and explain it all when we were on our own. Every time I spoke to him in front of the others I felt frozen and strange, like we were on display. Exhibit A: two teenagers, trying to interact.

Mia and Ash exchanged glances. 'Trouble in paradise?' Mia coughed out between giggles.

'Hey Jos!' Kate called from the other side of the auditorium, where she was setting up one of the set pieces to paint. 'Can you give me a hand with this for a second?'

He stayed for a moment longer, as if he was waiting for me to say something, but I didn't. I knew anything I said would probably make it worse.

'Sure, Kate,' he said eventually, and walked away.

'Wow, Loz, *cold*!' Ash said, before he'd taken two steps. 'I've heard of treat 'em mean, keep 'em keen, but that was rough.'

I forced myself to laugh, to try and make it seem like a joke. Almost immediately I wanted to take it back – but it was too late.

I saw Jos's shoulders stiffen.

'Maybe we should recast her as the ice queen.' Mia nudged Ash. 'She'll have all the boys after her, always want what they can't get.'

A cloud passed over Ash's face. 'The ice queen isn't even a character, Mia.' She caught herself. 'But you'd be perfect for it if it was, hey Loz?'

✻

After rehearsal, my phone dinged. A message from Jos. *Hey. Meet me out at the steps?*

Relieved that I could finally just hang out with him on our own, I dodged out the side door to the steps outside. Jos was leaning against the railing, twirling his phone between his fingers.

'Hey.' I leant next to him, felt my muscles relax now it was just us. 'Awful rehearsal today, right? I'm sorry I didn't get to talk to you properly.'

He didn't answer, didn't really look at me, just kept twirling the phone in his hands.

I felt a twinge of worry.

'Lara . . . do you like me?'

'What?' I was so relieved I smiled. Surely he wasn't seriously wondering.

Jos didn't smile back. I backtracked, quickly.

'Of course – I mean, yes, I like you.' How could he not think I liked him? Everyone in their right mind would like him.

'There's just been some pretty weird mixed signals at rehearsals lately. Or anytime that it's not just you, or you and Kate, actually.'

'Oh – that.'

'Yeah.'

'I just . . . I just didn't want to buy into that weird tradition of the musical gossip cycle, everyone knowing, everyone talking about it, you know? I wanted to enjoy this with just us, not anyone else involved.' I thought he'd get that. Surely, he'd get that it wasn't about him at all, or me, it was about *them*.

Jos looked at me, then away. 'Sure. But then you're still letting other people's opinion control what you do. If you need to hide it from them, they've still won. Why not just do what you want and screw what they think?'

'But I *don't* care what they think. That's why it's just easier to –'

'Easier.' Jos's voice was flat. 'Yeah, it's always easier to make Ashley happy. I'm sorry I'm just too difficult for you, Lara.'

'No – that's not what I –' I shook my head, trying to get my logic straight. I was sure he'd understand if I could just figure out how to explain. It was too hard to find the words. 'I'm sorry. It's not that simple.'

'It is simple. You didn't stand up for me, or yourself, because it was too hard to stand up to Ashley. Why not admit you're scared of that, if you're scared?'

I couldn't think of an answer.

'I guess I don't want to have to figure out . . . this . . . in a fishbowl, in front of everyone,' I said, at last.

Jos ran his hands over his curls, so they stuck up in crazy directions. 'Well, then I guess there's no "this" for you to figure out.' He opened his mouth to say something more, stopped, sighed. 'Okay. Bye, Lara.'

CHAPTER FORTY

It was the coldest day of the year so far. We were all wearing double layered tights, which turned our legs inky black. As Ash and I walked to the tram stop that night the wind picked up, one of those broken-glass-sharp Melbourne winds that felt like it dropped the temperature by ten degrees. It bit at my ears and face, snatching at the corners of my scarf. Like it had something against me. Like it was one more stupid thing in my life that wouldn't leave me alone.

'Why did you have to tell everyone about Jos and me and what happened at the beach?' I said, suddenly unable to hold it in.

'What?' Ash asked.

'I said –' the wind picked up again, a howl. No good having this conversation out here. I looked around and saw the old wooden seats by the oval. The first place I'd seen Mr Grant. They'd give us a bit of shelter, at least. I pulled her towards them and we slipped behind the structure.

I continued in the relative quiet, 'I said, why did you have to tell everyone about Jos and me?'

'Oh, so you admit there *is* a Jos and you, then? I had my bets on that you were too busy pining after the History teacher.'

I waved away the Mr Grant thing. 'No, there's *not* a Jos and me, that's the thing. He got sick of everyone giving him a hard time at rehearsal. He doesn't even look at me anymore.'

'Oh Lara, your life is so hard, the cute boys have momentarily stopped looking at you.' Ash dropped her bag on the ground, swung to face me. 'Did you ever think how it felt for me? Mia told me she saw someone on the beach, and I knew it was you and realised that my own best friend wasn't going to tell me?'

'No, that's not . . . that doesn't have anything to do with it . . .'

'This isn't how it was meant to GO!' Ash threw her head back in frustration. She looked more like the thwarted witch than she ever had in rehearsals. 'Ms Drummond will not get off my back about my part, the more I sing the more I feel my voice getting thinner and worse, and you're not even THERE.'

I could see tears in the edges of her eyes.

'Ash, I'm there. I'm here.'

'You're not, Lara. You're with Kate, you're with Jos, and Tim, and the others. Your head is too full of Mr Grant and this dumb project to have room for me. I can see it, you know, when we're hanging out.' She dropped her arms, defeated. 'Even when you're here, you're not really here.'

I reached out a cautious hand to her shoulder. 'I would have told you eventually about Jos . . . It's just that I didn't want to explain . . .'

Her anger was back, just like that. 'Yeah, I get it, because it would be so difficult to *explain* it to the girl who's never been kissed, right?'

And as she got angry, I felt myself go cold and hard. I pulled my hand back. 'I don't have to tell you anything. It's my thing, mine and his. Kate said I shouldn't have to explain it to anyone, and she was right.'

'Oh, *Kate* said. Yeah, I bet you and Kate have been enjoying that, talking about how backward I am, how I could never understand –'

It was like a chemistry equation. She took the heat, I was left with ice. My voice came out almost disinterested. 'We hardly even talk about you, actually. Not everyone is as obsessed with you as you think.'

'Oh, *I'm* self-obsessed? Me? Says the girl who is so caught up in her dumb boy dramas, who can't get over a *History teacher* enough to realise that she's lost her best friend.' She picked up her bag, slung it so violently over her shoulder her pencil case and diary spilled out from the top. She snatched them back with one hand, did not look at me, and left.

I sunk to the ground, leant back against the seats. The wind was whistling so loud around me it took me a second to realise it wasn't just the wind, it was the sound of my own erratic breathing, too. My chest had been tight all afternoon. I reached for my inhaler, felt the relief as my throat opened, my chest lightened.

I could breathe again.

CHAPTER FORTY-ONE

It was too quiet in my room. I used to get so annoyed when Hannah played her music loud enough for me to hear through the wall, and now I missed it. After reading the same Maths problem through again without taking it in I grabbed all my books and moved to the living room. Mum was watching a *Project Runway* rerun while flicking through her iPad, Dad was working on plans at his drafting table, working to a crazy deadline yet again.

I flopped down on the floor in front of the TV and spread out my books in front of me.

'Why don't you do that at a desk, sweetheart?' Mum asked.

'More comfortable here,' I replied from the ground. I didn't point out that she wasn't exactly the model of good posture herself, slumped on the couch. 'And you're double-screening Mum, isn't that forbidden?'

'I'm an adult, my brain is already in decline,' she said without looking up from her iPad. 'There's still hope for your young brain cells.'

'Does Maths and TV count as double-screening?' Dad asked from his table. Mum's love of *Project Runway* was a recurring battle in the house.

'I think she'll be okay,' Mum replied placidly.

'It's helpful white noise, Dad,' I said.

But I still couldn't focus. The fight with Ash was playing on loop in my brain. I sighed and faceplanted into my Maths book.

Mum muted the TV. 'What's up, love?'

'Nothing,' I mumbled into the book. 'Just stuff.'

'It's not Hannah again, is it?' Mum sounded concerned. 'You'd tell us if she sounded unhappy?'

Dad put down his pencil. 'Yes, Lara, we talked about this. You're not hiding anything else from us, are you?'

'No, chill guys.' I rolled over onto my back, feeling suddenly irritated. 'If you can believe it, this problem is actually about *me*.'

Dad stifled a laugh. Too late, I'd heard it. I turned to glare at him, but he was busy marking something on his plans. He shot a quick smile at Mum. 'Don't tell me we've got another teenager on our hands.'

Mum raised her eyebrows. 'It may have finally happened.'

'But I *am* a teenager,' I said to the ceiling.

'Oh, I know love, technically you are. But we thought that your sister was enough teenager for both of you – and so far, it had looked like we were right.'

'We definitely parented more than two teenagers' worth,' Dad muttered from the drafting table.

I closed my Maths book with a snap, and started to get up.

'Oh no, don't go Lara. Come on, tell me about it properly. What's going on?' Mum even put down her iPad.

Reluctantly, I sat back down, and shuffled over so I was leaning against the couch. 'Ash's mad at me.'

'Oh.' Mum sounded a little disappointed. 'But you girls always have these little tiffs and make up in the end.' Her gaze drifted back to the TV. 'I'm sure it will all be fine in a few days, love.'

'No, this time she's *really* mad. It was worse than usual. And – I think I'm mad at her too.'

'What's this about, Lara?' Dad asked.

'Um.' It seemed impossible to explain Jos, the kiss, the rumours. 'The musical, I guess?'

'But I thought Ashley wanted to do the musical.' Mum frowned. Something lit up behind her eyes. 'Oh! The boys, it must be to do with the boys, right?'

Dad groaned. 'I knew we should have stopped you from doing the musical. It's all coming back to me now.'

'Does Ashley have a boyfriend? Is it upsetting you, that she doesn't have as much time for you anymore?'

'Mum! No, why would you assume . . .' *Why would you assume that Ash would be the one with the boyfriend, not me,* I stopped myself from saying. I definitely did not want to bring up Jos with my parents. 'No, it's just that – I guess the musical isn't going that well for Ash. And she's frustrated about it.'

'Oh, right. Well, she probably needs you more than ever, then. I know you'll figure out a way to make it up to her.'

'Maybe . . .' I wondered if Mum was right. Maybe I'd been unfair on Ash.

Dad looked up from his table again. 'I'll tell you one thing, Lara. I'm still friends with my best friends from school. I know I could call them today and they'd drop everything and be there for me. The girls I had a crush on? I can hardly remember their names.' He paused, thoughtfully. 'Well – except for Flora, from my Year Seven class . . .'

Without looking away from the TV, Mum threw a cushion at him.

'What I mean is – your friends are more important than some boy.'

'I told you it wasn't about boys,' I said quickly. And it wasn't, really. I couldn't figure out how to explain what it felt like, knowing Ash had told everyone my secrets. How she looked during that fight, like she hated me. 'Do you really think I should apologise to her?'

Mum had already reclaimed her iPad. 'Hmm? Yes, sometimes you just have to be the bigger person, darling.' She unmuted the TV, just as the elimination was starting. 'Sleep on it. I'm sure it will all be much easier tomorrow.'

Ash's pinched, windswept face flashed in my mind. I wasn't sure Mum was right.

CHAPTER FORTY-TWO

I needed to release the tension from the fight with Ash somehow, so I squeezed in a run that Tuesday morning. By the time I made it to the Clam, I was late to rehearsal.

Something was up. The whole cast was gathered around Ash, watching something on her phone. People often shared online stuff at rehearsals, but it was never this . . . intense. The atmosphere felt like a game of Truth or Dare: everyone on edge, waiting for something funny or embarrassing to happen and hoping it wasn't going to happen to them.

It was some sort of music video, the voice weirdly familiar . . .

Kate rushed in behind me.

'What is that?' Her face was the palest I've ever seen it.

Ash looked over at her. When their eyes met, I saw something pass between them.

I was at the group so fast, I didn't remember walking across the hall. 'What is it, Ash?'

Ash passed me the phone, a terrible smirk on her face. 'Revisiting some ancient history.'

She pressed play to restart the video. It was an old reality TV clip. And I suddenly remembered why Kate had looked so familiar on that first night in the park . . .

Three years ago, Ash and I are sitting on her couch, waiting for our favourite contestant to perform on *The X*

Factor 'Katherine', the tiny girl – thirteen, just like us! – with the huge voice. It's a big week for her. It's her last chance to save herself.

She has wowed the judges in audition week with a performance that is shown in promo clips over and over again: the wide-eyed girl, flicking back her hair in an obviously self-conscious movement; the judges wearing long-suffering, faux polite smiles – and then she starts to sing, and they sit up in shock, like they've been slapped with the beauty of it.

But it all goes wrong: the more the judges push her to recapture the magic of that first audition, the worse she gets. She is tiny at the start of the show. Week on week, she shrinks, until she has almost disappeared.

Finally, there's this episode. A mega-star flies in from the states, one episode only, and sings a duet with Katherine. It gets the biggest audience of the year, bigger than the AFL Grand Final. It's her last chance.

Ash and I sit on her couch in matching pyjama shorts, share popcorn her mum made us, and watch, willing with all our might for Katherine to make it, to let loose that voice, belt out the song –

This was the clip that Ash was holding in front of me on the small screen of her iPhone. I couldn't help myself: even though I remembered what happened, as I watched it again, I willed the girl on the screen to sing –

But she chokes.

On stage, next to one of the biggest stars in the world, all of Australia watching: she opens her mouth and nothing comes out.

The music crashes to a halt. One of the judges throws his hands up in frustration, hoping, no doubt, that the image will be plastered over news stories the next day (it is). They start the song again. Ash and I hide behind couch cushions, we can't bear to watch.

Kate cannot sing. The celebrity swears audibly into her mic. And Kate starts to cry, ugly, face-scrunching tears that do not make for glamorous TV. The cameras zoom in anyway, capturing every awful moment, until she runs off stage, tripping over her costume.

The clip finished and the title faded up onto the screen. 'Kamikaze Katherine goes down in flames!!!' It had over one million views.

I turned, almost afraid to look. Kate was frozen in place. It was like a different girl was standing there – thirteen-year-old Katherine, from the past.

She was taller now, of course, and had filled out in the last three years. But the real reason I hadn't recognised her was her confidence: the nervousness, the uncertainty, the self-conscious mannerisms – all gone. I remembered with a flush of heat what I'd been like at that age. How awful to be thirteen all over national TV.

'What the *hell*, Ash?' I said at last.

'Blast from the past, right?' There was a slight tremor in her voice, like she was wondering if she'd gone too far. Around us, the cast were looking from Ash to Kate, shifting uncomfortably.

'What is going on here?' Ms Drummond's voice was cold and dangerous. No one had noticed her come in. She stalked to the front of the group, and held her hand out for Ash's phone. 'Since we are five weeks out from performance, none of you know your parts, and *several* of you are yet to justify my misplaced faith in casting you in the first place,' she shot a particularly venomous glare at Ash, 'I'd expect that *if* I am unavoidably detained from the start of rehearsal, I would find you hard at work giving me something to restore hope in this whole production. Not,' she held up the phone like it was something disgusting, 'watching YouTube.' She tried to read the title of the offending video.

'Don't play it again, please.' It was Tim who spoke up.

'I most certainly will, if I decide to see what has kept my cast so distracted –'

'No!' I stepped up, and held out my hand for the phone. I blinked. 'You can't. It's – it's a private video – I mean, it's – it's not . . . None of us should have watched it.'

Ms Drummond held my gaze. Then she let her hand drop. Thank God. 'Well, if it's off a TV show, I can't see how it can be private . . . but nevertheless. Ashley, would you care to explain why you felt the need to show this?'

Ash looked like the situation had escalated out of her control. She opened her mouth, but didn't say anything.

'I'm waiting.' Ms Drummond tapped the phone with one finger. The silence lengthened. I stared at Ash. Her face started to heat, and we made eye contact.

I was standing halfway between them, I realised. Ash in front of me, Kate behind. One step in either direction and I'd be standing next to either of them, in the face of Ms Drummond's glare, in front of the silent pity of the cast. I could choose which music to face.

A girl I thought at first was my sister, lying under my tree and stealing my clothes.

A spaceship lunchbox, a friend I needed, literally, to breathe.

I turned and took two steps to stand behind Kate. I reached out one hand and rested it on her shoulder. She was shaking.

And then, that voice.

Kate sang, full and strong.

The Witch's solo. Ash's song. The high point of the show.

The solo Ash's voice could never quite master, no matter how hard she tried.

And Kate was singing it as if three years of music had been stored up, ready to pour out of her.

She didn't break eye contact with Ash, the whole verse. She held the last note, true and powerful, for an extra beat, then let it fade.

The silence rang with the absence of her voice.

Jos stood up. 'Woo, Kate!' he started to clap. Tim joined in, contributing a noisy whistle. Ms Drummond hadn't yet moved. The rest of the cast cautiously applauded, some laughing, relieved at the break in tension. Ash alone stayed silent. I could feel Kate's shoulder, still trembling slightly, under my hand.

'Katherine Wong.' Ms Drummond's voice was faint. '*Why* did you not audition?'

Ash was gone. Ms Drummond didn't send her out, didn't even look at her after Kate started singing, so Ash left, her head high but her steps unsteady. For once, I didn't think about following her. Instead, I looked over at Jos, standing by Tim and Mia. Before I could lose my nerve I walked over.

'Hey.'

'Hey. That was . . . pretty epic,' he said.

'Right?' I nodded towards the stage, and his eyes followed mine to where Ms Drummond had pulled Kate to go through the other songs. 'Isn't she amazing?'

'She sure is.' He kept watching the stage.

Kate's strong voice reached all the edges of the room. It gave me courage. 'You know who else is amazing? You are,' I said in a rush, trying to ignore the others listening in.

Jos turned from the stage to look at me. Just keep talking, I thought. 'Look, I'm really sorry about before, Jos. I let Ash get in my head, she made me feel like I should be embarrassed for liking you when I wasn't, actually, at all. And I've never had a boyfriend before and I –'

'Hold up. Did you just call him your boyfriend?' Mia burst in, clearly delighted.

Oh God. The embarrassment curled up in my chest, making me want to cave in on myself, to be small. I forced myself to stay standing.

Jos's face was unreadable. We locked eyes. My face felt like it was burning hot enough to give him sunburn.

'Yeah, I think she did, Mia. Jealous?' His face broke open with that smile.

And he reached out and slipped his fingers around mine – and I was struck again by how *right* they felt together. He pulled me a step closer, and –

'Laylor! Ghazy! Do I *really* have to tell you kissing is not allowed in rehearsal?'

CHAPTER FORTY-THREE

The next month passed in a blur. Thankfully, the musical rehearsals took over our lives: I had no room to worry about what was going on with Ash, or even to think about Mr Grant. It was kind of incredible, really, how you could go from talking to someone all day every day to ignoring each other to the point you start doubting their existence. The only time she spoke to me was when she needed to get to her locker – cold little comments that always made me pull my school jumper closer around me.

Ms Drummond reassigned the role of the Witch to Kate. Other than a warning, Ash avoided any further consequences for showing the video, though under the school's new 'zero tolerance cyber-bullying program' (because YouTube was involved, Mrs Lamby was convinced it was cyber-bullying) she technically should have been suspended. Ms Drummond convinced them that losing the part was enough punishment. She was probably right.

With Kate's voice to hold it together, the musical was actually starting to feel like a real thing. I got goosebumps hearing her sing. Ms Drummond lost her calm exterior and started to look a little feverish with a kind of wild-eyed excitement – I think she was half glad it was all coming together at last and half scared that she'd actually have to show it to everyone.

'Don't you wish we could just finish rehearsals and skip the performance bit?' I asked Jos, after a particularly exhausting session.

'What, like Cinderella getting all dressed up and missing the ball?' He slung his bag closer over his shoulder. 'What an anticlimax. Anyway, then we couldn't have the afterparty.'

I thought of Hannah's gold dress, lying on her bed at home, and couldn't stop a smile. 'True.'

Jos paused. 'Look – Lara, can I ask you something?'

'Sure?'

'Things have been weird, with Ashley and Kate and everything, so I realised I hadn't even asked you yet. But . . . I'd love to go with you to the party, if you like?'

'Yes. Yeah, that would be . . . very cool.' Very cool? Where had that come from?

His grin widened. 'Well, great. Cool, then.'

I laughed. 'Oh – I'm an idiot though. I already said I'd get ready with Kate. Could we all go together, do you reckon?'

'Sure. I'll let Tim know. It'll save him the angst of asking Kate out himself.' Jos grinned and started walking off down the corridor.

'Okay – wait, what was that about Tim?'

He raised one arm in farewell, and didn't look back.

Suddenly, I couldn't wait for performance week.

Before I knew it, the last rehearsal was done, the audience was quietly seated, the final flicks of eyeliner applied, costume adjusted, and – here I was. Waiting by the side of the stage for my cue on opening night, as the orchestra started up the overture.

Kate stood next to me. She shook out her arms, shifted from foot to foot. For the first time since Ash showed that awful video, I saw a ghost of thirteen-year-old Katherine.

'Hey,' I whispered, 'want my shoe to vom in? I don't need it after the second act.'

Kate grinned, and some colour returned to her face. She reached out a hand and linked her pinkie with mine.

The orchestra stopped.

The curtain opened.

And when Kate made her entrance, she owned that stage.

Just as quickly – in a glittering, frantic, funny whirl – it was almost over. The nights blended together so it was hard to figure out we'd actually put on four separate performances. There were the weird moments, like when Tim accidentally sang words from the wrong reprise in his duet, and gave away the major plot twist of the second act, or when Ben Hurst, the kid playing Jack, who had most definitely not hit puberty yet, accidentally snapped a leg of his prop cow, and responded with 'Oh, *shit*.' He got the biggest laugh of the night, and I'm pretty sure it was the reason he ended up with a date to the afterparty.

And now it was Sunday night, our last performance, and I was in a rare moment of solitude in the dressing room. I had a bit longer before I had to get dressed. My laptop caught my eye, lying on the corner of the desk that was now my dressing table. I glanced around. No one else was here. I pulled it towards me and opened up my Mr Grant document; it had become as automatic for me as checking Facebook. Maybe, this time, there'd be something new I'd see. I did a search of his name on Google again, but nothing new came up. Nothing new ever came up. All I'd been able to find was that school in Adelaide, so I copied across the address and number, since it was the only real lead so far.

I heard footsteps on the corridor, the rest of the cast starting to get ready. Quickly, I shrugged into Cinderella's sooty apron outfit, and I caught sight of myself in the mirror. I was going to miss indecisive Cinderella, who gets what she wants, and then has it all blow up in her face. She's a survivor, in the end. She had the strength to figure out what to do after happily ever after. And I was glad being her, one last night.

'Not such a stupid princess after all, hey, Ash?' I said to the reflection, with a grin.

'What?'

I swung around. Ash was here – in the dressing room. She looked like I just slapped her – she must have heard me. 'You're not meant to be back here,' I said, stupidly.

Her face hardened. 'Thanks for the reminder. You know, I really think you're better suited for one of the ugly stepsister roles, hey?' She turned to leave.

'Woah – sorry, I was just surprised, that's all. You caught me in a bit of a spacey moment.'

'Whatever. I came to wish you luck, but I guess you don't need it. But break a leg, anyway. Break both, for all I care.' She opened the door to the corridor of cast members rushing back and forth, props being carried around. Someone yelled something about sequins.

I thought back to the hammock on the last day of the summer holidays, how badly she had wanted this, how I hadn't even wanted to audition.

'Wait, Ash, look . . . I really am sorry, that you're not here.'

She smiled her chilly smile. 'Maybe you will be.'

And she was gone.

CHAPTER FORTY-FOUR

'Okay Lara, be specific – he actually said Tim wanted to ask me out?'

'I told you, he was unclear. And then he left. Are these earrings too much?'

Kate groaned and threw a pillow at me. 'You're useless.'

'I guess you'll just have to see what happens tonight.' I grabbed the pillow and joined her on her bed. We were mid-party prep, makeup and jewellery spread in a colourful mess across Kate's desk and dresser. Both our outfits lay on the end of her bed.

'Okay.' I clapped my hands together. 'No more boy talk. Let's get our energy up.' I grabbed my phone and her speakers, put on our pre-party music of the minute – Lana Del Rey – and turned up the volume.

Kate jumped up off the bed. 'Yes. This is good. Now, lipstick.'

We'd left on our dramatic stage makeup, and Kate started adding to it, giving full reign to her artistic spirit. She gave me a look she called 'soot-chic' – smoky eyes, and two charcoal smudge marks on each cheekbone.

We pulled on our costumes to see the effect: I was in Hannah's dress, shimmery bronze folds, and perfect Cinderella-esque heels, but with my favourite black T-shirt over the dress, waist knotted with a hair tie, and pastel socks with the shoes. I observed the effect.

'Twisted enough?'

'Hmmm . . .' Kate scrunched one sock further down my ankle, so they were uneven. 'Perfect.'

She had decided to go as her version of a mermaid: she teased her hair into a fan around her face, and wore a tight green dress with a low back, perfect for her. She picked up a liquid eyeliner pen from the desk and, with intense concentration, began to ink silver scales, curling up around her neck. She went a bit cross-eyed, doing them in the mirror. They looked incredible.

'It's unfair, you know. That you're freakishly talented at singing *and* art. Most people just stick to one.'

'Says you, biggest all-rounder there ever was. You know, I think that's why Ashley was always jealous of you.'

'What? If anything, I was always jealous of *her*.'

'Whatever you say. Except you're not the jealous type. And hey, maybe now you two are not like this anymore,' Kate twisted two fingers together on her non-eyeliner hand, 'you can start letting yourself be the best at things. Like athletics, for example.'

'Maybe . . .'

'Anyway,' Kate continued, 'as her charming video showed, singing is not a reliable talent of mine.'

'Oh, shut up. You know you killed it tonight.'

Kate grinned. 'I did, didn't I?'

The doorbell rang. Jos was here.

'Here we go.' I grabbed her hand, and we went to answer.

CLIFTON GARDENS, SYDNEY, AUGUST 1945

No one ever arranged the meetings at the Clifton Gardens. They just happened, like flowers blooming overnight. Someone would tell someone, and they would tell you and then you were off. The hotel closed early, officially, but there was a way around – along the beach, up through the rocks, and into the beer garden, where you wouldn't be turned away for a drink, especially if you wore a nurse's cape or an army uniform.

Sometimes that was the best bit: scrambling up the rocks. Men swearing and tripping, leaning on each other and laughing as if they were already drunk. Maybe they were, or just drunk on the night air, the smell of salt, the crash of waves, and the knowledge of a secret path.

And then the nurses at the gardens! So free with their laughter, flushes of colour on their cheeks; or quiet and slow to smile – like one brought along by a friend, only twice, Jessica – 'call me Jess,' she said to him, then 'call me Tina,' so that, his words rushed by beer, the man's jumbled name for her came out as 'Jestyn' and it stuck.

Jestyn, who he tried to talk to once, but she drifted away, her eyes sliding over him as if they were separated by a glass window. He saw her talking to someone else later though, heads close – Alf Boxall, from intelligence, he recognised the man – what could they be speaking about, so intently, on a first meeting? – and then a soldier with blond curls pulled him away into a swirl of dance and noise.

Weeks later he saw them again, the stillness of the moment pulling his eyes to their corner: Jestyn and Boxall, and between them a book, pressed in their hands. A parting gift, he wondered? Boxall was leaving for active service the next day.

So many stories, he thought. All these stories on the rocks of the cliff, in leafy corners, in two hands linking in a dance, in eyes meeting each other over beers at the Clifton Gardens. All these stories, snatched in the spaces between the war; because where else could you find them, when you're young and alive?

CHAPTER FORTY-FIVE

Tim's house, location of the afterparty, was a short tram ride from Kate's. We stood in the middle, no hands, taking the corners like surfers, like snowboarders – Kate with her crazy hair, me in my gold dress, and Jos with a huge white chef's hat balanced on top of his curls. The tram put on speed and without thinking I grabbed his arms to steady myself.

'Who are you meant to be?'

'The Baker, graduated to Head Palace Chef, of course.' He gave a tiny bow, and the hat flew off into the lap of a businessman, coming home late from work. The man didn't even look up from his phone, he just passed back the hat with one hand.

Something about the man's resigned reaction, our ridiculous outfits, combined with the end of performance high, got to me, and I couldn't hold it in: a loud, snorting laugh burst out. And then Jos and Kate were laughing at the ridiculous sound that I made, and Kate, once she starts, can't stop giggling. The laughter loop grew and grew till we were almost falling on top of each other as we tried to keep our balance. As we got off at our stop I leant my head against Kate's shoulder. Every now and then I flicked my eyes to Jos and felt that tingle when he was looking at me too.

I wondered if this feeling had been there all along. I felt like I was discovering a whole other layer to life, a whole realm of things I had been missing. I felt like I was about to arrive.

The afterparty was already well underway when we arrived. The committee had leaned in hard to the theme – someone had brought in a tree from the set into the hallway, green fabric hung from the roof, and fake spider webs were strung around the doorway: it looked like the entrance from *Stranger Things*, only not as slimy. There were some pretty cool touches – I saw a projector showing the old Disney version of *Snow White* on one wall, there was a plate of fairy bread covered in black sprinkles, and hand-held masquerade masks on thin sticks stood in a vase on the hall table. Trust St Mags to make it way over the top.

But despite the decorations it felt a bit flat: groups of people stood awkwardly in groups by the walls or in corners, a few shivered on the deck outside, as the weather was definitely not warm enough yet for the outfits we were all wearing. Music was playing loud enough so you couldn't really talk, but no one was dancing. I immediately wanted to leave with Jos and Kate again, go roam the streets of Melbourne in our crazy costumes, just us.

'Oh – excellent, you're here.' Tim came to meet us, dressed in tights and bright silk boxers, for Prince Charming pantaloons. 'You're just in time. Kate, I'm going to need your assistance. Mood-lifting emergency.'

He turned up the music and pulled her onto the dance floor. Tim was definitely not one of those dancers who go into their own private world, just them and the music: his moves were ridiculous, limbs everywhere, and his face invited you to join in with his craziness. Kate played along instantly. They moved well together, she matched him with her own level of energy and seemed to take up much more room on the floor than her small body should have been able to.

Jos appeared at my shoulder with two drinks. 'It's meant to be spiked but I'm pretty sure it's just soft drink. Tim's Dad is taking manning the bar *very* seriously.' He touched his plastic glass to mine. 'Cheers.'

'Cheers.' I touched mine back.

Before I could even take a sip, Kate shot out an arm and tugged me onto the dance floor. I reached out and grabbed Jos's hand. If I was going down, I was taking him with me.

'Show us what you've got, Cinderella!' said Tim over the music, and I twisted and shimmied, moves I remembered doing with Hannah, with Ash, moves that were now mine.

Soon, the whole cast and crew joined us, a sweating, heaving mass dancing away the adrenaline high from the performance, dancing to be stupid and funny and sexy together.

Kate, Jos and I emerged, claimed a couch against one of the walls, and collapsed as one.

'Hey Kate, nice moves.' Jos raised his glass to her approvingly.

'Not so bad yourself, Baker.'

'By the way, my mum kept tying herself in knots, on the drive home, 'cause she'd try to compliment Lara and me – they loved you, Lara – but then she'd always have to finish on "That girl who played the Witch though, what an *extraordinary* voice." And then she'd go, "Oh but you were good too, dear, of course." And the whole cycle would start again. It was great.'

Kate rolled her eyes. 'Ah, stop.'

'You were amazing, Kate.' I swung my arm around her. 'I overheard Ms Drummond talking about your performance and she was weirdly close to *gushing*.'

The front doorbell rang. Kind of late for anyone to arrive.

I heard Tim's mum go to answer it. Murmured voices, then one loud enough to penetrate the music . . .

'Yeah, I wasn't part of the performance, but *technically* I was on the cast, so really . . . can I come in? Great.'

I knew that voice. No way.

'She wouldn't . . .' I said.

'What?' asked Kate. 'Oh.'

Ash stood in the doorway, swaying slightly. She'd come in the red dress we'd picked out, all those weeks ago, and done her makeup like the Queen of Hearts: white face, two red circles high on her cheeks, heart-shaped lipstick pattern over her mouth.

She saw me. 'Lara!' she called, and threw out her arms in greeting.

I leapt up off the couch. Jos stood beside me, took my hand.

'And Kate, the lovely Kate. The wonderful, amazing, talented Kate.'

Kate stood too, and joined us facing her. 'Ashley, are you drunk?'

Ash ignored her. 'Kate! You know what I've been hearing people say, all week? All the people in the corridors, the parents in the car park? They say you *stole the show*. And I can't help thinking, wow, they are *so* right.'

Her lipstick had smudged, leaving a red smear down her chin.

'Because you did steal the show, Kate! You stole a part that *wasn't even yours*.' Ash threw her head back in a trilling laugh. A few of the people dancing stopped to watch.

'Hey Ashley, why don't we go continue this in the kitchen?' Jos stepped in.

'Oh, you – Jos, I know all about *you*. You think she likes you?' Ash nodded at me. My stomach twisted. 'She doesn't like you. She's just pretending. She's good at it, did it with me for years but watch out because she'll get sick of you and move on to someone else, just wait!'

She turned to me and smiled. Her eyes were glittering, not quite focused on me. 'What did you say, Loz? When you were talking about kissing him?'

'Ash,' I begged her.

'Oh yeah, that's right. "Not a big deal", right? And you were *so* embarrassed that everyone knew! So ashamed of poor awkward *Jos*.'

Half the room was watching now.

I gritted my teeth to stop myself from yelling, even though I wanted to, I wanted to *scream*. 'Ash. WHY are you here?'

She stared straight into my eyes, and her voice went low and intense. 'You're always asking me that, aren't you, Lara? What am I doing here, at your party? In your dressing room? In your life? Well, you might have forgotten but I *was* part of the cast. And your life. Before anyone else showed up.' Her voice got higher, started to crack. 'I was here first, you know. *I was here first*. Before anyone else. Before the *only person* you seem to care about this year – oh wait, they don't know yet –'

She fumbled at her clutch, took a few goes to open it, and pulled out a crumpled white sheet.

'Mr Grant!'

I went still and cold. 'What is that?'

The entire room was watching us now. Some sadist had turned down the music.

I recognised the paper now. I could see my typewritten notes, the photo of Mr Grant's handwriting. 'Ash, please.'

Her eyes were hard, and cold. 'Hey, everyone, want to know a few fun facts about Lara the star?' She turned to the rest of the cast, waved the letter like a flag. 'She's been secretly obsessed with her History teacher with the –' She squinted to read the print out, 'blue-grey eyes, the one who disappeared,

but not before leaving her a *love letter*, here, there's *proof*.'
She stabbed at the paper with her finger. The red patches
of her makeup were blending into the rest of her face, puffy
and coloured with anger. 'He left her a love letter, and she
sent him chocolate, and who knows what was happening in
their special one-on-one after-school sessions.' She was almost
spitting the words now. 'So I think we all know why poor
little Jos just wasn't *enough* for her, right, Loz?'

Jos let go of my hand.

'Wait – what? *That's* why you hated the jokes about us at
rehearsal?'

'No – I just,' I turned to explain, but I stopped at the sight
of his face, creased in confusion.

'Told you so.' Ash laughed again.

There was a roaring in my ears. I thought I heard Kate – or
maybe Tim – swearing, then someone else turned the music
back up, and there was a hand on my shoulder – but I had
tunnel vision, all I could see was that paper, crumpled in
Ash's tight fist.

Two steps forward and I grabbed it, she didn't resist, she'd
done everything she wanted. I stumbled to the door, away
from the comforting hand, the watching faces, I took the
paper and I ran, faster than any Cinderella had run before,
away from the party and into the night.

CHAPTER FORTY-SIX

I stopped for a second in my driveway and looked up at the sky. The stars felt so close; the whole scene had a ringing sharpness to it, like everything was more *real* than usual. Like the time I'd kissed Jos on the beach. Only this time I didn't feel light and fizzy inside. The sky, the sharp edges of the plants dark in the night, all screamed at me that this was really happening.

I had a key somewhere in my bag, but my hands were shaking too much to open the clasp. Never mind. I leaned on the doorbell with one arm, heard it chime out again and again, the notes overlapping and clashing. No one came. I banged on the door with my other hand.

It swung open, and I almost fell in. Mum was there in a nightgown with an old, fuzzy jumper pulled over the top she must have grabbed to answer the door.

'What in the world – Lara! What's wrong?'

The jumper made me stop. It was the one from the laundry, from our family beach holidays. Snuggling up to that jumper at the end of a day covered in sand and sea salt. Warm, safe, family voices around me as I drifted off in Mum's arms, her hand absently smoothing my hair. For a second, all I wanted to do was collapse into that jumper and cry and cry.

'Did you just forget your key? Really, there was no need for such a fuss . . .'

It felt suddenly impossible to tell her about the afterparty, to make her understand. 'You *never* think there's need for a fuss.'

'What do you mean –' Mum paused, then continued '– anyway, forget about that for now – look who's here!' She took a step back, leaving the doorway open. I opened my mouth again to argue – when I saw her.

'Lara!'

Her hair hung lank and flat to her shoulders and her skin was a light shade of pale I'd never seen on her before. But she was here. Really here.

'Hannah?'

And then I ran through the door and even though she looked different she still smelled like her, like Hannah; and I squeezed and squeezed her as hard as I could.

'But how – when did you –' I stepped back. All my anger from the party drained away. It was too much to take in.

'Just tonight. Didn't tell anyone. Surprise!' Hannah gave a weak jazz-hands flourish.

'You didn't tell me –' I looked back to Mum and Dad.

'We didn't know either, darling. Why don't you two go have a tea? We just had one, kettle is still hot.' Mum rested her hand on my shoulder and squeezed gently.

Dad emerged from the living room, holding two mugs. 'Good idea. Hannah, we'll talk more in the morning. We'll let you girls catch up.' Mum and Dad turned to their bedroom.

'Yeah . . . tea.' Hannah walked into the kitchen. 'Want yours black, Lara? All the Europeans have theirs black. Means that milk doesn't drown out the taste.'

I held back a laugh at the fact she'd been back all of two minutes and was already making me feel inferior. For my tea choices.

'Sure, black is great,' I answered.

Hannah was watching the tea in her hands to make sure it didn't spill as she walked to the couch, and I had a chance to look at her properly. I'd seen Hannah at all spectrums of her mood, from bright and sharp to soul-achingly sad. And tonight her face looked . . . empty. As if this year had slowly taken her energy and personality and this was all that was left.

Hannah looked up. Her face jerked back, like she'd been slapped. She lifted her chin and I saw the old defensive flash in her eyes. She must have caught the pity on my face.

'Here.' She set the tea down on the table, a bit more force-fully than was necessary. 'So, little sister.' She waved an arm expansively. 'How are you? Because as you can see, I'm doing *great.*'

As I sat down, the afterparty was back in my head. I could hear Ash's voice, I could feel Jos's hand slipping away from mine – it was all I wanted to talk about, but this was Hannah, and she was home.

'I'm – I'm fine,' I replied, at last. 'So . . . you're back? What *happened?*'

'Just . . . sensed that it was the right time, I guess.'

'You mean you ran out of money?' I tried to stop judgement from creeping into my voice.

'I could have found work in a hostel or something, if I wanted, I'm sure.' Hannah waved a hand dismissively. 'It's pretty easy to keep travelling if you want.'

'Come on, Han – tell me, really.'

Hannah looked away from me, out the windows in front of us. 'I guess – I had this idea, that I had to let go of everything for this year. I just left. You know what happens when you leave all that behind – family, friends, expectations, personality – all the weight of your own history? You can be whoever you like.

It's like a mystery, who am I, really? And you finally get to figure it out.

'You're free. And without all that history – you're also small. What do you do when you're alone with yourself, and you suddenly wonder if that's enough?'

She turned back to me on the couch.

'I know the postcards weren't much. But they were something, right? They were all I could do. I couldn't get back in touch, because to go back to myself would be to give up. It would be admitting that I'm small. That I need my limits to feel big.'

Part of me did understand her. I imagined her writing those postcards, so breezy and colourful, that had felt to me like she was showing off, when really they were a thin tether holding her to home.

But I had needed her too. And it was her choice to leave herself so little to hold on to. I put my tea down. 'Yeah, well if it's that hard, why did you make it so complicated? Did you really need to create all this mystery, Hannah? Why couldn't you plan a trip properly, go with a friend, or keep in touch like a normal human?'

'Stop it, Lara. Just stop, I've already got all this from Mum and Dad.' Hannah leaned forward so her hair covered her face.

I was glad Mum and Dad hadn't let her get away with lying to them about where she was over the year. But it seemed so classic that Hannah would come back, take up all their attention, and then complain about it to me.

And still no one had asked me about the afterparty.

'Sure. Okay. But you couldn't even – I don't know – plan your return trip to arrive *one day earlier* to see me in the musical?'

'Wait – what musical?' Hannah frowned in confusion.

'The school musical, which you would know about if you'd replied to any of my emails instead of sending your too-cool postcards, or if you'd asked me a *single* question about where I've been tonight.'

'Hang on – you were in the Year Ten musical? Acting? In front of people? Ashley made you join the chorus or something, did she?' She smiled her infuriating older-sister smile. I knew she was remembering her own time in the musical, when she was a star. A wave of frustration rose in my chest.

'No. I had a main part. It was fun, actually. I was pretty good at it. And, uh – Ash wasn't in the musical at all in the end. Her voice wasn't good enough and she lost her part. We – we're not really friends anymore.'

Hannah's eyes widened. 'Ah. I get it, I think.' She was quiet for a while, then nudged me. 'Never liked her, anyway. Smiled too much. Should have known she was secretly a mega-bitch.'

'Yeah, well.' I had a flash of memory from first term, cleaning the girls' toilets with Ash, our spontaneous dance party. 'I didn't.'

Hannah continued, laughter in her voice. 'So, you really would have wanted me to come cheer you on in the musical? So unexpectedly needy of you.'

She still didn't get it. Still thought my problems were so adorable compared to hers. 'Needy? *Really?* Coming from you – even though you were overseas for the whole year, you still made sure everything revolved around you.' My tea was spilling over the edges of the cup, splashing hot drops on my arm. I put it down on the coffee table with an unsteady clunk. 'Yeah, I would have liked you to book your ticket a day earlier so you could see me perform. But I should have known it would be too much to ask for you to think about someone other than yourself, even for one night.'

Hannah's face was white. 'Come on. There's no way I would've been able to guess you'd sign up for the musical. This isn't all about you, Lara.'

I stood up. I suddenly couldn't bear to be in the house another second. 'It's *never* about me. And tonight, I needed it to be.'

I pushed past Hannah, back out the front door. I ran onto the lawn, and my heels sank into the grass. I pulled at them, feeling the straps strain into my feet, and I was too dizzy with anger and frustration to stop and undo them. I felt something snap and stumbled forward, in a lopsided limp. One shoe was left in the grass, as if I'd stabbed it in the lawn on purpose.

'Lara!' Mum called me from the doorway. As I whirled to face her, I saw her turn back to check on Hannah, still in the house behind her.

'What's going on?' Dad appeared beside Mum. 'Lara, what's happened to you?'

'Nothing has *happened* to me. You don't listen, you never listen –' I felt myself shaking. I still had one shoe left on and could feel my stupid ankle was about to roll. I pulled my remaining shoe off, stood there barefoot in front of them. I could see Mum's face twitch in disapproval, even with everything else going on. She'd always told me a real lady stays on heels until the end of the night.

I wouldn't be able to make them understand. Nothing would.

'Sorry, Mum. I'm done. I'm going to . . .' I stopped. Where could I go? Not to Jos, not with the memory of his crumpled face so clear. Not to Ash's. No. 'To a friend's,' I heard myself finish, and felt a rush of relief. I'd go to Kate's. Kate was safe. Kate would let me in. 'I'll be safe, I'll be fine. Just – let me go.'

I stumbled out of the driveway, single shoe in one hand, phone in the other. I started dialling. By now my sobs were making it difficult to talk.

CHAPTER FORTY-SEVEN

I loved her for the way she didn't ask any questions. For the way she met me at the park and walked the rest of the way with me. For the way she reached out and took my one shoe and murmured, 'Method acting?' in a way that made me laugh and hiccup at the same time, and for the way she then dropped the shoe and gave me a quick, fierce hug.

Kate showed me to a spare mattress laid out on the floor of her parents' study, slotted between a computer desk and piles of binders and paper that had clearly just been pushed out of the way. She loaned me a T-shirt and pyjama shorts without me asking. As we brushed our teeth – me with my finger, her with a toothbrush – she laid her head on my shoulder. I let my head rest to lie against hers. And part of me felt that everything was going to be okay. Ash hated me. Jos might never speak to me. But at least Kate was here. With her, I might just be able to get through.

I woke up at 6am, I'd forgotten to close the blinds last night. There was a disorientating second of trying to figure out where I was; my eyes tried to reconcile the piles of paper that lay in front of my face instead of my bedside lamp.

I remembered, and sat up, wide awake.

I reached for my phone to see if anyone had texted me overnight. The screen was blank. Dead battery – I hadn't brought my charger. Oh well. My Mr Grant notes were sticking out of my bag, a crumpled white triangle. My eyes skittered away from them, back to the stack of forms next to my makeshift bed.

Something about those forms niggled at my mind, something vaguely unsettling. The words came into focus.

Saraswati College: Application Form
Experience a new approach to education at Saraswati:
an alternative school on the outskirts of Melbourne. We
focus on the creative arts and a collaborative approach to
learning. No uniforms. No formal disciplinary system.
Excellent results.

The form was for next year's intake. It was filled in, in Kate's handwriting – she had even signed it. Attached were copies of her artwork, tiny inked line drawings: a portfolio submission, I guess. I flipped through the drawings – there was a man lying slumped on a beach, a feathered sandal, a single jewelled shoe, a fir tree . . .

So. She was leaving me too.

I dropped the portfolio. Only half aware of what I was doing, I dressed in the clothes I left here yesterday, when we were getting ready for the afterparty – a lifetime ago – and shoved my party clothes in my bag, along with my useless phone. I clicked the mouse of the computer on the desk; thankfully, it was still on. I looked up the flight I wanted, found a cheap one leaving that morning, filled out my details and printed the boarding pass. Minutes later I was out the door.

Out in the sleepy silence of dawn the light was soft and gentle, pinks blending into a brilliant blue overhead. It smelled

like spring: rain, the blossom tree in Kate's garden, freshly
cut grass.

I felt new, too. But not soft, or gentle. I felt hard, ready,
and, for one of the first times in my life, decisive.

I knew where I was going. I'd find him on my own, and
prove all of them wrong. I was going to Mr Grant, to the
Somerton Man. I didn't look back as the door swung shut
behind me.

I was going to Adelaide, and I was going alone.

PART 3
THE TRUTH

September

Thud thud my heart pumping blood
Whenever someone talks about my Taman Shud
He's gone and no one even cares at all
The earth won't answer and the sea don't mourn

THE DRONES

CHAPTER FORTY-EIGHT

I was out of Melbourne now, a blur of grey-green scrub and gum trees rolling out underneath the window. I watched the landscape go by hungrily, willing the plane to go further and further. It was like running, but better. All that distance, between me and home. More of it, please, more of it.

I'd never travelled this far alone before.

The Somerton Man would have taken a train, snaking its way somewhere along the land below. I imagined him sitting by a window, watching the trees shoot past, with his shined shoes and briefcase. Did he come from Melbourne? What was he running away from, or running towards?

It was kind of amazing that I could simply choose this. I took the bus from Southern Cross Station to the airport, gave my best polite St Margaret's girl smile to the flight attendant when she asked what I was up to in Adelaide – visiting family, I said – and she happily scanned my boarding pass. No one to stop me. Leaving, it turns out, is the easiest thing.

I leant my forehead against the cool plastic window, felt the rumbling of the plane in my body. My phone was still dead and without a book or anything to distract me my mind was beginning to settle, to wander. As I looked at all the land expanding out underneath me I thought back to when I was little, when Dad would sometimes bring back old plans from work and let me use them for colouring in. I liked the fluffy shapes of trees from above, which looked to me like clouds: the only softness between the straight lines. I used to colour the squares different shades, like a modernist painting.

'How can this be a building?' I would ask, holding up my crazy mosaic of colour.

He'd pull me up onto his lap and explain how the lines meant walls, how the measurements meant distances, twice as tall as me, three times the length of my arm, down to the width of windowsills – two of my small hands stretched wide.

'It's a pattern, Lara,' he'd say. 'It's like . . . a code, a map.'

'But why can't it be a picture of the actual house?'

He'd try again to explain the numbers, the representations, the difference between two and three dimensions.

'But wouldn't an exact picture be better?' I'd persist.

'Sometimes the exact picture doesn't tell you enough. Sometimes the map is the truth, the picture is a lie.'

'Drink for you, ma'am?'

I pulled away from the window with a start. A polite flight attendant had stopped next to me, wheeling a trolley.

'Just like in Harry Potter!'

He grinned. Oh. I'd said that out loud. The *ma'am* had thrown me.

'Well, no pumpkin pasties here. But we do have chips, chocolate, drinks? What would you like?'

I blinked. *Did* I want anything? I waited, tried to let the answer float up from somewhere inside. From the Lara who was separate from Kate and Ash and Hannah, separate from my parents, separate from Mr Grant. If she even existed, if I even knew her.

I wanted to be going to Adelaide. I wanted to visit the Somerton Man. I wanted to know what happened to Mr Grant. And I wanted orange juice.

The man had a slightly glazed look. I had maybe kept him waiting too long.

'Orange juice,' I heard myself say, firmly. 'Definitely. Orange juice. That's what I'd like.'

'Uh . . . right. Four-twenty, then.'

I didn't care if he thought I was weird. I knew what I wanted to drink. It was a start.

CHAPTER FORTY-NINE

The shuttle bus from the airport dropped me off outside the main train station. Thinking again of the Somerton Man, I stepped inside. The arrival hall ceiling was high, morning light filtering through the windows and casting the sandstone walls golden-brown. The ceiling was big enough to absorb the sound of trains, clacking shoes, rolling suitcases, conversations and guard whistles – I could hear all that, but as though it were far away, echoing down a tunnel, or coming from a different time. The noise of the station dropped away, and I thought instead of the hush of libraries, cathedrals, of places with history.

He would have stepped off his train into this room. The bones of the building wouldn't have changed much. A medium height, well-put-together man, holding a briefcase – I could almost see him, trotting purposefully in front of me to check in his luggage.

Where were you going, that day? What were you thinking?

'I don't know, there's a bus involved somehow, there's always a bus,' a woman said into her phone as she pushed past me. She jostled my bag and shoulder. 'Sorry!' she mouthed, with a wave, and kept going.

I pulled my bag closer to me, suddenly back in twenty-first century Adelaide, rather than 1948 with the Somerton Man.

I was the only one standing still, the crowd parting around me. What was I *doing* here? I felt a bubble of panic start to rise in my chest. Getting out of Melbourne had felt so important, and now I was here, what was I going to do?

I pulled out my phone, out of reflex, and stared blankly at the black screen. Where could I go to charge it? Did I even want to turn it back on, and be in contact with Melbourne again? Would anyone be looking for me by now? The panic bubble grew. Okay. Deep breaths, if I kept moving, I'd be okay. I shoved my phone back in my bag, and pulled out the sheets of notes on Mr Grant. The past school's address, I had that at least. If they'd tell me what happened to him, I could prove to Ash that I'd been right to investigate his disappearance, it didn't mean I was crazy – and I'd know for myself. It was as much of a plan as any that I had.

I knew the school was in central Adelaide. I should be able to get there pretty easily. There, up ahead in the station, was a brightly lit tourist office. I took a breath, and joined the stream of people moving around me; I headed to the office for a map.

CHAPTER FIFTY

I checked the address on the printout of my Mr Grant notes. Yes, this was it. Kingswood Grammar. I was struck by how familiar it felt, even though I'd never been there. There was the same imposing entrance – here, it was two pillars topped with statues, instead of the stone archway of St Mags. Different place, same attempts to impress. It made me smile and feel confident enough to go on. I walked up the drive, past the impeccable green lawns. I followed a tasteful plaque labelled 'Reception' into a room where a woman was typing non-stop.

'You have to use the student entrance, even if you're late,' she said, without looking up. 'It's Term Three, you should know that by now.'

'Oh – I don't – I'm not a student.'

She looked up, took in my crumpled clothes from the day before, my messy hair. Her lips pursed in distaste. 'If you're a prospective student you need to book in a tour time and come back then, with a parent or guardian.' She pushed a leaflet across the counter to me and went back to typing.

'Just, since I'm here, I did have a question.'

'Really, it's better if you come back with your parents. We can't accommodate school tours for walk-ins.'

'I don't want a tour.' She still wasn't looking at me. I pushed my shoulders back, stood up tall. I raised my voice. 'I have a question. One. Question.'

The woman sighed, and glanced behind her. I could see more offices through a glass door, lots of soft carpet, muted colours on the walls, faint sounds of murmured conversations. Not a place for loud, poorly dressed teenagers. I could see her mental calculations on which would make me leave quicker: continuing to be blandly unhelpful, or humouring me.

'How can I assist, then?' she said, at last, as if she'd rather scrape dog poo off the ground than help. Her fingers still hovered over her keyboard, ready to go back to work as soon as she got rid of me.

'It's about a teacher who was here last year – Mr Grant? I'm, uh, really interested in history and heard he was really good, so I wanted to know why he left and if . . . if he might come back?'

She pushed her chair away from her desk. She leant over the counter to look at me, really look at me, for the first time. Her face was pinched and angry. I took a step back in surprise.

'Are you press?' She hissed. 'I can tell you, we've had enough tabloid reporters hovering around, *none* of whom went to print because of our excellent legal team, just so you know – but to impersonate a teenager, that's a new low. Tell me why I shouldn't call security *right now.*'

'No, no – I –' My head was spinning. Her reaction was so fast and intense I couldn't figure out what it meant. Before I realised what I was doing, I started telling the truth. 'It's just, he was a teacher at my school too, and I knew him pretty well, but now he's gone and no one will tell me where he is, so I just hoped you could – I just want someone to tell me *what's going on.*' I was almost shouting the last words. My hands were balled into fists.

One of the doors in the tasteful offices behind reception opened, a curious head poked out.

The receptionist was still staring at me, but her look was a different kind of horrified now. 'You knew him? You're one of his students – do you –' She stopped herself from finishing that sentence. 'I have to –' She reached out for the phone.

But I didn't wait for her to call security on me, or whatever she was going to do. I suddenly felt claustrophobic in that neat office, all the carpet and rules and dignified hush. I pushed open the door and left before she could come after me, past the drive, past the perfect lawns, and back out into the city.

ELEPHANT AND CASTLE HOTEL, ADELAIDE, JUNE 1949

Leo Kenny, publican of the Elephant and Castle Hotel, moved closer to the two men discussing the latest development in the case.

'You hear they've finally set a funeral date?'

'That's right, two weeks from now. Going to be a pauper's grave, poor sod.'

'What's that?' Leo asked.

'Haven't you heard? The Somerton body, finally going to be buried. Thought you'd know, Leo. You've been following the case that closely.'

'But – surely not – a pauper's grave?' He asked.

'Imagine that, buried with no name, no family, no money.'

Leo felt suddenly faint, and pulled out a cleaning cloth so he could inconspicuously steady himself on the bar as he wiped it down. The man found at Somerton Beach had been all he and his patrons, many from the cemetery across the road, had talked about these last six months. And now the man was going to be buried, alone.

The network Leo had built around himself – his regular customers who he knew by name, drink order, and recurring marital problems; the weekly conversation and complaint about the weather with the delivery man from the brewery; the gentle jibes and fatherly advice (always ignored) he gave the girls on his staff; even his own family name, known throughout Adelaide – all this suddenly felt as tenuous and fragile as a spider web. Could he end up in an unfamiliar city, unclaimed, unloved, and alone? Left lying on the beach, as if the sea itself had spat him out in rejection? (This was an early theory about the body on Somerton Beach, that he had simply washed in with the tide: until newspaper articles confirmed the man and his clothes were bone-dry, the sand around him undisturbed.)

'No.' Leo stopped cleaning and dropped his fist on the bar with a thud. Both men looked up from their beers. 'Not as a pauper.'

'Well, no one knows who he is. Who'd pay for it?'

'We will.' Leo felt the decision crystallise as he said it. 'Yes, why not? God knows, the poor man's given us ample entertainment over the last six months. I've pulled enough beers as you lot have picked over each latest article, ghouls that you are.' He attempted a laugh at this last comment, but couldn't quite pull it off. One of the men watching, Al, from the Bookmakers' Association, smirked at his friend.

'Your lot can put in a chunk towards the funeral, right Al?' Leo said, suddenly fierce. 'You're often giving to all kinds of causes, and I know there's been more than a few racing bets placed in my pub over these last weeks as everyone's discussed the case. Really, I should be getting a cut myself.' He did not bother to put any humour in his voice. 'Least you can do is chuck in some of that profit to bury the man.'

Al looked around for support, eyes wide with panic. But he wasn't going to find anyone who'd disagree with the man pulling the beers. 'I'll have to take it to the other Association members,' he muttered. 'Interesting idea, Leo.'

Leo turned to the man sitting at the other end of the bar, a stonemason. 'And you could do a headstone, right, Archie?'

Archie frowned. 'How do you figure, a headstone without a name?'

Leo felt his panic building. 'Well, put down where he was found. And when.'

Archie still looked doubtful.

'Just say "The Unknown Man", for a name,' Leo said. 'He's still a man, name or no, right?'

Archie nodded slowly. 'The Unknown Man. I could swing that. May not have it ready by the funeral date, but could do it for a few days after.'

'Thanks, Arch.' Leo felt his shoulders relax. He gave the bar a final wipe and put the cloth in his pocket. 'Can't give him a name or family, but he won't be buried a pauper.'

CHAPTER FIFTY-ONE

I ran from the school until I was back on Rundle Mall, where I stopped, bent over, panting. What now? My mind was still whirring from the school visit. I needed to find somewhere quiet, somewhere I could think properly.

The wide, open street wasn't that busy, for a weekday. Over one wall, I could see the tops of trees of a city park, and in another direction, a laneway looked like it led to more shops, maybe a café. I could go any way I wanted. Instead of freedom, I started to feel panicky again. The hours of the day stretched ahead of me, saggy and shapeless. I began to understand what Hannah had meant, the night before. How did she do it, travelling on her own? How did she fill those hours, without anyone to fill them with her?

All I needed was a plan, I thought, ignoring my growing anxiety. A next step, it didn't matter what. I pulled out my Adelaide map. There – in the corner – a suggestion for tourists: *Why not catch Adelaide's one remaining tram, from the city centre to the seaside suburb of Glenelg?*

A tram wasn't exactly a novelty for me, considering I took one to school every day in Melbourne. But Glenelg, and Somerton Beach – yes, that would be worth visiting. If I couldn't find Mr Grant, maybe I could find the Somerton Man.

❄

I took the long way around from the tram stop, and ended up walking along Moseley Street, where the nurse whose phone number was in the back of the *Rubaiyat* would have lived. The one real lead the police had, never followed through because of their nervousness exposing a single mother. One of these houses was hers – just five minutes' walk from where the body was found on the beach. I wondered if the house had changed since, or not.

Slowly I sank to my knees and sat on the footpath, feet in the gutter. No one was around. The street was quiet, I could hear a seagull cawing and the rustle of gum trees. In the yard of a house in front of me, a Hills Hoist creaked in the wind, weighed down by washing. Could this have been her house?

I imagined the nurse, a young mum, living in this little house. I had no idea what it would have been like to have a toddler and be unmarried. I imagined her strong, resilient, unbreakable – but she could have been terrified, underneath it all. It must have felt like a pretty precarious situation, living with a man she wasn't married to, while raising a two-year-old, before 1950. What went through her mind, when the police knocked on her door and asked her about the book of Persian poetry? Did she answer the door with a toddler balanced on her hip? Was she expecting them? Was she scared? Had she already passed on a secret message through a chain of command?

I pulled out a tuft of weeds growing between the concrete. I couldn't imagine her, I realised. Because she was as much a mystery as the Somerton Man. If she was a spy – a spy who used the *Rubaiyat* to pass secret messages, maybe – then he was, too. If she was an old friend, or a lover, of a perfectly ordinary man, then that's his identity. But there's no way of knowing his story through hers, because she did not want it to be told. She died telling no one, no reporters, no police. He couldn't help becoming a mystery, but she chose to remain one. I found myself respecting that. She didn't let anyone else define her story – she kept it for herself.

I stood up, and walked out towards the beach.

CHAPTER FIFTY-TWO

I leant over the esplanade railings, looking out across Somerton Beach. Somewhere along here must be the place where he was found. The wind whipped the waves to white peaks, and caught at the edges of people's jackets and coats. I liked it. The breeze felt cleansing somehow: for a moment, I didn't have to think.

'Lara!'

I looked up from the esplanade. Two figures were waving from the tram stop, calling my name. I felt a rush of panic – had security from the Adelaide school come after me? And how would they know my name?

'Lara? Yes, it's her! Lara!' They were running towards me, close now. Suddenly I recognised them.

'Kate? How did you –' and with her, really, was it '– Jos?'

Before I could say anything more, Kate pulled me into a bone-crushing hug. She pulled away, and pummelled my shoulder with her fists.

'Oi! That hurts!'

'If you run off like this again, I'm going to be forced to murder you.'

'How – where did you even –' I shook my head, to try and get the questions out. I felt like I should be glad to see them, but all I felt was the anxiety of the reality of Melbourne crashing back onto me now they were here. I couldn't escape it, after all.

'You left the flight booking open on my computer, you dork,' Kate said. She was still holding my arm, as if she was scared to let me go again.

'You wouldn't have made a great spy after all, Laylor,' Jos added. His voice was shaking, slightly.

'It was Jos's idea to come to the beach,' Kate said.

'Just in case you wanted to visit the Somerton Man, too.'

'Too? How did you know – did you know I was looking for Mr Grant?' I looked from Kate to Jos. There was something wrong. Neither of them was quite meeting my eyes.

Kate opened her mouth to say something, stopped. She looked down at her feet.

'Because,' I said, 'I think I was right, something strange is going on. I went to the school, you know, the one we found in that search in the library?' I was babbling, but I just wanted Kate to look at me, for that awful expression to come off her face. 'The receptionist at the school was really aggressive and strange – she thought I was a reporter – they're covering something up there for sure –'

'Lara.' Kate met my eyes. 'We know about Mr Grant. We know what happened.'

'What – what do you mean?' And why was she looking at me like that, like *I* was the one who was hiding something?

'There isn't something you're not telling me, is there?' Kate asked, gently. 'He didn't ask you to meet him here, or something –'

'Lara, you can tell us, it's okay,' Jos said, also in that hushed tone.

'Guys – I've told you everything – you clearly know more than I do.' I could feel my pulse increasing, an impatient fluttering in my chest. 'What is it? What's happened?'

Kate gave me a searching look.

'She really doesn't know,' Jos said. He sounded – relieved?

'Kate – just tell me –' I felt like I couldn't stand another second of this.

She reached in her bag and handed me something – a letter.

'One was delivered to every family in the school today. This is my parents' one.'

I opened my mouth to ask more but she shook her head. 'Read it, Lara. It's all in there.'

Dr Matilda Taplin
Principal
St Margaret's Girls' School
Greenfields, Melbourne

To: All Parents
CC: Members of the Board, Entire Staff
Re: Mr David Grant

Dear Mr and Mrs Wong,
A former teacher of the school, Mr David Grant, has been disqualified from teaching and had his registration cancelled by the Victorian Institute of Teaching at a hearing this week. This is due to conduct unbefitting a teacher, as per Section 2.6.46 of the Education Act (2006).

The conduct relates to a relationship with a student, which took place last year during his previous position at a school in Adelaide.

St Margaret's Girls' School was unaware of the incident when we hired Mr Grant, who came with excellent recommendations from previous employers and high praise from student testimonials.

Mr Grant taught History at St Margaret's for two terms at the start of this year before leaving the role. There is no indication of inappropriate behaviour during his brief period at the school. However, the Board and the office of the Principal take the incident extremely seriously and felt it important to inform the school community of events.

Should you have further questions, please contact us.

Regards,

Dr Matilda Taplin   Mr Paul Dalton
Principal   Chairman of the Board
St Margaret's Girls' School   St Margaret's Girls' School

CHAPTER FIFTY-THREE

I stared at the letter. How unfair that it should look so ordinary – the faint green letterhead of the school, like all the term bills and permission slips I'd collected from my letterbox over the years, concerning me but addressed always to my parents.

'The "no indication" thing is a bit of a lie though, isn't it?' Kate's eyes were wide with worry. 'There were those private sessions with you after school, and Mrs Lamby seemed freaked out about them.'

'And the note,' I said, blankly. 'The note he left me in my locker was probably inappropriate.'

'Wait, that part was true?' Jos asked. 'He did leave you a love letter before he left?'

I didn't answer. The whole trip was reshaping in my mind, the whole year.

Mr Grant said once that studying history was like a map to the past. The more you know – the more facts, figures, and motivations you can gather – the more accurate the map, and the clearer you can draw the lines of what happened: the roads and landmarks of where, and who, and why. But get in too close – learn too much of what Robespierre's hairdresser thought or what the peasants had eaten that morning or why the weather on 14 July changed everything – and you can get lost in the detail. All you can see is minutiae, a satellite picture of the land that blurs into greens and greys and endless rooftops, which is no help at all to navigation.

A map is a metaphor. Close enough and distant enough to what it describes so that you can understand it. It is not the thing itself, despite the trick of language.

I stopped reading and let the letter fall. A gust of wind snatched it away, it landed against a stair rail leading down towards the beach. Somerton Beach, where the Somerton Man had died.

I guess I'd begun to think of the Somerton Man and Mr Grant as a metaphor, a map. That if I solved the mystery of who this unknown man was, if I found my teacher, it could help me figure out who I was, too. But I was too close now, I had lost them in the detail, I was no longer sure what I was trying to interpret.

I stood up and walked unsteadily to retrieve the letter.

'Lara? Are you okay?' Kate's voice sounded like it was coming from far away. All I could hear was the rush of wind, the caw of seagulls, and a cold official voice . . . *disqualified from teaching* . . .

I took a few steps, but the wind changed, whisked the letter down the stairs. I followed.

'Lara? Lara, it's okay, leave it!'

. . . his registration cancelled . . .

A figure standing at the side of an oval on the first day of school. A trail of smoke from a forbidden cigarette. The flash of interest in his eyes when I said something surprising.

I could see the letter flapping along the beach. It flew upwards in a sudden twist of the sea breeze. A small dog on a lead barked, his owner pulled him away, the straining lead forcing the dog into an awkward standing position. It kept barking, and barking.

If I didn't go now the letter would be gone.

I started to run.

The sand was wet and firm here, my sandals stuck with each step. I kicked them off. And then I didn't notice much else. I passed the small dog, I picked up speed, the letter dancing ahead of me, a roaring in my ears, or maybe that was the crash of the waves.

And I was in my rhythm, running faster and stronger than in the park, than playing frisbee on the cast weekend away, I could feel a new power flowing through my legs, a power that scared me, that made me move too fast, a power that came from Mum's frozen face at the door as I left, from Ash's bright cheeks at the afterparty, Jos's silence, Kate's admission forms to leave me behind, and – Mr Grant.

Mr Grant in the car park, comparing sunsets with me, his half-smile, talking about the boys in the musical.

I can see the letter from the school fluttering up ahead, or is it a plastic bag? No – the letter, it is, it tangles with the string of a kite, floats down a few steps in front of me and I sweep it up, crumple it in my hand like a baton, and I have it now, but I don't care, I'm running just to run, running because if I run fast enough maybe I can stop hearing that voice echoing around in my head . . .

waves crash –

. . . *inappropriate relationship* . . .

seagulls call –

the tide sucks out –

a small shell catches in the soft arch of my foot –

my breath getting short, my lungs screaming, my head spinning –

and then I see up ahead:

A staircase leading down to the beach. Just the same as the photograph Mr Grant had handed to me and Kate, that first class, an X in the sand where the stairs meet the beach.

And I swear I almost see him, I see a figure, someone, lying in the sand, I smell the smoke of a dying cigarette, and he lifts one arm to me, as if to tell me something, as if to wave, and then lets it fall.

I hear the rasping of my lungs, something inside pulling tighter and tighter –

And I see another picture in my head now, a memory – my bag dropped at Kate and Jos's feet, and lying in my bag, my inhaler.

So far away now.

And my vision starts to close in on itself, down to a pinprick –

My knees hit the sand –

I wish that gasping noise would stop –

I wish my chest would tear open, to stop the squeezing, I feel my hand pull uselessly at my T-shirt –

I see the stairs, the beach, there's no one there after all.

I hear footsteps and think I see Kate's face, her hair whipping around in the wind, and Jos, looking more serious than I've ever seen him –

It's so hard to breathe –

And then I don't see anything at all.

CHAPTER FIFTY-FOUR

I took four deep puffs of the inhaler, waited a few minutes, and took four more. My chest started to open up, my breathing became a little easier. I focused on that, on each breath, instead of thinking how close that had been. That was the worst asthma attack I could remember. Kate and Jos sat either side of me, a hand on each of my shoulders.

'Can we get away from this beach?' I said, when my breathing was steady enough to talk. The crash of the waves felt way too loud.

'Sure.' Kate looked around. 'We're not far from my grand-parents' place. I know a café.'

It was a fish and chip shop that also did coffee, rather than a café, and we were the only ones there – perfect. I sat on the metal folding chair outside with relief – even the short walk was too much right now.

'Long black?' Jos asked.

He remembered. 'I think caffeine would be a very bad idea at this point.' I held out my hand, which was shaking a little from the asthma medication. I'd had to take more than usual. 'Just water.'

'Well, I definitely want a coffee,' said Kate. 'Jos?'

'Flat white, please.'

She went up to order, leaving me alone with Jos. I suddenly realised I hadn't talked to him properly since the afterparty last night.

I looked down at the table, unsure how to start. 'I really didn't know until Kate showed me the letter,' I said in a rush. 'I mean – there wasn't anything – or at least, *I* didn't think there was anything . . .'

'Who *cares* about him, Lara?' Jos interrupted me. He turned red, ran a hand through his curls. 'I don't. I just care about you.'

For a second, I couldn't say anything. 'I thought you were meant to hate me – after the party, and Ash –'

'You should know by now that no one listens to anything Ashley says.' He offered me a version of his heart-stopping smile, just a flash.

I smiled back.

Jos reached his hand over the café table, let it sit there by the tin of sugar sachets. After a moment, I reached out my hand and hooked my pinkie around his.

'You know, this is still the first time I've had a boyfriend. And apparently I'm a slow learner. So, there's a high possibility I'll keep stuffing it up.'

'Well, I'm happy to be the subject of that experiment as long as you'll let me.' He looked serious. 'For scientific purposes.' His thumb drew a slow circle over my hand, and I felt it all again: that shiver, electricity, the gaps between the stars.

'Kate's taking a while with the order, hey?' I said at last, though I could have sat there looking at him for longer.

Jos half-turned in his seat. 'She's on the phone, looks like.'

Kate stood by the counter, talking quickly into her mobile. She came back and put it down on the table. 'Your mum,' she said in explanation. 'I managed to convince her I'd spirited you away for an overnight trip to Adelaide.'

'And she was okay with that?' I asked, surprised.

'Not exactly. But she calmed down when I told her I'd already bought our tickets back and I agreed to forward them to her, so she knows when to come pick you up. She's going to ask you a lot of questions once you get home.' Kate frowned. 'And she said something about definitely having *two* teenagers now, which is confusing, since you already were a teenager.'

I managed a shaky laugh at that. 'I know, right?'

'Oh,' Kate added. 'Your sister – apparently she's home? – also told me to make you check your email, immediately.' Kate slid her phone across the table. 'Sign in there if you like.'

TO: laylor.l@stmargarets.vic.edu.au
FROM: Hannah_tacocat@gmail.com

Oh, Lara. As the queen of dramatic disasters, I have to applaud you, but next time start a little smaller, hey? Just kiss a boy or sneak out to a party, don't run away interstate. I've heard teenagers lack perspective, and from my vastly more mature age of almost twenty I agree you need a bit of scale here.

But seriously: I get it. I'm sorry. I was a jerk this year. And I hereby give you permission to screenshot this and use it against me at ANY time you see fit. (Okay, with a limit of once a month and never valid for vetoing a movie choice, please.)

I've finally read all your emails. I saw them there, each time I logged in at those internet cafés, your name appearing on the fuzzy computer screens that took forever to load. It was hard not to read them. But I really thought I couldn't (I know, I know, it sounds like I'm making it about me again – I'm trying not to, I promise). I wanted to push myself to last the year without you. I knew the moment I opened one of those emails, heard your voice, the whole structure of rules I'd built around myself, everything that was keeping me there, would collapse. So I sent you postcards instead.

I think you've always been so centred, so self-contained, like you had your life under control when mine *never* was – that I missed the fact you could need me too. I'll always look up to you, Lara, even though it's meant to be the other way around.

I can report that you've given Mum and Dad a sufficient rattling, too – hope you're prepared for a significant increase in parental attention on your return. Funny how all this time they probably needed to let go of me more, and hold on to you tighter.

They are also mildly freaking out over the letter about that teacher – he taught you History, right? Dad was saying that you mentioned History a LOT this year and had been doing some 'special project', so if there's anything sinister to that, you let me know right away, and I'll make sure this teacher loses two things more valuable to him than his teaching licence. I'll hunt him down myself and twist them off with pliers.

I miss you, Lara. Please hurry back from Adelaide.

Also, you'd better come back soon because Mum and Dad are bugging me about what course I'm going to study next year, etc., and I'm too vulnerable to fight back, so if you're not quick to come distract them I'll start making well-thought-out, sensible decisions and end up doing something like Commerce. HURRY.

Xxxxxxxxxxxxxxxxxxxx

(extra x's because I really am worried and can't wait to see you again)

I opened my emails and read quickly. Hannah – listening to me, at last. I gave my first real smile of the trip, one big enough to split my face in half, and I read her message again, slowly. I tapped out a quick reply, to reassure her, and turned to Kate. 'You've already bought our tickets home?'

'Yep. Already called my grandparents, they'll take us in tonight. There weren't any cheap flights for tomorrow, but I thought it could be cool to catch the train instead.' She looked at me as if to check if I was ready for the joke, then continued. 'I thought the Somerton Man would approve of that choice of transport. It leaves tomorrow morning.'

A whole train trip with Jos and Kate sounded like the perfect buffer between here and home. Suddenly I couldn't wait for tomorrow.

I passed the phone back to Kate, grinning at her. Then I remembered – we only had one more term together. I felt some of my elation seep away.

'I, uh – I haven't had a chance to say – I found the forms for your new school. So I guess you won't be around to rescue me if I run away again.' I tried to smile, to say the words lightly, but they sounded like an accusation.

Kate took a deep breath. 'Yeah, I kind of figured you would have seen those. I found the application left out in the study when I was looking for you.'

'Congratulations,' I added quickly, fighting the heaviness settling in my chest. 'It looks really cool.'

'Lara – I didn't apply. I'm not going.'

'What?' I felt a flash of fear. 'If this is because of me, don't worry, I'll be fine. That school looks really great for you, and I'll find new friends at St Mags, some of the people from the musical seemed cool . . .'

'That's just it, Lara, that school is way too perfect for me. If I moved there, I'd become my worst fear: normal. Can you imagine a whole school of arty creative types? It'd be hell.'

Her voice was bright, but I didn't buy it.

Kate sighed. 'Look, I wrote the application ages ago. Right after the rehearsal when Ashley told everyone about – well, you know.' Her face turned fierce. 'But then I stayed. The worst had happened, my secret was out in the most horrible way and – I was okay. It was kind of a relief, actually. I never sent the application in.'

I looked at her for a long while. 'You're really staying?'

'Really. Much more fun to stay and try to bring down the St Margaret's establishment from the inside.'

The waiter came and dropped off our order.

'Hey, can we eat and walk?' I asked suddenly. 'There's one more spot I want to visit.'

CHAPTER FIFTY-FIVE

It took us a long time to find him. The cemetery was huge, laid out in irregularly shaped sections that were hard to follow. I ended up wandering aimlessly through rows on the edge of the cemetery. The noise of the main road just over the wall was loud and intrusive; it felt unnatural that something as everyday as traffic and exhaust fumes and the honk of horns could be so close.

'Lara! Over here.'

Kate had spotted him, just a few rows back and across from where I'd been looking. Jos and I hurried over.

I don't know what I was expecting, but it was a shock to see it: a neat, small grave bordered by concrete, filled in with reddish gravel. The tombstone read, in block capitals:

> *HERE LIES*
> *THE UNKNOWN MAN*
> *WHO WAS FOUND AT*
> *SOMERTON BEACH*
> *1ST DEC. 1948.*

There was a small, cheery sign next to the grave that had obviously been set up recently, giving a brief overview of the case and offering speculation about his possible identity. Other than that, nothing marked the grave apart. There was a brass vase at the headstone, holding a few fake roses that had faded under a layer of dirt.

I looked away to the grave next to his. 'Elizabeth Fellowes, died eighth November 1889, aged eighty-six,' I read aloud. 'And Edward Fellowes, died eighteenth August 1903, aged fifty-six. *We bring our years to an end as if it were a tale that is told.*' I looked at Kate and Jos. 'That quote works fine for Elizabeth and Edward. But what about the Somerton Man? His years ended and the story's not finished. It might never be.'

Jos paused. 'I don't know. For him, the story's pretty well told.' He rummaged in his pockets for a minute, then pulled out a few shells, tiny white and pink fans. He placed them on the grave, next to the vase. 'Picked them up on Somerton Beach,' he murmured, when he saw me staring at him.

'Huh.' Kate nodded in approval. She turned back to the path we'd walked along and picked a few dandelion flowers growing up through the gravel. She tucked them into the vase, stood back.

I didn't know what to say.

All this time, I'd been trying to figure out who this guy was, without ever really thinking of him as a person. A person with a real, physical body lying there under the dirt. I'd thought of his identity as a mystery to be solved – and I'd thought of Mr Grant that way too. But it doesn't work like that. He's a person: and maybe to be human, with all our friendships and connections and thoughts and fears and joys, is to be a web of unsolvable mysteries.

I reached into my pocket for the note I knew was there – Mr Grant's note, the one he'd left in my locker. I pushed down a flush of embarrassment that I'd kept it with me all this time. I curled it up tight, knelt down and tucked it in between Kate's weeds and the fake roses. 'Tamam Shud,' I said quietly, to the grave. Tamam Shud. It is finished.

As I stood up, I felt a lightness, like the mixture of relief and exhaustion at the end of a long-distance run. I turned from the grave, walked towards the arched gate of the cemetery.

✿

The three of us were quiet as we walked towards the exit, so the buzzing sound of Kate's phone made me jump.

'Ugh.' She pulled it out and hung up. A message popped up on the screen: thirty-six missed calls from the same number.

'Who is it?'

Kate glanced at Jos, then back at me. 'Ashley,' she said. 'Finally found her conscience and is worried about you, I guess.'

The phone buzzed again.

'Here.' I reached for it.

'Are you sure?' Kate asked. 'You don't have to speak to her.'

After the run on the beach I felt numb, which also made me feel invincible. I nodded at Kate and took the phone. I walked a few steps down the path, out of earshot of Kate and Jos, and answered.

'Kate? I know you must completely hate me, and whatever, that's fine, but please don't hang up – I just need to know where Lara is –'

Hearing her voice, tinny and panicked over the phone, I felt like I was transported straight back to Melbourne, straight back to before the afterparty, before everything. A wave of exhaustion hit me and I closed my eyes. 'Hey, Ash.'

'Loz? You're okay? Where *are* you?'

'Adelaide.'

'Crap, seriously? Adelaide? Oh God, I've been freaking out. I tried your phone so many times, then finally your house, and your mum said you'd gone to stay with a friend and she'd assumed it was me, and then *she* started freaking out, and I had to tell her that the friend wasn't me, it was probably Kate, and – well, I guess I was right. But, Adelaide?'

'I came here looking for . . . for the Somerton Man.' I stopped myself from saying his name. I did not want to talk to her about Mr Grant, not now.

Ash paused. When she spoke again her voice was calmer, softer. 'Anyway. I'm so glad I've got you. Listen, I wanted to explain about the afterparty. I was just so mad about Kate taking the part, and you guys all having fun without me, when you know that I always wanted that much more than you did – whatever. I got into some of Mum's Baileys and thought, why shouldn't I join the party? And – look, I did some things that weren't okay, especially now.' Her voice took on a hushed, careful tone. 'Oh, but since you're away of course, you wouldn't know – oh, Lara, I've got something terrible to tell you about Mr –'

'I know about Mr Grant, Ash.'

She paused. 'What?'

'Kate brought up the letter for me. I know.'

'Of course she did.' Ash's voice was flat, totally different from her breathy apology.

'She wanted to make sure I knew. She was looking out for me.' I felt a rush of anger. 'Jos is here too, by the way. In case you were wondering.'

It was a few seconds before she spoke. 'Loz. I am sorry. I shouldn't have done the party thing.'

I said nothing. I couldn't remember another time she'd apologised to me. Funny then, how it still didn't feel like enough.

She continued. 'Look, I've said sorry. And you have to admit, in a way, I was right about him, wasn't I? Yes, I got caught up in it all, but really, I was just trying to protect you.

Turns out, I was totally right, he was a creep. And he never took me in.'

I felt a pull, like a rip in the ocean that tugs at your ankles and threatens to drag you out to sea. I could agree with her, if I wanted. Her voice would go sunny and sweet, and she'd forgive me, even if I didn't really say sorry. I'd know exactly where I stood, and we'd go on, maybe not quite as before, but without breaking stride. Ash and Loz, always together, always in that order.

Maybe before I'd taken the plane to Adelaide on my own, maybe before I'd looked for the Somerton Man and realised he couldn't be found. Maybe before Kate drew me on the map on her arm, or before Jos's smile, before Hannah missed me enough to leave Europe and come home.

Maybe then. Not now.

'Ash.'

'Yeah?'

'I'm sorry you lost your part. It wasn't my fault, or even Kate's, but it sucked. And thank you for apologising for the afterparty. I'm going to be completely fine. I hope you will too, really, I do.'

'But, Lara –'

'Goodbye, Ashley.'

I hung up the phone. In the end, it was as easy as that.

CHAPTER FIFTY-SIX

I could see where Kate got her calm demeanour from: both her grandparents seemed unfazed by anything, including three dishevelled teenagers unexpectedly descending on their seaside home. They settled us on their lounge room floor without missing a beat. I slept better than I expected on the pushed-together couch cushions, the sound of the sea just audible through the window. Kate's grandad dropped us off early in the morning to the station.

Over an hour into our train journey to Melbourne, Jos held out his book to me, his finger marking a passage. The book was a slim vintage classic, a battered paperback. I could picture him pulling it out of his bookcase at home.

'What's this?' The lines were hard to focus on.

'It's the *Rubaiyat*, Lara.'

I didn't want to think about the *Rubaiyat*, or the mystery, ever again. 'No thanks.'

'No really – this bit.' When he saw I really wasn't going to take the book, he read aloud. His voice was soft.

'And after many days my Soul return'd / And said, "Behold, Myself am Heav'n and Hell".

'Maybe it makes sense of Mr Grant a bit,' Jos explained, when I didn't say anything. 'Maybe there isn't an answer. He was good and bad, all together – "Heav'n and Hell", like in all of us.'

'No,' Kate interrupted. 'Some things are black and white, Jos. Not in all of us. Not like that.'

'I'm not excusing him, I just mean – you can think of him as a good teacher, and recognise that, even though –'

I put my head to the window; I let the juddering movement vibrate through my forehead, drowning them out.

'Lara.' Jos's arm on my shoulder.

'I don't know if I can think about him like that yet.' I leant back. Suddenly the words all came at once. 'I wish I knew – did he really think of me as a smart and a good student? Did he really like me, as me, or was it all part of his act? And if he *did* really like me, does that make it better or worse? What does it say about me, if –'

'No.' Kate gripped my arm until I looked at her. Her eyes were fierce. 'None of this is your fault, Lara. None of it.'

'Okay.' She kept hold of my arm. 'Okay, I get it.' I felt something loosen in my chest, and tried a small smile. Tears began to smart in the corners of my eyes instead.

'Ahem.' Jos held out his phone. 'Emergency YouTube party? Have you seen the puppy eating a lemon?'

I coughed out a laugh and shook my head. He pressed play.

The train churned along, bringing us closer to home.

WEST TERRACE CEMETERY, ADELAIDE, JUNE 1949

There were no flowers. The austere kindness of the SA Grandstand Bookmakers' Association, who volunteered to fund the funeral, had not stretched to flowers. Perhaps they had not thought of it.

There was no funeral notice published in the paper, either. This was deliberate. The police did not want curious members of the public – 'ghoulish onlookers', as they called them – to come. Perhaps as a mark of respect to the man, because the occasion should be one of dignity, not gossip. Or, perhaps it was because they wanted to dispose of him quietly, before anyone could ask more questions. It is hard to say.

So, it was a small funeral. A publican and a journalist had to be called on to be pallbearers, along with two gravediggers. And, though the man's identity was as insubstantial and impossible to grasp as air, his body was still heavy: their faces braced with the weight of him, their shoulders strained.

The young priest from the Salvation Army gave a short sermon, and read the rites as he did at every funeral. It was nearly over now. The priest closed his prayer book. The gravedigger came forward and tipped a spadeful of dirt over the coffin. It made a pattering noise that blended with the sound of the light rain.

Although there were no wreaths at the funeral, his grave was not left bare. In the weeks to follow, a small bunch of violets appeared, their blooms a soft pool of colour against the grey headstone.

The cemetery caretaker was never able to say who it was who left the tribute, although he did notice that the flowers appeared each year on the anniversary of the man's death: the first day of summer.

TAMAM SHUD

AUTHOR'S NOTE

The story of the Somerton Man is true, and one of the great unsolved mysteries of our time. Many of the scenes recreated in this book are based loosely on fact, though I have imagined my own version of the case. Some timelines or facts have been changed or simplified for the sake of the story, and some unknowns I filled in by imagining my own possibilities. For instance, the funeral was really paid for by the SA Grandstand Bookmakers' Association and a headstone donated a few days after the burial, but the conversation in the pub is entirely invented. The man who found the *Rubaiyat* in his car did ask to remain anonymous, but was later revealed to be a chemist (George and Elena are fictional, but I liked their story better).

There are many, many people who have investigated and reported on the case over the years, and some of the resources I drew on for my research included *The Unknown Man* by Gerry Feltus; the work of Derek Abbott at Adelaide University, including his lectures on the case on YouTube and his discussions on Reddit; the 1978 ABC documentary episode of *Inside Story* 'The Somerton Beach Mystery'; Kerry Greenwood's book *Tamam Shud: The Somerton Man Mystery*; and the relevant episodes from the *Casefile*, *My Favorite Murder* and *Astonishing Legends* podcasts. There are also countless blogs and online articles for readers who would like to go further down the rabbit hole.

Like Lara, at times I was in danger of getting so involved in the mystery of the Somerton Man that I could forget he was, in the end, a man: a human being with dignity and worth. I hope that I did him justice in my story. I pay my respects to the Unknown Man, whoever he was. May he rest in peace.

ACKNOWLEDGEMENTS

In some ways, the biggest mystery for me is that this story which existed only in my mind for so long is now out in the world as a book. None of it would have happened without these people.

Thank you to everyone at The Bent Agency and most of all to my agent Gemma Cooper: thank you for shaping Lara's story with me and becoming our champion, for your patience, and for all the reassuring FaceTime calls. Team Cooper forever!

Hachette Australia have made the experience of being published a dream. Thank you to my publisher Suzanne O'Sullivan for your enthusiasm for the book and for making it better. Many thanks to my editor Brigid Mullane, and to Jeanmarie Morosin, Jenny Topham, Amy Dobson, Rebecca Hamilton, Aleesha Paz, and the rest of the team at Hachette.

Thank you to Fiona Wood for reading an early copy and for your kind words. Thanks also to the LoveOzYA community for your welcome, and for writing all my favourite books.

The Bath Spa MA in Writing for Young People was my first step in becoming a writer – thanks to my tutors and classmates who were there at the very beginning of Lara's story. I am especially grateful to Julia Green, and to Anna Hoghton, whose postcard 'review' kept me going in tricky times. Thank you Jessica Dowling Bonaddio for proofreading an early draft and providing motivational memes in the years since as required, and to Imme Visser for coffees on the balcony. Thanks to my friends for your support and for knowing when not to ask how the writing is going.

Thank you Jon and Caleb (I hope I haven't been quite as overbearing an older sibling as Hannah!) and Charice, for always cheering on me and Lara. To Allison, David, Nat, James, Scarlett and little Pretzel: thank you for love, biryani and 'family hugs'.

I am grateful to my grandparents, Patricia Nicholson and Bev and Ken Morgan for their support of my writing, and for their enthusiasm for the book – showing how wide the readership for YA really is.

Thank you to Mum and Dad for everything; and thank you especially for giving me books every birthday and Christmas, for diagnosing the condition of 'I need something to read' as seriously as you diagnose medical conditions (perhaps more so?), and for teaching me to be empathetic and curious about the world.

Finally, thank you Evan: the best husband, friend, first reader, plot-problem-sounding-board, and live-in barista I know. Thanks for holding my hand under the stars (and the gaps between the stars) that night.

CHILDREN'S BOOKS

If you would like to find out more about Hachette Children's Books, our authors, upcoming events and new releases you can visit our website, Facebook or follow us on Twitter:

hachettechildrens.com.au
twitter.com/HCBoz
facebook.com/hcboz